Cries of the Orchids

By

Terri Bailey

1663 LIBERTY DRIVE, SUITE 200
BLOOMINGTON, INDIANA 47403
(800) 839-8640
WWW.AUTHORHOUSE.COM

This book is a work of fiction. Places, events, and situations in this story are purely fictional and any resemblance to actual persons, living or dead, is coincidental.

© 2004 Terri Bailey.
All Rights Reserved.

No part of this book may be reproduced, stored in a retrieval system, or transmitted by any means without the written permission of the author.

First published by AuthorHouse 10/26/04

ISBN: 1-4184-9441-0 (sc)

Printed in the United States of America
Bloomington, Indiana

This book is printed on acid-free paper.

Acknowledgements

  I find myself unable to express the depth of my gratitude to those who supported the creation of this story. The collaboration of encouragement I received from friends and family was so monumental, I fear I will unwittingly fail to acknowledge someone of importance to this work. Ahead of time, I express my apologies.

  A special "thank you" to Karen Houser-Malcom who with a mother's love read each draft with encouragement and constructive criticism. And to my grandfather, Dale Houser, whose words of wisdom I hold dear.

  For their brutal honesty and editorial guidance, I want to thank my sister, Shea Le`on and my aunt, Kay Jackson. Further editorial advice came with much appreciation from Michelle Brown, Doyle Wayne Malcom, Debbie Perret, and Lorie Mitchell.

  I would like to express my gratitude to Joe Paul Owens, Jim Bailey, and Kirk MClellehan for sharing their expertise in law enforcement and to Ernie Cox, who saved me endless hours of research in the medical field. A special thanks to members of the Malvern Fire Department for being patient with my infinite questions.

  To my partner in crime, Mary Lou Mathis, thank you for pushing me past each occasion of writer's block.

  To "the real" Kenny Thomas, whose gift of art leaves other designers paling by comparison.

  To the "children" in my life: Kaleb, Kaci, Emmarie, Madison, Malarie, Piersen, Hannah, Christian, Christina and Kaleb Tyler for teaching my soul how to love on a different level, thus providing inspiration for this book.

For my sisters and cheerleaders: Kelli Hathcock, Traci Garrett, and Shea Le'on. (Where would I be without you?)

To my precious Carl Jackson who inspired the character of Nelson.

To my niece, Malarie Garrett, for all of her special prayers.

And to John, my husband & cover designer, I express my gratitude for the endless hours of patience and encouragement you bestowed upon me until the very last word was written.

This book is dedicated to my children, Kaleb and Kaci. With all of my imagination, I am unable to picture my life without you.

And to my foster daughter, Christina, who should have been mine from birth.

Chapter One

The man leaned against the hood of his car in the middle of the woods. It was a good spot. No one could see him. The nearest neighbor was a mile away, and the house would be completely consumed before anyone noticed. He chewed the end of a long piece of grass and studied the tiny house, as he'd done several times before. He knew the routine now. It was always the same: first one light would go out, then another. By now she was putting the kids to bed.

He assumed this case would be a little harder than the one he'd done six months ago, because this family was white: *Niggers don't feel pain like white people do.* He'd brought chloroform for this job, unlike the other, because he didn't want the kids to wake up after he set the house on fire.

It was dark, and he couldn't see his watch. The kids weren't asleep yet, because he could still see the light glowing through the shades of both windows on the far right-hand side of the house. It was probably getting close to eight, and the wait was just about over. He walked to the passenger's side of the car to get his things and put his cowboy hat in the front seat. The grass dangled carelessly from his mouth as he repositioned himself in front of the car. Watching closely, he waited until he saw the first light go out.

It was eight o'clock, and Carol had just tucked in the boys. They had played hard today, and it wouldn't be long before they would be fast asleep. Emily was a different story. The three-year-old was bouncing up and down on the living room couch, her long brown hair tangled from endless bouts of activities, singing a song she had just made up about "crunchy cars."

Carol had developed a routine for getting all four kids to sleep by nine: the boys, ages nine and seven, went down first because they were the easiest; Emily was next, which generally took a good thirty minutes; by eight-thirty, it was time for three-week-old Sarah's bottle. It was important to get Emily down before the baby's feeding; otherwise, when Sarah went back to sleep, Emily would wake her up.

When the baby was fed, diapered, and back asleep, Carol got to take a bath and watch some television. It was the only time of the day that she could be alone. With four children, she needed brief moments of solitude if she were to remain sane. Getting the children coordinated and adjusted to the new routine was an exhaustive effort, but it seemed that everyone, including her newborn was settling in nicely. And Carol was happy.

She had been so scared when her husband left eight months ago. Because Carol spent most of her adult years at home with her children, she had no job and no education. Abandoned and alone, Carol felt empty, as though part of her body had been amputated and discarded. The fear of not being able to support her children was crippling, causing her to battle chronic depression for the first three months following the divorce. At times she had to force herself to do such simple tasks as getting out of bed or brushing her teeth. But by the grace of God, she was now able to see that she and the kids could make it just fine on their own.

Emily was riding the arm of the couch as if it were a horse. Her mother walked in and swooped her up. "Okay, young lady, time for bed."

Emily fussed and pouted. When that didn't work, she went into a full-blown temper tantrum. Carol sat her down. Before the baby came, she would have relented and let the girl stay up another half hour or so, which was now part of the problem. Her history of relenting to the three-year-old had only reinforced the tantrums.

Emily was now on her back kicking her legs and screaming, "*No*, Mommy. I don't *want* to go to bed."

Carol was patient, "If you go back there and lie down, I'll come tell you a story."

Emily didn't budge, so Carol added, "And if you don't, I'll give you a spanking, and you'll go to bed without the story."

That's all it took. Emily was up and off to her room. Smiling at her daughter's tenacity, Carol went into the kitchen and put a bottle of formula in a cup of hot water. The stranger watched through the window as Carol checked her watch. It was twenty minutes after eight.

Leaving the kitchen, Carol went to the girls' room, where she found Emily pouting beneath the covers. Carol ignored her and began a lengthy fairytale about the Princess Emily and her magical flying horse. Together, they saved the kingdom from Granddaddy Long Legs, the most feared creatures in all the land.

Carol had almost run out of imagination when the child's eyes drooped. She continued the story until Emily was fast asleep, having learned that if she tried to sneak out before Emily was completely asleep there would be another temper tantrum, and she, Emily, and the baby would be up for another two hours.

It was now the baby's turn, and as Carol looked over the bars of the crib, she saw the small bundle all curled up and sound asleep. She decided to go ahead and wake her so that Sarah would stay on schedule. Carol changed the baby's diaper and went to the kitchen to get the bottle. She didn't know that the stranger was inside the house, watching her quietly from his position at the back door.

She situated the baby in her right arm and carried her and the warm bottle of milk to the living room. Loving this time of the evening when everything began to unwind, she could reflect on another successful day; a day they had all made it without John. Sitting in the rocking chair, she held the bottle to the baby's mouth and giggled as Sarah's little mouth jerked around the nipple as if she were a newborn puppy instinctively searching for its mother's milk. Carol rocked until the baby began to drift off to sleep. Putting a burp rag over her shoulder, she lifted Sarah up and patted her back gently. "My sweet little Sarah," she cooed. "My sweet, sweet baby."

Carol's head snapped back and slammed against the rocking chair when the man shoved the chloroform-tainted cloth over her mouth and nose. Clutching to the baby, Carol jerked and twisted violently, choking in terror as she thought of her children. Desperately trying to pull away, the man held the cloth tightly to her mouth, causing every gasp to fill her lungs with the toxic vapors emanating from the cloth. She tried to cry out, *My babies! Please don't hurt my babies!* But the fumes were too strong, and she felt herself slipping away, helpless to protect the children.

When Carol was unconscious, the man lifted the baby from her slumped body and let her smell the fumes, until she too was unconscious. He put the baby on Carol's chest, draping her arms around the infant. Standing to the side, he stared, amazed at how peaceful they looked; mother and child asleep, holding on to one another. *It would have made a lovely portrait*, he thought.

Next, he went to the boys' room and held the cloth to their mouths and noses. There was no struggle. They were already asleep, but now he needn't be concerned they'd wake up when the house was burning. After all, he had a heart.

He went to the little girl's room. As she stirred in her sleep, he moved quickly to render her unconscious. The toddler's eyes opened and filled with fear, but the vapor worked quickly, knocking her out before she had time to struggle. He continued to hold the cloth firmly to her face until he was certain that she wouldn't wake up. *Sweet little thing*, he thought, as he paved the way to her death. He didn't like killing white kids, but it had to be done. There was too much money at stake.

Walking back into the kitchen where he had left the extra-large plastic bags filled with fabric softener sheets, he picked them up and went into the laundry room. It was in a good location, tucked into a cubby in the middle of the hallway. There were no windows to worry about. He opened each bag and emptied the fabric softener behind and around the dryer. When the bags were empty, the sheets littered the whole of the small area. Fabric softener was completely combustible. It left nothing for the arson dogs to find. The fire department would blame it on faulty wiring from the dryer. They wouldn't be able to prove anything to the contrary.

He lit a match and set the sheets on fire. They burned quickly, and he grabbed dirty clothes from the laundry basket and added them to the blaze. In a matter of minutes, the fire had consumed the wall behind the dryer and had begun eating away at the highly flammable cleaning products on the shelf above it, thus further fueling the fire. He waited until the flame burned ravenously and began seeping into the hallway.

Walking through the living room to the kitchen, he caught another glimpse of Carol and the baby. The smoke billowed from the laundry room and down the hallway, encircling the two of them like a dusty cloud.

The man slipped out through the kitchen, the same way he'd come in, thinking the job had almost been too easy. *The stupid woman shouldn't have left the back door unlocked.* No matter, he would have gotten in anyway.

Back at the car, he grabbed his hat and then reached down to find another piece of grass to chew on. He had angled the car such that he could watch the blaze from the hood. The show was about to begin.

The fire began as a dim flicker behind the shades in the living room. He leaned against the car and waited. In no time at all, the fire became a frenzied inferno that broke through the living room windows and lapped at the house's exterior. The woman and her baby would surely be dead by now. It only took another five minutes before the fire reached the back bedrooms and developed into a blazing fury.

Confident that all five were dead, he knew it was time to leave the woods. As soon as someone became aware of the blaze they would call it in, and he needed to be prepared for action. Plopping behind the wheel, he crept through the path in the woods, turning his lights on only when he was sure no one would see him from the highway. He headed back toward town, noticing the amber-colored sky growing vividly brighter in his rearview mirror.

The C.B. crackled just as he hit the city limits. "Code 810 just off Highway Five. All units respond."

That was quick, he thought, as he turned around and clicked his sirens on, reflecting again on how easy the job had been. There was only the minor struggle with the mother and the brief moment that the toddler awakened. Thinking of the little girl, he smiled with twisted grandfatherly adoration. *She was such a pretty little thing.*

Chapter Two

Well, here we are again, Shy thought, as her nostrils and stomach adjusted to the stench of Mattie's home. Sharon "Shy" Sauze had received a Bachelor's Degree in social work from the University of Arkansas in Little Rock but received most of her education by watching five consecutive years of Oprah Winfrey. She knew everything about homosexual discrimination, tragic accident survivors, oppression, depression, abused children and Oprah's fiftieth birthday party. What she didn't know was how to get Mattie to clean her damn house.

"Mattie, this is it. I've been coming here every week for eight months and look at this house. I don't understand it. You do well for awhile and then *this*."

She flung her hands up and around the room, as if Mattie needed a personal tour guide to see the magnitude of her own squalor. Dirty clothes were scattered about the yellowed, linoleum floor and piled up beside Mattie on the couch. A glass lay toppled over with thick chunks of curdled milk splattered beside it. In some places of the living room, Shy couldn't see the floor for all the trash, which made it difficult to even walk around.

Mattie sat blithely- her fat behind on the fifty-dollar sofa the Department of Human Services (DHS) had bought for her two months ago. Her lime green sleeveless shirt was entirely too small- white flesh engulfed the stained blouse and protruded through every opening. Her legs were sprawled out in front of her with little display of modesty. Chigger bites covered her calves and thigh area and looked magnified against her pasty, white legs.

Mattie looked thoughtful as if pondering the next few brilliant words to be launched from her mouth. Squirming a bit, she moved to scratch a chigger bite under her arm. The finger that was momentarily lost in her armpit was moved quickly to her mouth. As she chewed the tip of the nail completely off, Shy fought the urge to vomit.

Pulling the finger from her mouth, Mattie said, "Miss Shy, you know I been sick," her poor grammar accentuated by her thick southern drawl, befitting her to the stereotypical Arkansas hillbilly.

Brilliant, Shy thought sarcastically. "That's what you told me last week. I'm tired of these excuses, Mattie. Do you want Jake to live in a foster home with strangers?"

"No, ma'am," Mattie answered, unmoved by the idea that Jake might be taken from her. She didn't believe it for a second.

Shy could hardly blame her. Mattie's son, Jake, would have been put in foster care months ago if not for the new Welfare Reforms Act passed last year. Arkansas had been sued three years ago for allegedly taking poor care of its neglected or abused children. An investigation conducted by the federal government concluded that the accusations were true. Not only were children being left in homes with pedophiles and heinously abusive foster parents, children who were placed in custody were often forgotten, moved from home to home and eventually lost in the system.

Though new regulations were now in place for monitoring and investigating cases, the departments were often understaffed to the extent that they couldn't comply with policy. The entire Child Protective Services division continued to be lacking. That, coupled with meager salaries and fifty to sixty hour workweeks, led to quick burnout, making it hard to keep quality people in the workforce.

One new regulation held that all possible measures had to be taken to keep a child in his or her home. Rehabilitate, educate, assist the family in getting services, and/or remove the perpetrator before removing the child. Long-term studies showed that the trauma of a child being removed from everything and everyone he or she had ever known was often worse than living in an abusive home.

So far, Mattie had shown the ability to care for and nurture her baby. There was never any evidence of abuse and there seemed to be a strong bond between the two of them, but she was a pig, plain and simple. Shy took a deep breath and tried another approach. "Listen, Mattie, I know you can do this; I've seen you do it. You were keeping your house clean two months ago. In fact, you were doing so well I almost closed the case. I don't understand what happened. Help me understand."

Mattie chewed another nail as if she hadn't heard a word. There was a moment of silence, and then she suddenly lowered her eyebrows, squinted her eyes, looked to be deep in thought. "Miss Shy," she said, and then paused as if trying to think of the best words to use. "Do you want a Sprike?"

"No, Mattie, I do not want a Sprite," Shy said with restrained frustration. Mattie appeared much like a child who had just gotten her candy taken away.

It was a Monday ritual. Shy would come over and teach Mattie some type of domestic skill, inspect the home for Mattie's progress, and then they would sit together and drink a "Sprike." They would talk and laugh at something cute Jake was doing, and they would make plans to meet again the following week. Today was different. Mattie could see that Miss Shy was angry. She didn't like the way this made her feel, and she wanted to cry. Miss Shy was her best friend.

Jake began to cry in the back room. Mattie's heartbroken expression lit up as she chirped, "There's my baby," while struggling up off the couch, tugging and pulling her shorts from every unmentionable nook and cranny. She tromped clumsily down the hallway to tend to Jake.

Shy moved a hand to the side of her head and massaged her temple. She'd been on call the night before and hadn't slept well, thinking her beeper would go off any minute. She was tired, frustrated, and woozy from the stench of the house. Lifting her head, she could hear Mattie cooing and giggling with Jake in the back room. She smiled in spite of her exasperation.

Mattie's interaction with her baby was a joy to watch. Shy had rarely seen a mother who took such sheer delight in her child.

With the help of a few parenting classes, Mattie had learned to care for Jake marvelously. Unfortunately, the filthy living conditions were unacceptable and spelled neglect regardless of how well Mattie tended to Jake.

Shy looked toward the partitioned door that separated the living room from the kitchen. It was open about two inches, giving her a glimpse of the baby-blue wallpaper with yellow sunflowers above the white counters. A faint smell of bleach mingled with the stench of the living room. Shy moved closer and pushed open the door to get a better look in the kitchen. A stack of dishes lay drying in the drainer beside the sink; the counters were clean; the floor was clean. The entire *room* was spotless. A cloth lay folded neatly over the divider between the sinks; a broom and dustpan stood in the corner beside the refrigerator.

Staring with confusion, Shy wondered why the kitchen was meticulously clean and the living room such a disaster. Was Mattie keeping her living room a mess on purpose? Why? When she heard Mattie tumbling back down the hallway, she quickly shut the door and moved away from it. Mattie was grinning from ear to ear, still chirping baby talk, with Jake babbling on her hip.

"Well, hi there, Jake. Did you wake up from your nap?" Her voice and Mattie's melded until both women were cooing in unison. Mattie brought the baby over to her, and Shy held out her arms. Baby Jake squealed and held out his chubby hands.

"You're a big boy aren't you, little man?" Shy smiled as Jake gurgled and kicked his legs. His left eye crossed as he tried to focus on the pearl beads draped around her neck, making Shy and Mattie laugh. Shy's beeper went off. She jostled Jake to her left hip in order to read the numbers on her pager. It was Bill, her supervisor.

"Mattie, I've got to go." She pulled Jake up so that he stood, still a bit shaky, on her thighs. He reached for the beads again and struggled to put them in his mouth. Shy kissed him quickly on the forehead and said, "You be a good boy for Mommy." She handed him over, legs kicking gingerly in the air.

"I'll be back next week."

"Okay, Miss Shy. I'll do better next time, I promise."

Cries of the Orchids

As Shy turned to walk away, she thought about the kitchen again. She turned back around. "Mattie, I just want you to know," she sat down in the wooden chair across from Mattie and looked directly into her eyes, "I want you to know that eventually, when you meet all of your goals on the case plan, we can close your case, and I won't have to be coming over, checking on you every week."

Mattie immediately averted her eyes and shifted in her seat. Baby Jake played quietly with a gold button loosely fastened to the top of his mother's shirt.

"But we can still be friends," Shy said.

Mattie's eyes moved from the floor back to Shy, her solemn expression turning cheerful. "Okay." A Cheshire Cat grin quickly brightened her face. "I think that's a real good idear, Miss Shy, yes ma'am I do!"

Shy stood up and Mattie barreled off the couch, throwing a heavy arm around Shy and embracing her forcefully. Jake dangled from her other arm, confused by the sudden change in motion. Shy smiled, feeling a general sense of warmth for Mattie, but a strong need to put some distance between herself and Mattie's sweaty armpit. Pulling away from the embrace she smiled, "Okay, you two." Patting Jake on the head, she brushed a solitary eyelash from his cheek saying, "I'll see you next Monday. And my turn to bring the Sprites," she added with a wink.

Shy closed the door behind her and walked quickly down the porch steps and opened the door to her blue Grand Am, almost spilling her purse in the process. Clicking her cell phone on, she managed to back out of Mattie's weed-infested driveway and dial the office at the same time. It was the third day of July and summer had long since made its presence known. Dust from the parched country road billowed from the car and formed a cloud of golden powder behind her.

After thirty seconds of B-rated music, Shy heard the familiar voice of her boss and said, "Hi, it's me. You beeped? ... Yeah, sure, I'm famished. Anything sounds good to me. ... Sounds great. I'll be there in about twenty minutes."

She continued to drive, processing the events that had just occurred with Mattie. Amazing, she thought. It had never dawned

Terri Bailey

on her before how lonely Mattie must be out here all alone with no family or friends. She must look forward to Shy's weekly visits. It was no wonder Mattie stopped doing so well with her house cleaning when she was told her case would be closed. Most people would jump at the idea of no longer having a social worker intrude upon their family each week, but Mattie's story was a bit different. As Shy drove down the dusty road, she reflected on the hardships that she and Mattie had worked through since she became Mattie's social worker nine months ago.

Just prior to Jake's birth, a trucker just outside of Texarkana on I-30 picked up Mattie. Apparently, Mattie told the kind trucker that she was trying to get to Beverly Hills so she could raise her baby in a big house with nice things. Mattie, who was mildly retarded, saw a television program featuring a child who was raised in a luxurious Beverly Hills mansion. The child's friends, subsequently, all had similar homes. Mattie's child-like vision sought the land of milk and honey. She thought that if she could only get there all the riches and glory would befall her and her baby. The trucker had compassion and listened to Mattie rattle on and on about her baby and what all she would be giving it as soon as she reached her destination.

He took her as far as Maburn where he knew a friend of a friend who ran a homeless shelter. The shelter contacted DHS, and Shy subsequently became Mattie's caseworker. When a small, two-bedroom house became available through the local housing authority, Shy assisted Mattie with the application. While Mattie was happy with her new home, she continued to talk of "Beberly Hills."

Shy told her that her baby would be so lucky to have her as a mother and that it wouldn't care if it lived in a mansion or a one-room shack. With that said, Mattie determined that Miss Shy was her best friend in the whole world.

Shy tapped the Department of Human Services Emergency Relief Fund and was able to furnish the house with a bed, sheets, two blankets, and a few dishes. She assisted Mattie with the Medicaid application so that Mattie could receive what was left of prenatal care. Medicaid would also cover the birth of the baby and any medical care the baby would need until he turned eighteen. Mattie also met the criteria for emergency relief and therefore received two hundred and eighteen dollars in food stamps just three days after she turned in her application.

Shy took her to the grocery store, helped her buy staple items, sandwich meat, and a few other items. She then showed Mattie how to use her food stamp card as the checker waited patiently. A local flea market donated four changes of clothes for Mattie, as well as a thick winter coat. Shy worked with Mattie two hours a week on parenting skills, personal hygiene, and housekeeping. Mattie was eager to learn and progressed quickly.

Living her entire childhood in Louisiana, Mattie stayed with the last of her six foster families until she was eighteen. She said the family was "like all the rest" and felt that she was never loved by anyone except a girl named Christina, her seventeen-year-old foster sister of her third foster home. Apparently, Christina gave Mattie more attention and affection than she had ever received.

Mattie recalled numerous afternoons of Christina sitting on the floor with her as they played with an old collection of Barbie's that Christina had stashed away in her closet. She also said that Christina would take her to the Sonic and buy them each a "Sprike," and they would go to the park and swing. Shy thought that this was probably the reason Mattie loved Sprite.

When Mattie was nine, her foster dad was transferred to Arkansas. The family did everything in their power to adopt Mattie so that she could go with them. Unfortunately, the state of Louisiana would not permit Mattie to leave the state. Mattie was placed in yet another home and torn from the only friend she had ever known. This cycle continued until Mattie turned eighteen and was able to move out on her own.

Mattie's baby, Jacob Ray Johnson, was born on October twelfth at two o'clock in the morning. He weighed eight pounds and six ounces. Mattie did well through the eleven-hour labor, as well as the delivery. Shy was the only one waiting in the receiving area. She remembered seeing Jake for the first time. He was wrinkled, pink, and beautiful. Mattie was beaming, cradling the baby gently as if she'd held the infant a hundred times. She chose to bottle feed the baby and when it was time to leave the hospital, the nurse gave her a two-week supply of formula with instructions to feed the baby one to two ounces every four hours. Mattie nodded eagerly, anticipating the opportunity to start caring for the baby all by herself. When the nurse left the room Mattie looked at Shy earnestly and said, "I need to go to the grocery store, cuz I don't have ounces at my house." Shy was confused at first by what Mattie could be talking about. She then realized that when the nurse told Mattie to feed the baby one to two ounces every four hours, Mattie thought she was talking about some type of food. Shy explained to Mattie what an ounce was and showed her where the measures were on the bottle. Mattie's eyes lit up like she'd solved a great mystery. "Oh. So when I hold the bottle up and the formal, I mean formra--"

"Formula," Shy enunciated.

"Right, formrula comes down one line or two lines, he's had enough."

"That's right. You catch on quickly." Shy couldn't help but get caught up in the excitement that encompassed Mattie. The following week, Shy assisted Mattie in the Women, Infants, and Children Program (WIC), which would provide formula for the baby, as well as milk, cheese, and eggs for Mattie. As the baby grew older, WIC would provide cereal and juice for him also.

Because of her low mental aptitude, Mattie began receiving Supplemental Security Income checks in the amount of five hundred and sixty dollars a month. Shy periodically took Mattie to yard sales where Mattie bought baby clothes and toys for Jake. She used the rest of her money each month to begin stocking her house with sheets, towels and other necessities.

By the time Jake was three and a half months old, Mattie had managed to purchase a used oak table with four chairs, a playpen, and two chests of drawers. She put a used refrigerator on layaway, and was hoping that in two months she would have it paid off and would no longer have to put her food in an ice chest. She was excited that she would even be able to freeze some of her food.

In many ways Mattie behaved like a five-year-old child. She sought praise and attention and often asked, "Did I do good?" She was naive and required much education about managing money, cooking, and basic hygiene. Shy put a great deal of effort into

Mattie's case and often found herself working well into the night to manage the rest of her caseload. It was necessary, she thought, if this little family were going to stay intact. She was grateful that she currently had no other cases as demanding as Mattie's.

Mattie continued to manage her mothering skills like a pro. Shy often thought the world would be altogether different if all children were afforded the type of affection Mattie gave her baby.

Shy checked on Mattie and Jake for several weeks following the birth. In spite of Mattie's occasional bouts of poor hygiene, she kept Jake clean and dry. She would feed him and then hold him up on her knee, gently cradling his chin in one hand, and pat him on the back. When Jake finally burped she would praise and praise him, then cradle him in her arms again for more feeding.

When Jake was about four months old, Shy began reducing her visits to one time per week. All was well until one cold February morning. Shy went to work and learned that most of the electricity in the northern part of the county had been out since midnight due to a freeze that moved in earlier that evening.

Shy went to check on Mattie and the baby and found Mattie naked and in hypothermic shock. The house was so bitterly cold that frost had begun to develop on the insides of the windows. A pile of thin blankets, sheets, and clothes lay beside Mattie. Shy noticed a small tunnel burrowed through the clothes such that it resembled a cave. Uncovering it, she found the baby snuggly wrapped in Mattie's winter coat.

"Mattie, honey, can you hear me?" Shy remembered Mattie looking at her but giving no response. She appeared confused and disoriented. Shy felt panic sweep throughout her body but quickly oriented her thoughts.

"Mattie, I'm going to take Jake outside to my car where it's warm, and I'll be right back in to get you." She took two of the blankets and one of the sheets, wrapped them tightly around Mattie. She then grabbed the baby and rushed him to the car, carefully watching for inconspicuous patches of ice. With no time to locate the car seat, she laid the baby on the passenger's side, making sure the coat was wrapped snugly around him. She hoped that this would secure him and keep him from rolling off the seat. She wove the seatbelt around the thick coat and fastened it snuggly. Jake cooed and gurgled as Shy hurried out of the car.

Inside the house, Mattie had not moved from her position, and Shy could not get her to respond verbally. "Mattie, it's going to be okay." Shy was petite but strong, nonetheless trying to move Mattie's enormous body without any assistance would test even the strongest of men. She began to feel panic rush through her veins again. Having left her cell phone at the Department of Human Services, Shy had no way of calling for help.

"Mattie," she cupped Mattie's face in her hands, forcing Mattie to look at her, "We're going to get up now. I need you to try to stand up." Mattie's face was glazed and unresponsive. Her breathing was slow and labored.

"Mattie!" Shy's voice had become louder and rang of authority. "Mattie, we're going to get up, now. I need you to try to stand so we can go to the car and check on Jake." She knew if anything could re-orient Mattie it would be Jake. Mattie stirred and then made eye contact. Her voice was hoarse and barely audible, "My baby?"

"He's just fine, Mattie, you took very good care of him. But he's in the car. Now, I need you to stand up so we can get out there and be with him." Mattie nodded and slowly began shifting to stand. She was shaky and had difficulty adjusting her body to a position where her legs could manage the brunt of her weight.

Shy used every muscle in her body to help support Mattie. When Mattie finally got to her feet, the blankets and sheet toppled to the floor. Shy had one of Mattie's arms draped over her shoulders to offer support and now had Mattie's large, naked, left breast right smack in her face.

Mattie tried sluggishly to reach for a cover, but Shy stopped her. "It's okay, Mattie, lets just get you and Jake to the hospital."

Shy managed to get Mattie through the front door and halfway to the car when Mattie stumbled, causing Shy to fall hard on one knee. She quickly regained stability and together they managed to make it to the warmth of the car. Mattie immediately lay down in the back seat. The car had become quite toasty, and Shy feeling frantic to get Mattie immediate medical attention, decided to not waste any more time by going back and getting the blankets to cover Mattie's naked body.

She drove carefully on the way to the hospital, watching for any signs of black ice. Traffic was extremely light, probably because of the weather. She periodically tried to get Mattie to talk but to no avail, so she opted to simply try to comfort her. Shy could only imagine what Mattie must have gone through last night in the bitter cold. She was moved to tears when she thought of how Mattie took every meager thing she owned, including her own clothes, to cover the baby and keep him warm. She almost died for her baby. A real mama, Shy thought.

Shy pulled into the parking lot of the emergency room with a loud screech as her tires tried to make contact with the slushy pavement. She grabbed Jake and hurried inside. A nurse, about fifty-five years old with dyed red hair pulled high up on her head was walking down the hallway, thumbing through a chart as Shy rushed in. Her black rimmed, cat-like eyeglasses were perched just on the tip of her nose.

Shy ran up to her. "I need help!"

She forced the baby on to the nurse causing the woman to drop the file she had been reading. She hollered, "I have a woman out in my car in hypothermic shock." Shy immediately turned and ran back outside grabbing a blanket from a linen rack on the way. The nurse left the file in the floor and rushed to the nurse's station.

"We need a team on deck STAT!" She handed the baby to another nurse and said, "Take him into One. Check him over and stay with him until we can find out what's going on."

The subordinate nurse took Jake carefully into her arms and carried him down the hall. The older nurse hurriedly picked up the file as a group of men and women rushed by her. The men hurried through the door with a gurney and the women went into room Two and began setting it up for Mattie.

Shy was in the car trying to talk to Mattie and drape the sheet around her. She thought Mattie would be embarrassed to someday know she was hauled out of the car and into the hospital naked as a jaybird. Or maybe she wouldn't be embarrassed. Mattie had a tendency to be extremely uncouth. All Shy knew was that she would be embarrassed if faced with a similar situation, and someone would have hell to pay if they didn't cover her bare body. The medical team rushed up to the car. Shy moved out of the way quickly so they could get to Mattie. It took a full fifteen minutes for the men to get Mattie onto the gurney and into the hospital.

Shy took a seat in the waiting area. Now that Mattie and the baby were in expert care, relief settled in so strongly that she began to cry. She waited another hour and then left word for Mattie that she was going back to the office and would be back around five o'clock. The red haired nurse asked her if she was family. Shy was very careful to protect the confidentiality of her clients and didn't want to tell the woman that she was Mattie's social worker. If Mattie chose to give this information that would be fine, but she would not. She opted to tell the nurse that she was a friend. She told the nurse that she was happy to be the emergency contact and gave her the number to her beeper.

At five-fifteen Shy returned to the hospital. The red haired nurse was at the desk.

"Hi," Shy said, "I've come back to check on Mattie and her son."

"Yes," the woman said with a smile. "We've been waiting for you to come back. I was just going to page you. Everything's fine Miss, uh," she looked down at the chart hoping to find Shy's name, but Shy bailed her out.

"Sauze"

"Ah, yes, Miss Sauze, Miss Johnson is doing just fine. We've moved her to a room, and we'll be keeping her overnight. Her vitals are all normal, but the doctor wants to keep her 'til morning just to be certain. She's a very lucky woman. The doctor said she wouldn't have survived three more hours."

The idea that Mattie could have died was sobering to say the least. "What about the baby?"

"Oh, he's the cutest thing, isn't he?" Shy nodded in agreement but was anxious for the nurse to get on with it.

"He's perfectly fine and ready to be released. Will you be taking him? Ms. Johnson informed us that she had no family."

Cries of the Orchids

"Umm, could I please see Mattie for a moment?" She was scratching her forehead, trying to think of what to do.

"Sure. She's on the second floor in room 209."

Shy headed down the hallway and stopped by the gift shop. She purchased a ten-dollar bouquet of fresh flowers. Finding the elevator, she punched the number two, and waited for what seemed like an eternity for the elevator to creep up one floor. When the doors opened she immediately saw a burgundy sign with white numbers showing that rooms two hundred to two hundred and fifteen were to the right. Locating Mattie's room, she peeked in.

Mattie was asleep. A small-framed nurse sat in a rocking chair to one side of Mattie's bed. Jake gurgled and cooed in her arms. The nurse smiled sweetly at her and whispered, "You must be Shy Sauze."

"Yes ma'am."

"We've been waiting for you." She spoke with a higher tone as if portraying Jake's thoughts too. The nurse handed the baby over to Shy and told her that all the paperwork had been completed for discharge and that the baby was ready to go. She also stated that this had been the most delightful shift she'd ever worked. After stroking Jake's head and giving him a quick kiss on the cheek, the nurse left the room. Shy rocked Jake until Mattie began to stir in her sleep. Holding the baby up to her shoulder, Shy went to Mattie's bedside just in time for her eyes to flutter and open. Mattie smiled weakly.

"How are you feeling?" Shy asked as she balanced Jake with one arm and used her free hand to hold Mattie's. The nightstand beside the bed was adorned with the colorful bouquet Shy had bought for her. Mattie tried to speak but had to clear her throat twice before anything audible could come out. Her voice was raspy.

"No one's ever brung me flowers before."

"Do you like them?" Mattie nodded and smiled.

"They gave me an I.B." She held her arm up much like a child showing off a recent boo-boo. The I.V. tubing ran from her left wrist to a bag of heated saline solution.

"I see that," Shy said, tickled at Mattie's mispronunciation of I.V. "Did it hurt?"

Mattie shook her head to show Shy how brave she was. Shy smiled at her and patted Jake who had fallen asleep on her shoulder.

"They say my baby's just fine. They say I took good care of him in that cold. It was so awful cold, Miss Shy." Mattie's eyes began to water, as she recalled the freezing night. Shy reached out for her hand again.

"I can't imagine how awful that must have been for you." Mattie nodded and brushed away the tear that had rolled down her cheek.

"You gonna keep my Jake until tomorrow?"

Shy had not prepared for this question. In fact, she hadn't even thought about the baby being discharged before Mattie and where he might stay. Mattie had no one to keep him, and it was against state policy for a caseworker to house a client, even for one night. She would have to find a foster family to keep Jake for the night but pondered on the best way to present this to Mattie.

"Mattie, it's against policy for me to keep Jake at my house, but I know some really nice people--"

Mattie interrupted with a strong shake of her head. She was becoming weaker, and her voice was difficult to understand.

"Please don't put him with strangers. You're all he knows 'sides me. Please, Miss Shy." With this, her eyes drooped shut. Shy brushed her hand against Mattie's forehead. She understood Mattie's reluctance. Mattie knew more than anyone what it was like to live with strangers.

"Okay, Mattie," Shy relented, "I'll take good care of him. I'll call you a bit later." Mattie opened her eyes once more, but they were heavy. She smiled and then fell back asleep.

Shy ran by Mattie's house to make sure the heat had been restored. She packed Jake an overnight bag and made sure both doors were locked. At home, she fed and bathed the baby. Later that evening, Shy called the hospital to ease Mattie's anxiety over having been separated from Jake. She allowed Mattie to chatter and coo with Jake until she felt comfortable and ready to go back to sleep.

Putting Jake on a blanket in the living room floor with several little plastic toys, she called Bill, but no one answered. She paged him and then sat the phone down and waited for his call. Shy played with Jake another half hour until his eyes began to droop. He rubbed his chubby cheeks and cried crankily. She picked the baby up and cradled him in her arms as she went to the kitchen for a bottle. Shy let the bottle sit in a cup of hot water and went upstairs to get a blanket from Jake's things. He fussed, becoming increasingly anxious for his bottle.

"Shh," she bounced up and down gently and talked to him soothingly. "You miss your mommy don't you?" She grabbed his blanket and headed back downstairs. The bottle had warmed nicely, and Shy shook it several seconds to evenly distribute its temperature. Jake kicked hard and tried desperately to coordinate his hands to grab the bottle.

Shy stuck it in his mouth. "That's better isn't it?" Jake slurped the bottle greedily. "My goodness you were hungry."

Sitting in the blue rocker beside the large picture window in the living room, Shy held the baby close, rocking slowly, back and forth until Jake's eyes closed wearily and his breath slowed to a soft, steady rhythm. After a few minutes, she slowly pulled the bottle from his mouth. Milk covered his chin and dribbled down his neck. His lips, tongue, and cheeks were still working together in a reflexive sucking motion as if the bottle were still in his mouth. Shy took the end of the blanket and wiped the milk from his chin and neck. She stared at him, cradling him affectionately against her chest and stroking his soft, velvety hair. What a beautiful little angel. Who could have guessed that something so precious could emerge from the birth canal of Mattie Johnson?

She had actually started to like Mattie and her child-like spirit. Shy continued to be amazed that in all of Mattie's twenty three years, she'd never learned anything about caring for her own body or a home, much less another human being. In spite of her shortcomings, Mattie had managed to learn a great deal in four short months.

The lights were out in the living room. Shy held the baby until the room turned from a dusky glow, to light blue, and finally to total darkness, where the only light was the full moon shimmering through the large picture window. Until now, Shy had not realized how much she'd fallen in love with this little boy.

It all haunted her in a way, and made her grieve for the child she would never have. As Shy looked down onto the cherub, she sighed bitterly. The slow rhythm of baby breath sounds was music to a song she would never call her own. A cruel thing fate is, that it would bring this child into her life and thrust him against her breast for the duration of one night, tormenting her with only a glimmer of how motherhood might feel.

She shook her head as if to physically remove the memory of the painful surgery that removed endometriosis, along with her fallopian tubes and both ovaries. It was a necessary surgery, but it shattered so many dreams- dreams of cradling her own baby, a baby just like little Jake. She wiped a tear that stained her left cheek.

Shy went upstairs to the makeshift crib she'd made from a compilation of pillows and blankets. She lay Jake down gently. He wiggled objectionably then nestled down with a quiet drone. The breathing slowed its pace again and soon it was apparent that Jake had moved back into the unconscious world of baby dreams.

Exhausted from such an eventful day, Shy began to move from her knees to the bed. She took one last look at the sleeping baby and found his aura drawing her back to him. Something was wrong. Shy laid her hand gently on Jake's back and felt his soft, shallow, baby breath. She then touched his cheek lightly to see if he had a fever. After convincing herself that Jake was fine, Shy moved up to the side of the bed and sat there, hands folded in her lap, unable to take her eyes off him. Trepidation began to stir so deeply within her soul that her skin began to dimple with goose bumps. She couldn't pinpoint the fear, but it surrounded the infant. The child was fine, she thought, but something seemed to tell her that he would not always be. There was an element of danger and chaos in the child's fate. She tried to rationalize it but found panic instead, sweeping through her veins with such a jolt that she found herself once again on her knees beside him.

She picked the baby up and held him to her chest tightly as if to shelter him from his own fate. Overwhelming feelings of fear and desperation filled her lungs and threatened to suffocate her. She closed her eyes and uttered, "God, please." Her voice rang with an urgency that only a mother might feel for her child. As she fought back tears of helplessness, she tried to calm down from a fear that she could neither see nor hear- a fear that had no logical rationale but was no less real or terrifying.

Shy swiped at the tears that had begun to spill over her lashes and dribble about her cheeks. As she sat in the darkened room rocking Jake gently, her plea was formed as a whisper, but her soul was screaming, "God, please protect this child."

Shy shook back to reality as a car pulled out in front of her. She had been driving a full twenty minutes since she left Mattie's and realized that she was now almost to the city limits. Had she been reminiscing that long? Amazing, she thought, how one could operate a complex automobile and stay on track of directions while completely lost in thought.

It was hard to believe that it had only been five short months ago that she had kept Jake the night Mattie went into the hospital. He's grown and changed so much since then. Shy wondered what had frightened her so badly that night. Now and again she still prayed about it.

Mattie had waited until she could no longer see Shy down the highway before she took Jake back to his room and laid him in his playpen. She put some large colored blocks in there with him to keep him entertained. Jake's room was small and could hardly contain his playpen, the small chest of drawers, and an array of toys that she'd bought with Shy at various yard sales and flea markets.

The brown carpeting on the floor was worn and appeared to be over thirty years old. A small closet with rolling doors stood adjacent to the playpen. One of the doors fell off the track two weeks ago, and instead of getting the door repaired, Mattie chose to tear it completely off. Half of the closet's contents were now exposed at all times. Four outfits hung neatly on wire hangers inside the tiny closet. One of Mattie's kitchen chairs sat in the corner with a collage of diapers, baby wipes, socks, and pajamas beside it. The room was as neat as her room, the bathroom, and the kitchen.

For weeks Mattie applauded herself at the ingenious plan she had come up with to keep Shy from closing her case. All she had to do was make Shy think that she still needed help learning to keep her house clean. Knowing that Shy would be coming on Monday's, Mattie would spend all day Sunday destroying her kitchen and living room. Shy never went into the back part of the house so Mattie would leave those rooms clean. She loaded the sink and counters with dishes after dirtying them up with ketchup, mustard, milk, and anything else she could find. She put trash and dirty clothes all over the floor and furniture.

This week she even planned ahead. She kept a glass of milk under her kitchen sink and let it curdle all week. When she heard Shy's car pull up, she poured it on the linoleum floor in the living room. She was very proud of her plan. She knew it made Shy mad at her. *But she kept coming back now, didn't she?*

Mattie began picking up the newspaper, paper towels, and plastic sacks she'd strewn about the room, and she collected all of the dirty clothes and placed them in the laundry basket. She worked hard and fast except for the breaks she took to tend to Jake. After the laundry was picked up, she adjusted her weight on one knee so that she could clean up the soured milk and wipe the area down with bleach. Streams of sweat poured from Mattie's forehead as she scanned the room and examined her progress. The room was as clean as it was yesterday.

Mattie was thankful she didn't mess up the kitchen this time. She was tired yesterday and decided to wait until this morning to start demolishing. Mattie had been so busy in the living room that she lost track of time and wasn't able to disassemble the kitchen. She closed the door to the kitchen and planned to work extra hard at keeping Shy in the living room. And when it was time for the Sprikes, Mattie would just slip into the kitchen and then back out before Shy could see. The whole plan worked beautifully.

Shy didn't want a Sprite today. This normally would have upset Mattie, but not today. Mattie went to the back to check on Jake again. He was happily chewing on a green plastic block.

She walked back into the kitchen, fixed herself a glass of iced tea, and held it briefly to the stream of sunlight shining through the window. It was perfect- the color and everything. She brought it to her lips and took a sip. And it tasted just right, too. *Ain't no tea anywhere's any better than what's in my glass, and I made it all by myself.* Not just anybody could make a good glass of tea like she could. She even gave Jake a sip in his bottle the other day, and she could tell that he was proud that his mama knew how to make it.

   She grabbed a clean cloth from the drawer under the sink, and wiped it across her forehead, exposing the sweat-drenched fabric under her arm. She thought about what Shy had said- that they would still be friends even after the case was closed. This made her extremely happy. She would have kept messing up the house if she had to but now she wouldn't need to. Shy would still be her friend, no matter what. She took another hard gulp of her tea and smiled gleefully. *Ain't life grand?*

Chapter Three

Bill Williams sat in the café style dining area of Maburn's only Asian restaurant. He tapped his fingers impatiently when a "not so Asian" freckled, red head chirped, "Whatcha gonna have today, hon?"

"I'm waiting on someone, but I'll go ahead and take an iced tea now. Matter of fact, make it two iced teas." He knew that Shy would want tea- tea with extra ice, half a packet of sweetener, and no lemon to be exact.

"Sure thing." The waitress scribbled on a note pad and off she went, swinging her hips in a pendulum fashion. Bill thought she reminded him of Flo on the 'seventies' sitcom, "Alice." He was sure that any moment he would hear her say, "Kiss my grits."

Shy was to arrive any minute. He looked at his watch and thought he'd go ahead and fix his salad. The bar was laden with numerous grazing items. Bill put a bit of lettuce on his plate and then covered it with mounds of potato salad, cottage cheese and chunks of sharp cheddar. He spooned on ranch dressing until it oozed off the side of the plate and onto his finger. He sprinkled bacon bits and croutons and then headed back to his chair.

The jingle of the bell fastened to the inside of the door caught Bill's attention. Shy saw him immediately and smiled as she pulled off her sunglasses. Her dark brown hair fell about her shoulders evenly. She had an hourglass figure but looked particularly slender in her short black dress. Bill always felt like her dark brown eyes saw right through to his core. He made a strong effort to suck in his stomach.

"Hey, starting without me?" she asked as she moved the chair to sit down, placing her purse to the side.

He smiled back at her. "You know me. How's your day so far?"

"Pretty good for a Monday. I think I may have accomplished a breakthrough with Mattie. I'll tell you all about it in just a second. I'm gonna go ahead and fix myself a salad. Would you order me an iced tea?"

"Done."

"Thanks. Be right back."

Shy began filling her plate with lettuce, dainty carrots, and morsels of mixed vegetables. She dribbled low calorie vinaigrette then headed back to the table.

"Fit for a rabbit," Bill chuckled, feeling somewhat embarrassed by his mountain of a salad that had already begun to ooze off his plate and onto the table. Flo came back with two iced teas.

"What can I get for you two, today?"

"I think I'm just going to have a salad. And can I get some extra ice?" Shy asked.

Bill smiled at his forethought when Shy ordered the extra ice. He thought he probably knew more about Sharon Sauze than she knew about herself.

"Sure," the waitress said as she chomped on a bright pink piece of bubble gum that seemed entirely too big for her mouth. "What about you, hon?"

"I think I'll just have a salad, also," Bill said. The waitress scribbled on her pad, tucked her pencil behind her ear and bounced off.

"Did I just step into the Twilight Zone?" Shy said, taking a sip of her tea.

"Mel's Diner?" Bill asked with a grin.

Shy choked, laughing so hard that tea came out of her nose. All she could do was point at him and nod her head, holding her mouth to keep the remaining portion of tea in her mouth.

Bill was thrilled that he could make her laugh that hard and thought he would milk it for what it was worth.

He continued, "She looks like Flo, doesn't she? I thought the very same thing. Funny the things we remember." Shy nodded, still snickering a bit. She wiped the tears from the corner of her eyes and emptied half a packet of sweetener into her tea and then stirred the mixture slowly.

Shy always said grace before she ate, and today was no exception. She was a devout Christian, or tried to be. She never intruded on anyone else's beliefs or asked others to join her in prayer. It just wasn't in her nature. She simply bowed her head discreetly, said a quick "thanks" and that was it.

Bill had grown accustomed, although not entirely comfortable with this ritual. Having never grown up in a "churchy" home, he couldn't completely understand the concept of prayer. He knew that she would respect him no less if he didn't bow his head, but he did it anyway. After a moment of uncomfortable silence, Bill would watch her in his peripheral for the cue when he could look up. Once the prayer was over, Bill immediately engaged her in conversation.

"So, tell me about this alleged breakthrough with Mattie Johnson." His cynicism had always annoyed Shy, and she fought the urge to tell him. Bill had worked for the agency over fifteen years. The effects of working in a field with such emotional intensity were renowned and somewhat dangerous for a man in his position. He rarely showed any emotion on even the most heinous abuse cases.

One time he came back from the hospital after a three month old had been shaken fiercely by the mother's boyfriend. The child had lived for three days but died due to a hemorrhage in his brain. Shy immediately went to Bill's office to see if he was okay. She assumed the experience had been emotionally traumatic for him as it would have been for her. In fact, Bill showed so little emotion that it made her feel uneasy. At one point in the conversation he made the comment, "If you've seen one dead baby, you've seen them all."

Shy immediately lost all control of emotion. She said more curse words than she had said in all of her twenty-four years. Among other things, she told him that the children of Maburn County would never be effectively safeguarded as long as he was the supervisor of child protective services. She also told him that she wouldn't be a part of any team led by him. She ranted a bit more then stormed out of his office. After twenty minutes, she came to Bill's office with resignation in hand, slammed it on his desk and left without saying a word.

Bill felt disgusted with himself. He remembered the way he used to be before the visions of cruelty to children took its toll. He too thought he could save the world. Now he was much more a realist then a hero. As much as he admired her stoicism, he knew that eventually, even she would harden to the cold realities of the real world.

He made arrangements to go see her after work that day. Because of the freeze placed on state employee positions, Shy was his only worker, and he couldn't afford to lose her. Besides that, he didn't want to lose her. She was the best in the field. He was also becoming well aware that he had feelings for her. He knew he shouldn't, but he nonetheless did. At her home that evening, hat in hand, he apologized, telling her some nonsense about the whole experience of the baby dying being quite traumatic, and he just felt like he would better be able to cope with it by acting as if he didn't care. She fell for it and even apologized for not seeing through it. This made him feel like an even bigger jerk. But that was two years ago, and he had promised himself that he would be more guarded with his rough exterior around Shy.

"So, let me take an educated guess about what Mattie's house looked like."

"Okay, but you might be surprised," she said. Bill squinted his eyes and looked at her inquisitively.

Shy swallowed what little she'd put in her mouth. "I think Mattie teaches me something new every time I go out there. I'm thinking she's been intentionally messing up her house to keep me from closing her case." Shy's eyebrows were raised a bit. Her lips hinted of a smile.

"No kidding? Did she tell you that?"

"No, not exactly." She proceeded to tell Bill about the filth in the living room and then the spotless kitchen.

"So, what's your take on that?" He shoveled a mound full of salad concoction in his mouth. A bit of white dressing decorated his beard. Shy continued to talk but had a difficult time taking her eyes off of the creamy smudge.

"Well, Mattie kept the entire house clean until I told her that she was doing well enough that I could close her case and stop coming out every week. Mattie has no friends or family here in Arkansas, and I'm wondering if she hasn't been sabotaging the closure of the case so that I'll continue to come and see her each week."

"Hmmm, maybe. So, whatcha gonna do?"

"I told Mattie today that I will still be her friend and come see her, even if the case closes."

"What? You can't mean that."

"I do mean it, Bill. Mattie has no one. If giving up a bit of my time to visit with her now and then will make her life a bit brighter, I'm happy to do it. In the mean time, I'm going to look into local functions that Mattie can be involved with to increase her social supports. Maybe then she won't feel so dependent on me. She just needs friends, Bill. She's lonely for adult companionship."

"She's a client, Shy."

"She won't be when the case is closed."

"I think you're over-invested. Why would you want to spend your free time with people like that, anyway?" He crinkled his nose and shuddered as if he'd just gotten a whiff of rotten meat.

Shy felt the slow rise of irritation that she had come to expect in her discussions with Bill. Any expression of feeling for clients was "over-investment" where he was concerned.

"Bill, you and I look at things differently. I'd like to not discuss this any further."

"Okay. Geez. Calm down. I didn't mean to upset you. Please continue with what you were saying. Please."

She began speaking with a tone of reluctance in her voice. "I just think that if my theory holds true, Mattie's house will be clean on Monday." She dabbled at a carrot dripping with vinaigrette, not even looking at him. Bill squinted his eyes and smiled at her.

"And what if it isn't?"

"If it isn't, I ..." her eyes roamed as if searching for something to say. She finally fell back in her chair in resignation.

"I don't want to put Jake in foster care, Bill. I can't imagine what kind of psychological damage it would do to him. I mean, if I hold him for any length of time, he starts crying for his mother. There's a strong bond between them." She looked at Bill with genuine concern. "He doesn't need to be with strangers." She sighed heavily, "I just hope I'm right about Mattie." She shrugged away from the topic before Bill could speak.

"So," she said forking at a cucumber, "how has your day been so far? Any new reports?"

"Just one but it turned out to be a custody dispute."

Shy shook her head in disgust. She found it amazing how some people used their kids for retribution against an estranged spouse, even to the point of making false child abuse allegations. As if the kids hadn't been through enough from mom and dad splitting up. Let's throw in an intrusive interview and full body inspection by a complete stranger. No big deal. A child's emotional trauma is a small price to pay for sweet revenge. Shy wondered how kids these days even had a chance.

The ding of the door caught Bill's attention. "Oh look," Bill said with his face appearing somewhat bemused, "your boyfriend just walked in."

Shy turned and saw Sheriff Tills walk into the restaurant with a new cop she'd never seen before. Sheriff Tills was a tall, big-bellied man who made a huge appearance, and often a jackass of himself, wherever he went. Tills was constantly creating opportunities to win future votes.

Shy couldn't remember a single time when he wasn't a complete glutton for attention. His face was in the newspaper every other day. And if it wasn't, he made sure to call the Maburn Dailey and let them in on some heroic deed he'd performed for the citizens of this great community. In Shy's opinion, he single handedly topped the charts of egoistic masturbation. Just looking at him made her cringe, and Bill knew this all too well.

"We're in luck," Bill said under his breath, "he's coming this way." Shy rolled her eyes.

Cries of the Orchids

"Well, hi there folks," Tills bellowed from across the room as he walked toward them, "who'duv guessed I'd run into two of my favorite people today?"

Shy felt a sudden tug at her stomach as it began to knot. Her shoulders tensed. Bill stood up to shake Tills' hand. Shy continued to sit, barely even making eye contact. The wave of cigars and cheap cologne permeated the air around their table. She wondered if "Flo" would be willing to open a window.

Tills directed their attention to the man beside him.

"This here's my new rookie, Ben Crossno. I'm tryin' to teach him a thing or two about Maburn."

Tills stuck his chest out as if he were the all-knowing vessel of erudition, teaching the less fortunate. Shy wanted to puke. Bill shook the stranger's hand. "Nice to have you in Maburn. Where are you from?"

"San Diego and thank you, I'm happy to be here."

"Wow, you've traveled some distance. What brings you to these parts?"

"Family. I was actually born in Little Rock. My folks moved to California when I was two."

"This must be quite a change for you."

"Certainly is."

"You were a cop out there, were ya?"

"Yes, sir."

"I bet you have a lot less to do here, with the crime rate being so much lower and all."

Tills seemed almost offended by this. He wanted the world to think that he constantly and humbly puts his life on the line for the good citizens of Maburn. He jumped in before Ben could answer.

"Well, " he grunted, "we have to give a lot of credit to the sheriff's office for our low crime rate." He tugged at his belt, which barely sat atop the crack of his rear end, and immediately changed the subject, lest anyone challenge the density of crime in Maburn.

"Have you met Miss Sauze?" Tills put his hand on Shy's shoulder as he spoke. It took a great deal of self-control on Shy's part not to jerk her shoulder away and smack him in the face. She took in a deep breath. *Just be polite.* She smiled at Ben.

"You ever have a problem that involves a kid and this little lady a help ya out." Shy grimaced at "little lady" but managed to hold her hand out politely for a handshake.

"These two work for the Department of Human Services. They get involved with all the child abuse stuff. And we couldn't have two finer people doing the job." After a moment of grinning, nodding, and looking like a complete idiot, Tills turned his attention to Ben. "Well, boy, we better get to eatin'. We've got a big day ahead of us. Good to see you two." He displayed his "don't forget to vote for me" smile and then barked at the waitress.

"Young lady, we'll have a couple of iced teas over at that table by the window." He gave Shy a final pat causing her neck and shoulders to prickle in complete annoyance.

"So nice to meet you." Ben shook Bill's hand again.

"You too. If there's anything we can do to help you get settled in just let us know."

"I certainly will. Thanks." He turned to Shy. "And what did you say your name was?"

She smiled politely, "Sharon Sauze. My friends call me 'Shy.'"

"Shy," he pondered, "that's interesting. I'd like to hear the history behind that, sometime."

"All right," she said with a chuckle, "maybe I'll share it with you sometime." He grinned at her, looking hard into her eyes and then turned and walked away. Bill felt a twinge of jealousy rising in his belly. Ben was a young guy, about twenty-nine, who still had a full head of hair. And unlike Bill, his stomach stayed well within the waistline of his britches. He tried to dismiss it.

In the far corner of the restaurant, Sheriff Tills' voice boomed loudly as he "Hey, good buddied" every other man that walked in.

"I wonder if Tills can talk any louder over there."

Shy let out a quick giggle. "He fits the politician prototype, doesn't he?"

Bill agreed. "Speaking of politicians, Mayor Kult was on the local news station at ten o'clock this morning. He says that he's working on a plan that will drastically lower the need for state welfare services in our city."

Cries of the Orchids

"Really? What's the plan?" She put a medium sized chunk of iceberg lettuce in her mouth.

"Something about a grant given by the federal government to develop services to help unemployed mothers get back into the work force."

"Like what kind of services?"

"I don't know. He said that he would go into more detail about the specifics at a later time. I can only assume that it would involve education and job skills training."

"It's a wonderful idea," Shy said, forking at her food, "imagine what that would do for our economy if it were successful on a national level. Even still, I'll have to see it to believe it. There's something I don't like about that guy. I can't put my finger on it."

Jack Kult ran for mayor of Maburn some ten years ago but lost miserably. Having grown up with extensive familial wealth, Jack assumed that his deceased father's fine reputation as a state senator would prime him for the position. He had felt publicly humiliated by the miniscule amount of votes he'd accumulated at the polls. With numbers that small, he wasn't even sure if his own mother voted for him. Three years ago he pulled himself up by the bootstraps and decided to run for City Council Chairman. There were no other candidates running and he, subsequently, won the position. Two years after swearing into office the current mayor, as luck would have it, was indicted for extortion and Kult became the new mayor. Having fought long and hard to get where he was, he would do whatever was necessary to stay there.

"All that to say," Shy continued with a smile, "I will try to keep an open mind."

"Yeah, me too." Bill was unaware that a large chunk of potato salad laden with ranch dressing had fallen down his shirt and onto his pants.

"Bill, you spilled something on your shirt."

"Dadgummit." He grabbed a napkin and began cleaning up.

"Hey," he said putting the dirty napkin on the table, "you hear about the Watsons?"

"Carol Watson?"

"Yeah, their house burned down last night."

"What? No, I didn't hear. I've been at Mattie's all morning. Are they all okay?"

Bill loved having Shy's undivided attention even when he was the provider of bad news. She stared at him, waiting for an answer.

"Afraid not." He spooned an enormous amount of salad concoction in his mouth and continued to chew with his mouth open.

"Are they hurt?" Shy was growing impatient. She said this with a combination of both concern and irritation.

Bill shook his head. "All dead."

Shy held both hands to her face. "What!" She looked at him wide-eyed. "Oh, dear God." Her stomach ground itself into a large knot and threatened to regurgitate what little she had in it.

"How, uh," she could hardly speak. Her words were slow and barely audible, "how did it happen?" Her body felt weak with shock.

"Not sure. Hey, are you all right?"

"No, I guess I'm not."

Bill displayed an apologetic expression. "Because of this? I'm sorry to have upset you again. I guess I'm on a roll."

"No," Shy held her hands back up to her face, "I just, uh, I didn't sleep well last night and I …"

Bill interrupted with a swallow of guilt. "Why don't you go home and rest? I can cover the rest of the day."

"I think I'll take you up on that." She dug in her purse and left a five-dollar bill on the table. She worked hard to fight back inevitable tears and was anxious to make it to her car before her emotions broke.

"I'll see you tomorrow," Bill said. She turned away from him as he tenderly added, "Call me if you need anything."

She nodded without looking back. Bill watched her walk away. The skirt of her black dress was immediately entangled in a quick tuft of wind as she walked through the door into the elements. Bill caught a glimpse of her upper thigh, and it gave him goose bumps.

He wondered if he would ever have the courage to tell Shy how much he loved her. Her dark eyes seemed to penetrate his soul and made him wonder if she already knew his secret. Seeing her five days a week for the last two years has brought back the spirit that he'd left for dead during his early thirties.

Bill and his wife divorced almost twenty years ago. Since that time, he's never found anyone that stirred his hormones like Shy Sauze. He tried not to let it show but sometimes just thinking of her reduced him to the pimply faced teenager of his youth, unable to even concentrate on matters at hand. All too often he found himself in an important meeting or investigation, drifting off with her to a secret place where she loved him as much as he loved her. And yet his daydreams always drew him to the same miserable question. What would an intelligent, beautiful, twenty-six year old want with a short, balding man in his late forties? He sighed heavily as he always did when pining for her.

As he watched her get into her car he was suddenly aware that he had let his belly return to its natural state, comparable to six months gestation. He turned back to see if there was a line at the food bar. Sheriff Tills was returning to his table. Bill noticed the rookie staring out the window, curiously consumed with something on the parking lot. Bill felt the tease of the green-eyed monster he'd learned to cope with since he had met Shy. He tried to shrug it away, but jealousy didn't shrug easily for him. The new deputy continued to watch Shy as she pulled out of the parking lot. Bill suddenly found that his appetite had ceased. "Waitress, could I please get my check?"

Shy pulled into the drive of her two-bedroom apartment. Her head had begun to pound and she feared the beginnings of another migraine headache. Maybe not, perhaps it was just tension, and she would be able to avoid the pounding jolts of pain that crippled her with each debilitating migraine. She'd stopped and bought a paper on the way home and now clutched it under her left arm as she struggled to get the door open.

The neighbor kids were playing basketball at the side of the apartment. They all stopped and waved at her. Malarie and Kaci were twins. They were seven years old. Their older brother, Kaleb, was nine. The girls' bedroom was directly across from Shy's, and she would often see them in the window, lift hers up and talk with them across the brief expanse of yard. They were all sweet kids. Normally, Shy would have put her things down and played with them. Today, she just wanted to get inside quickly before they had a chance to run over and chat with her.

Inside she went straight to the kitchen to get some Tylenol. She knew that trying to get a migraine stopped with Tylenol was a joke but hoped that maybe she would only have a mild headache rather than the crippling sort. She choked down two pills with a hard gulp of water, made an ice pack, and closed all the shades in the living room. After thirty minutes of lying on the couch in the dark, the pressure in her head had eased just a bit. No migraine this time. The phone rang and she reached behind her to the receiver on the end table.

"Hi, Nelson. Not really. It's been a long day."

Nelson had been one of her best friends since childhood. His family had moved in to her all white neighborhood when they were both seven years old. Maburn was known for being anti-black, anti-gay, anti-Jew, anti-anything but "white male, happy to invite you to church on Sunday" community. Nelson's family was the only black family that had the grit to withstand it.

Unfortunately, Nelson had endured the brunt of it. She'd watched him being tortured on the playground, and saw the teachers turn their heads. One day, a group of four kids had him down on the ground, brutalizing him. Shy and three of her girlfriends jumped in the middle and started hitting back. Two of the girls drew blood and one of the perpetrators left with a broken nose.

All three of the girls were sent to the principal's office. They were given hard paddlings that blistered their bottoms and legs. None of them cried. The principal expelled them and called their parents to come get them from school.

Shy's dad was the first to show. He was a tall brute of a man who could easily intimidate by appearance alone. He let few people know that he was a teddy bear at heart. He listened to the principal tell the story of the girls' attack.

Cries of the Orchids

"This was all over a black boy, huh?" Shy nodded but didn't speak. He squatted down low where he could look her squarely in the eyes. The principal stood beside him with his hands on his hips, trying hard not to smile at the scolding to come. Her dad was staring at her. His voice was stern, but his eyes were kind. He spoke slowly and distinctly.

"Was it worth it?"

Shy didn't hesitate with the answer. Her voice was also strong and distinct. "Yes, sir."

He stood and patted her on the head. "That's my girl."

The principal, of course, was infuriated by this and tried to intervene by telling Shy's dad that she needed to be disciplined. Shy's father asked her to stand out in the hall. When she was out of sight, her father grabbed the principal by the collar, pinned him against the wall and said, "If you ever put your hands on my daughter again, I'm going to discipline you."

From that day forward, she and Nelson were the best of friends. And none of the other kids messed with them for fear of what she and the other girls might do. They graduated high school together, started college together, and both became social workers.

Nelson worked two counties away from her in Saline where he'd been the supervisor now for two years. They didn't dare work in the same county together. Over the years the relationship had developed into a brother/sister kinship, and Nelson often accused Shy of being too bossy about everything including his personal life. He always said that if they worked in the same county they would end up killing each other. But that didn't stop them from trading war stories.

Even by telephone Shy could sense the concern in Nelson's voice as he said, "That sounds like an understatement to me."

"You heard about the Watsons?"

"Read it in the paper. Was it your case?"

"Yeah."

"I'm sorry, baby girl. You want me to come over?"

"No, my head's hurting. I just want to lie still for awhile."

"Are you having another migraine?"

"I don't think so. It's easing up a little."
"I wish you would go back to the doctor."
"I'll be fine. Can I call you later?"
"Sure. Promise to call if I can do anything?"
"Promise."

Hanging up the phone, she let it drop to the floor beside her. She wished she could sleep the headache off but there was probably no chance of that. She lay still for two hours, until the pressure had dropped to a tolerable level and she felt able to take a hot bath.

She walked upstairs, feeling groggy from the "would be" migraine. Her bedroom was spotless as always. It contained a queen size bed, a chest of drawers, and a throw rug. That was it. She could afford little more on a social worker's salary, and quite frankly that was all she wanted. Less to dust.

She went to her closet, grabbed her white, terrycloth bathrobe, took it into the bathroom and laid it across the counter. She lit an unscented candle on the back of the toilet and turned out the bathroom light, hoping this would further ease the pressure in her head. Starting the water in the bathtub, she held her hand under the faucet while she adjusted the temperature. She kept the towels under the sink but had forgotten that she'd just washed them this morning. They were all sitting in the dryer downstairs. *Damn.*

The walk back down the stairs felt almost like walking a marathon. The laundry room was just on the other side of the kitchen. She wondered why the blueprint person couldn't have made her life easier and just put it upstairs. Grabbing one towel, not wanting to fool with the rest, she started heading toward the stairs.

She saw the paper sitting on the kitchen table where she had left it. She knew the story about the Watsons was in there. That was the reason why she had bought it. She wanted to know the facts without hearing them from Bill.

She walked past it, thinking that she simply couldn't bear the grisly details right now. Before she reached the stairs, her curiosity had gotten the better of her, so she went back to the kitchen, sat at the table, and opened the paper. There was nothing about it on the front page. She flipped through until she saw a small insert on the fourth page headlined, "Five Burn to Death in House Fire."

The right side of Shy's head thumped harder as she continued to read. The paper listed the names and ages of the deceased. "Carol Watson 31, Daryl 8, Sean 6, Emily 3, and Sarah 3 weeks." The paper stated that the initial findings concluded only four deaths but then gave the gruesome details of having found three-week-old Sarah fused to her mother's body. The paper continued by saying that the infant's body had to be forcibly detached. Shy's eyes watered heavily. Carol was probably rocking the baby to sleep, she thought. How could this have happened? She read further that the cause of the fire was unknown and continued to be under investigation.

Shy had come to know Carol eight months prior to the baby's birth when she assisted the middle aged mother with a Medicaid application. During the initial intake Shy met the children: Daryl, Sean, and Emily, Carol's children. They all had a head full of dark brown hair with matching brown eyes. Carol frequently had to stop the intake to interrupt an argument between the boys or to stop Emily from jumping on the couch. Shy was impressed with Carol's ability to manage the kids so patiently considering all that she had gone through and the immense stress that she must have been dealing with as a single mother.

Carol's husband abandoned all of them after ten years of marriage but not before getting her pregnant one more time. Carol spent more than a decade staying at home and tending to her children. Although the family often lived paycheck to paycheck, she and the children had never wanted for anything.

Abandoned and pregnant, Carol felt devastated but determined to make it for her children. Abortion was not an option for Carol. She considered adoption until she began to feel the baby move. With government assistance, Carol was able to provide a home, food, and medical care for all of her children.

The day the baby was born; Shy stopped at a local thrift shop and found a beautiful layette set with white eyelet lace. It was used but looked brand new. Shy wrapped it in pink paper and put a large white bow on top. Carol loved the outfit. Shy remembered her saying, "I can't wait to put it on her."

Just before Shy opened the door to leave, Carol stopped her and said, "You know, Ms. Sauze," she looked sweetly from Shy to her baby, the serene glow of motherhood about her face, "we're going to make it."

Three short weeks later the mother's courage and promise of hope were incinerated, along with her four children. Shy put the paper down and went to the cabinet for another Tylenol. Tears spilled out about her cheeks, and her head felt as if it would explode. She walked upstairs as the headache continued with vicious pangs down the left side of her head. Each step felt as if a brick were rhythmically pounding against her skull.

The sunlight coming in from the bedroom window seemed ten times brighter than usual and caused her to squint. Any hope of avoiding a migraine was now gone. She pulled down the shade and stumbled into the bathroom to turn off the water. Tears emptied about her face and dripped down on her neck. She brushed them away only to have them replaced by others. The nausea hit, and she made it to the toilet just in time to throw up and heave until her stomach muscles were aching.

She grabbed the robe from the counter to wipe her face, took off her shoes, and climbed into bed fully dressed. She covered her head with a pillow and tried desperately not to think of the Watsons.

The candle in the bathroom burned all night.

Chapter Four

Kayline Hathcock sat behind an enormous oak desk and sighed heavily. The work continued to pile up and yet the state was taking its dear sweet time replacing her computer. Her work hours had almost doubled since her old Macintosh had broken down almost three weeks ago. The professional but annoying voice from central office repeated the same blanket statement the last four times she had called to see when it would be ready.

"It will be there in the next day or so." She thought she would throw the phone across the room if she had to hear that one more time.

Kayline had been working for the state crime lab for just over ten years. She'd worked her way up from answering the phone in the file room to assisting the medical examiner. She balanced her full-time job and two years of continuing education to get where she was and finally felt like a real human being within the system. The state crime lab examiner, Doctor John C. Collins, was an arrogant man but she'd gotten used to him and was thankful that her only boss was THE boss.

Collins' luxurious office sat directly behind Kayline's desk. No one could get to Collins without going through her first. She really didn't mind being his bulldog. It gave her a sense of authority where she would otherwise hunker in her low self-esteem. Sometimes she even enjoyed getting to be "firm" with people, especially those who had been rude to her at one time or another during her tenure at the crime lab, probably not even remembering her name. With pursed lips and arched eyebrows she would say, "Dr. Collins is a very busy man. Do you have an appointment?" This gave her a strange sense of pleasure.

Her job duties continued to increase with each passing year while her salary continued to stagnate at the maximum salary allowed for her education level. She was glad to learn new things, though, and figured the experience would benefit her someday.

On several occasions she actually assisted Collins with autopsies. A big feat, considering there was a time when just being in a funeral home gave her the willies. Now she was touching and handling cadavers on a regular basis. She'd grown accustomed to the stale chemical smell of the morgue along with the sterile atmosphere. She no longer had nightmares of dead bodies coming to life with blank, zombie-like stares, reaching for her, trying to avenge her for mutilating their bodies. Being in the morgue was now like any other day. In fact, it wasn't uncommon for Collins and her to stop an autopsy, break for lunch and return to complete the exam after filling their stomachs.

Kayline looked at the miniature clock sitting on the side of her desk. The brass timepiece had such tiny hands that she had to lean forward and squint to see the time. It was forty-five minutes after four and time to start wrapping things up. She shuffled and organized papers into her file cabinet, and then she put some lab work in Collins' box for review. She tidied up her desk and prepared to leave.

Collins opened the door behind her. He was a tall, handsome man who always wore expensive suits. His dark hair had only a touch of gray for his forty-six years and seemed to match his charcoal eyes identically.

"We've got five crispy critters on the way," he said without smiling. He dropped a thick manila folder in front of her.

"Where from?"

"Maburn. They'll be here first thing in the morning, so I'll need you to be on time."

This annoyed her. Her record for days missed was impeccable. In the three and a half years she'd worked for Collins, she had always been at least twenty minutes early each day and had only missed four days of work. She'd accumulated almost forty vacation days and knew she would probably never get to use them.

"I'll be here with bells on," she chirped as she grabbed her purse and prepared to leave.

"Go ahead and review the chart before you leave. And separate it out. Make one chart for each of them." He turned and walked back into his office.

Kayline immediately began to feel the prickles of anger about her neck and shoulders. Collins never failed to dump work on her at the last minute. He had probably received the chart hours ago and inevitably waited until four forty-five to heap it on her. She slouched back in the chair and flung the chart open so hard that it hit her desk with a hefty smack. Collins opened the door to his office with the jacket of his Armani suite lying neatly over his right arm.

"Everything okay in here?" His eyebrows were arched suspiciously.

"Everything's fine. I just dropped my purse." Her bright blue eyes helped mask the anger.

"All right, then, I'll see you in the morning." He grabbed his briefcase and walked, chin up, out of the office.

"Jackass," Kayline uttered aloud after he left. Her shoulders and neck began to ache in frustration.

For two seconds she thought about leaving the chart until morning. Collins would often have her do paperwork, sort, and file as if he were going to do the procedure the moment the cadaver entered the building. It never happened. She would stay late in the office the night before, getting everything prepped and ready for him to start the next morning, and he would inevitably wait a week or more before he started. It really pissed her off. She knew it would be the same this time. But with her luck, the first time she did anything against her boss' wishes, he'd find out and she sure wasn't going to give him the satisfaction of reprimanding her.

She read the first page to get the general demographics. The fire occurred on 1617 Troll Street in Maburn. According to the coroner's report, a woman in her early thirties, three small children and an infant were in the home. All were burned beyond recognition. The chart also contained reports from the sheriff's office, the coroner, and the local fire department. All reports indicated accidental death.

How sad, she thought, putting the chart to the side and cringing at Collins' reference to burned bodies as "crispy critters." She could only assume that two decades of examining disfigured corpses would naturally produce an apathetic creature like Collins.

She filed the chart under M for Maburn. How odd, she thought, noticing Maburn's ratio of cases to the others. Maybe the bureaucrats in Maburn were insecure about their own diagnostic skills. Why else would Maburn have nearly three times the cases sent to the crime lab as the other counties? She noticed that the S section was large also. Out of curiosity she thumbed through to find that Saline also had a disproportionate number of cases. But still less than Maburn.

She shut the drawer and turned to get her purse, thankful Collins wasn't there to give her something else to do. "Jerk," she uttered, feeling a strong sense of assertion now that she was alone. She took a deep breath as she turned to lock the office door and looked at her watch. It was almost six. She would run by McDonald's on the way home and curl up to the television with a pile of salted fries.

She felt depressed that a re-run of Alley McBeal was all she had to look forward to this evening. Kayline was a large-framed beauty with long, blonde hair and an impeccable taste for clothes. Unfortunately, she had a very low self-esteem and often let it interfere with her social life.

She walked to the elevator and sighed heavily, "Me and my mundane life."

Collins drove down Marizone Avenue with the top down on his red Porsche. The wind gusted violently through his thinning hair. At the stoplight, he looked over at a pretty blonde in a white Trans Am next to him. He put on a cocky grin and gave a half nod. She looked away without smiling. *Dyke*, he thought and gunned the accelerator just before the light turned green. That any skirt would not, at the very least, give him a smile was enough to determine that she was a lesbian.

Cries of the Orchids

Collins grabbed his cell phone and punched in several numbers without looking. He ran his fingers through his hair and adjusted his sun glasses. "Hey, Buddy, yeah, I got off about twenty minutes ago. They'll be here in the morning. Don't worry, man, I got it all covered. Sure, a stiff one sounds great about now. Okay, I'll see you in about fifteen." He hung up the phone and turned left on Clark Street heading toward the capitol.

Collins and Mayor Kult had been friends long before Kult came into office. During the preliminaries, Collins gave large financial contributions to his friend's campaign. Kult returned the favor by using his father's connections to keep Collins at the crime lab. They made a pact to keep each other in office no matter what it took.

When Kult learned of the five billion dollar federal grant to reduce state welfare services, he devised a plan to further fund his political campaign without tapping into his family's resources. The plan was ingenious in its simplicity in that it would also make the citizens of Maburn grateful to him- the one who miraculously increased the bulk of the town's wallet. It was crucial; however, to find folks that could be trusted to keep their mouths shut. This wasn't too difficult. Once the pallet was wet with the receiving end of extortion, most of his friends could keep a secret.

Kult made a public announcement that he was currently working on a way to balance the budget in Maburn. He said the town could expect to feel the rewards of the plan by the middle of next year. Collins and Kult, along with the club members of Maburn and Saline, were coming up with the fictitious scheme that would be shared with the public. And they would have to launder the money they made. Not too difficult, but they had to be careful- no paper trails.

Collins veered onto Interstate 10 toward Maburn. He and Kult would have another long talk about their future endeavors. He was due to make a great deal of money, especially if a couple of other towns in Arkansas became committed to the program- and who wouldn't? The collective collaboration of all of the liberals in the country could never daunt the potential benefits the plan could have on the nation. It would take a lot of time and careful planning,

Terri Bailey

but with the right leader, the remuneration- seen in black and white- would certainly keep the bleeding hearts in check. It was a win-win situation, he reminded himself.

Chapter Five

Ben Crossno left the courthouse with a bounce in his walk. He'd stayed after his shift with some of the other deputies to watch the hyped up boxing match on HBO. The excitement coupled with the high density of testosterone permeated the air as he opened the door to his red Jeep Wrangler. It was a good match. And a good time to bond with his fellow colleagues.

He was finally getting settled in Maburn, Arkansas. He felt legends away from his roots, but found himself growing a liking to the quiet town. The other deputies were beginning to warm up to him. It was important that they befriend him. Trust was crucial in his line of work.

He spent the first four weeks of his new job learning the likes and dislikes of his colleagues, inviting them over for cookouts, and staying late at work to help. It didn't take long before the deputies started inviting him for a beer after work. He even heard Sheriff Tills making a nice comment or two.

He was still not quite used to the air of central Arkansas. Maburn was a far cry from being the cultural center of the earth. It had the local Wal-Mart and a Sonic Drive In, and that was pretty much it. Being born and raised just outside of Los Angeles, he was accustomed to an area of heavily congested liberals, where people pranced about half-clothed and did just about anything they wanted. The most exciting thing to do in Maburn was to decipher what type of road kill lay up ahead before getting to it.

Ben got his education from the University of California at Berkley in criminal justice. His career was booming, and he found his life out "in the real world" to be thrilling and satisfying. Working the streets of L.A. kept him on his toes. A mere traffic stop could lead to serious danger, and he was always aware of this.

After four years of working for the Los Angeles Police Department, he was promoted to sergeant. Then the Fed came, and the roller coaster ride began. He was transferred to Arkansas last year and endured four months of intensive training. After preparing and polishing another two months, he took the Civil Service exam, passed it, and sent out five applications to various counties in the southern portion of Arkansas. He was hired by the Hot Spring County Sheriff's office six weeks ago and was given a physical and a psychological exam. Everything was go, and he was now an official deputy.

He longed to go back home, missing his family and the beach. Outside of his job, he found his life here at Maburn to be fairly boring. Until today. Today he'd found the first woman in years to make his heart flutter.

Ben was never much on love at first sight, but there was something about this Sharon Sauze. As he watched her at lunch today, he made every effort to be inconspicuous but felt sure Tills must have noticed his periodic waning. He caught a glimpse of her license plate as she left the parking lot and ran the tags back at the office when none of the others were looking. Apparently Miss Sauze lives only blocks from him at a small apartment complex called The Meadows.

Ben looked up at the second floor of the courthouse. He could see an orange clad inmate sweeping the floor as a bailiff solemnly stared at a television and chomped on a donut. When the bailiff got up and left the room, the inmate rushed to the box of donuts on the desk and crammed an entire pastry in his mouth. When the bailiff returned, the inmate turned his back quickly and began sweeping the far corner of the room as he gulped down large lumps of evidence.

Ben grinned at the inmate's tenacity and put on his Razorback cap. He felt unusually serene and giddy. Try as he might, he couldn't get Sharon out of his mind. She said that her friends call her Shy. He thought maybe they called her that because she was timid. But who knows? Sometimes people get a nickname that's opposite of who they are, like calling a large man "Tiny."

He hopped behind the wheel of his jeep and started the ignition. He didn't really care if she was shy or not. He just wanted to get to know her. An impish smile came over his lips as he remembered her address tucked away in the pocket of his jeans. He'd make sure their paths crossed again.

Somehow, just driving down the road managed to put Kayline's mind at ease. She was two blocks from McDonald's when she looked in the rearview mirror and noticed the same crème-colored sedan behind her. She pulled into McDonald's to the drive through menu. The sedan followed but pulled into a parking slot behind her. The driver didn't get out of the car. Dusk had fallen heavily across Little Rock and there wasn't enough light to distinguish whether or not she knew the person.

"Can I help you, please?" The voice came over the box with a charge of fuzzy static. The only coherent words were, "can, help, and please." Kayline ordered a hamburger, fries, and a medium coke. Looking frequently in her rearview mirror, she could see the outline of what seemed to be a large framed man. He seemed to be looking straight ahead.

"Please pull around to the second window," the voice said.

Kayline put her car in gear and began rounding the corner when she noticed the man's head turn and his break lights engage. A blanket of paranoia engulfed her. Without thinking about possible rationales for the car behind her, she gunned her accelerator and jetted by a stunned employee at the second window holding a coke in one hand and fries in the other.

She pulled out onto Main Street and headed south with such a roar that her tires squalled objectionably. After seven minutes of jutting around corners and racing through traffic lights, she managed to find herself on a service road heading south toward Benton. She checked her rearview mirror. She had lost him. Lost who? After another five minutes of contemplating who might have possibly deemed her worthy of stalking, she'd chalked the whole thing up to a silly delusion. Why would anyone be following her? She flushed at the ridiculous notion.

She located a quaint little Italian restaurant on the corner of Third and Jefferson, continuing to feel a bit paranoid and unable to shake the compulsion to cast an occasional glimpse in the rearview mirror. No one was behind her. She located a vacant parking spot near the entrance of the restaurant and slipped her car into it.

Inside the restaurant, she selected a booth in the far corner, out of the way. It was perfect for eating and reading. She sat and waited for the waitress to take her drink order and return with a coke, silverware, and napkins before she got up to wash her hands. The items on the table would declare the booth taken should other customers try to sit there. She left her book and stood up, scanning the restaurant for a bathroom sign. A large buffet of pizzas, lasagna, and pasta stood adjacent to a salad bar in the middle of the dining area. The steamy aroma of melted cheese, oregano, and spicy meats infiltrated her nostrils and made her forget how afraid she had been just twenty-five minutes ago.

She found the bathrooms in the far left-hand corner of the restaurant and stepped inside to wash her hands. Normally, she would have cringed as she walked through the bathroom door. She hated few things more than public restrooms, but this one wasn't too bad. The restaurant obviously used a professional deodorizer and did a nice job of keeping it clean.

Lathering her hands and holding them under the tap, she looked briefly in the mirror, noticing the delicate lines forming under her eyes and around her mouth. Growing old right before her very eyes, she gazed at the sad, pathetic reflection staring back at her and suddenly felt sodden with a deep sense of loneliness. She smiled and held her face in various different positions, but they all gave the same feedback….pathetic. Digging in her purse for her compact, she dabbled powder around her eyes, mouth, and forehead. It didn't help much. She sighed heavily from the burden of knowing she was getting older, and that she was doing it alone, without benefit of husband or companion or children.

She stepped out of the bathroom resolute on drowning her misery in the comfort of everything displayed on the two buffets in the center of the restaurant. Tonight, pizza was her companion, and the thought of gorging on a massive load of carbohydrates perked her mood quickly.

Grabbing a plate at the end of the food line, her stomach growled. She scooped up a thick slice of pepperoni pizza with gummy cheese stretching from the pan all the way to her plate. Winding the spatula around the strings of cheese until they broke free, she then headed for the salad bar. Scooping a small bed of lettuce, she placed it on the remaining half of her plate. Dressing it with her favorite assortment of pickles, olives, and cherry tomatoes, she topped it off with a dribble of her favorite dressing and croutons.

With no more room on her plate, she headed back to her booth, intermittently weaving between other people and a maze of chairs and tables in the middle of the room. Just before reaching her booth, a young boy, about four, ran right into her causing her to stumble ungracefully and drop her plate. Her cheeks burned with embarrassment as everyone in the room turned and stared.

A man who was sitting alone in the booth just in front of hers immediately lent her his assistance. He was kind and offered a bit of humor that made her smile. She picked up the plate and the pizza that now seemed partially wedged in the carpet. Bits of pickle and lettuce lay in a two-yard radius around her and covered the kind man's table and chair.

The waitress, who was carrying a cup of coffee and Kayline's coke, immediately assessed the situation and bid them to let her finish cleaning it up. She sat Kayline's coke down and told the man she would find him another place to sit while she cleaned his table. Kayline insisted that he sit at her booth. The waitress sat the coffee at the booth and took Kayline's plate of dismembered pizza with her as she headed back for a washcloth and cleaner.

"I'm gonna have to tip that girl BIG," Kayline said, her cheeks still flushed. The stranger who seemed to be in his early sixties was nicely dressed in a tasteful gray suit. He was a handsome man with a firm jaw line and kind eyes. He had a gentle smile and a rough throaty voice that accentuated a novel, southern drawl.

"I'm Alex Malcom." He extended his hand.

"Kayline," she shook his hand firmly, "Kayline Hathcock."

"Kayline, what do you say we tackle that food bar again. And we'll watch out for those pint-sized stumbling blocks."

She laughed. "It's a deal."

They went to the bar, loaded their plates with the finest Italian delicacies that an American-owned pub in Benton could possibly offer, then headed back to the booth. Kayline walked steadily with both hands on her plate, on guard for running toddlers.

"What are you reading?" Malcom asked, nodding toward the book on the table as he plopped into his seat. Kayline shrugged as she grabbed the book and put it in her purse.

"Just a stupid romance novel."

"Stupid? Since when did romance become stupid?"

This made her smile a bit. To Kayline's relief, the conversation with the stranger came easily. She came to learn that Mr. Malcom was from Eudora, some five hours away from Little Rock. He was married for thirty-nine years to his wife who had died three years earlier from a stroke. He had five children, seven grandchildren, and a keen sense of humor that gave Kayline two or three good belly laughs.

To Kayline, who often felt extremely lonely, people who have experienced a life full of marriage, babies, and grandbabies were far superior in things to talk about than people like herself. The most she had to look forward to was television, and she didn't think Malcom would care much about the trials and tribulations of her favorite characters. In an effort to not bore the poor man, she said little about herself. That he didn't ask was another quality she found endearing.

"So do you work in Benton?" she asked.

"No, I do a bit of work in Little Rock when necessary," he answered.

"What kind of work do you do?" She hoped she wasn't being too personal.

"Well, lets just say I'm in the business of helping folks in a fix."

"Oh." A curious answer, she thought. She suspected there might be a reason why the man wasn't being more explicit and chose not to pry any further.

In spite of the one awkward moment, she found the entire conversation with Malcom to be utterly delightful. He was funny, charming, and didn't once even insinuate an advance. It was such a nice respite from her usual routine. By the end of the conversation Kayline thought that if she'd ever had a dad, she would have wanted him to be just like Malcom.

The only other customers left in the room besides them were at the register getting ready to leave. The four-year-old who had tripped her earlier was fast asleep in his daddy's arms. The bell on the door chimed quietly as they exited.

"I guess I didn't realize how long we had been talking," she said.

Malcom looked around a bit bewildered by the empty restaurant and looked at his watch. "Well, I'll be!" he said, "Looks like we've been talkin' almost two hours."

The waitress came by to see if they needed anything else. Malcom shook his head and gave the woman enough money to cover both their meals and a sizeable tip. Kayline resisted, but Malcom held a hand out and said he didn't want to hear another word. Before the waitress turned to leave, Kayline asked her for some water to go.

"Miss Hathcock, there's two things a person can't get enough of: good food and good company." She giggled but felt a bit sad that she would likely never see Malcom again. She told him how sincerely she'd enjoyed meeting him.

"Well, let me tell you what I'm gonna do. I'm gonna write my name and number down on this napkin, that way if you should ever need a 'Mr. Fix It', you'll know who to call."

They exchanged goodbyes and Malcom turned to leave the restaurant. He walked with a bit of a bounce and was singing a funny jingle about some nonsense. Kayline couldn't help but laugh. Malcom was a charming, jovial man, and she hated to see him go. He walked out the door just as the waitress returned with the water. Kayline thanked her for all of her trouble and gave the woman another four dollars.

The parking lot was lit with orange florescent lights. It was empty except for her white Explorer. She was confused as to how

Malcom could have left so quickly. She heard an ignition start around the corner where the employees parked and wondered why he would park all the way back there. She didn't think the restaurant was that crowded. She walked three yards to the corner of the building to give Malcom a final wave but froze and pressed up against the wall. Her breathing became labored in panic.

    She took one more peek and watched the crème colored sedan leave the back exit.

Chapter Six

Shy awoke the next morning, still clad in her dress and pantyhose, feeling groggy but much better. One time she had had a severe headache that lasted a whole day and well into the next evening. It was miserable, and she was thankful that this day she only felt the residue of last night's pain.

Taking off the severely wrinkled dress, she threw it, along with her pantyhose and underwear, in the bathroom floor and ran the water until it was about five inches from spilling over. She soaked for thirty minutes and got out, realizing that the towel she'd gotten last night was still sitting on the kitchen table. Slightly irritated, she threw on her robe and headed downstairs.

The towel and the paper were just as she had left them. She grabbed the towel and threw her head over, wrapping it around the back and twisting it up until she had it tightly piled on the top of her head. The phone rang and she ran to the living room to get it.

"Hello."

"Hi, friend." It was Nelson. "Just wanted to see how you were doing before I left for work. You okay?"

"I think so." She took a deep breath.

"I figured you probably knew them well."

"I did."

"I'm so glad you did."

She was perplexed by his response. "Why?"

"Because I know you. And I know that family got the best of care if they were in your hands." Shy wanted to cry. It was true.

Nelson did know her. There had never been a romantic interest between them, but she always considered him to be her soul mate. He understood without her ever having to say a word.

"I love you, Nelson."

"I love you too, baby girl." He paused briefly and then added, "And if you weren't mean as hell, I'd probably marry you."

He always had a way of adding humor in the middle of disaster. She laughed and said, "I thought you didn't date white girls."

"Watch it, girl." They were both laughing by now, and the humor made her feel better. They chatted a bit more and then Shy remembered a story she'd read in the paper several weeks ago.

"Didn't I see a story recently about a family of three dying in a house fire. It was in your county, I think, in Staton maybe?"

"Yeah. It wasn't a Division of Children and Family Services (DCFS) case, though. I didn't know them. A couple of food stamp and Medicaid workers knew them, though. It was a sad story."

"How old were the kids?"

"I think they were two and five. Awful, isn't it?"

"Tragic."

Nelson tried to change the subject. "Mom keeps asking me when you're coming over for dinner."

Shy had a lot of affection for Nelson's mom, Glorie. She had spent the majority of her childhood at Nelson's house, and she got to go to church with them whenever her mom and dad would let her. She was the only white person in the entire church, but no one made her feel any different.

Nelson had a baby brother named Samuel. Miss Glorie would always let Shy hold him during church, and it made her feel big. Glorie spent a lot of alone time with Shy, teaching her about Jesus and how He loves all of His children. Shy wouldn't be the person she was today without Nelson's mom, and she was so grateful to have had someone like Glorie in her life.

"Tell her I miss her, and I'll get there as soon as things slow down a bit."

They finished the conversation, and Shy rushed upstairs to dry her hair and put on her makeup. She was ready in about thirty minutes and headed out the door. Juvenile court was in session at nine, and she never knew where her cases fell on the docket.

She made it to court by five after, and the Department of Human Services' attorney, Lynn Fowler, immediately flagged her down. Shy had no respect for Ms. Fowler, and it probably showed all over her face.

"So, are we ready to send this kid back to the family?"

"Which kid?" Shy asked.

Lynn gave her a scolding look for not being more prepared. "Brice Korla, the only one we have on the docket."

Shy ignored the comment. It was no secret that her cases were piled up to the ceiling. The attorney knew that there was a government freeze on worker positions. Shy worked long, hard hours, and would not apologize for not being able to manage the impossible.

"No," Shy said, "it's not my recommendation that he be returned." The attorney rolled her eyes. She was well known throughout the department for wanting things to be short and sweet. Send the kids home, close the case, and wash your hands of them.

"Why not? The goal is to reunite the family."

"Because the *family* has made no effort to rehabilitate themselves. They've not attended parenting classes as the court ordered, and they've not gone to counseling. In addition to that, they've missed two out of every three of their weekly visits with Brice. You know what that means? I stand there trying to console a grieving six year old and try to explain to him why mommy and daddy don't give a damn about him."

The lawyer was looking at her with eyebrows arched, "I don't like your tone, Miss Sauze."

Shy didn't respond to the last comment. "My recommendation is no, Lynn. When the family complies with the court order and the case plan, we'll look at reunification. Until then you can forget it." She walked away.

The judge had a great deal of respect for Shy because she never seemed to have her own agenda. The child's best interest was always at the forefront. She was articulate and could always support her reasons for wanting a child returned or removed from a home.

She made his job easier, and he was always happy to see her in his courtroom. Ms. Fowler knew this. There was no point in arguing.

It wasn't a difficult case anyway. No decent judge would send an abused child back into a volatile situation. Because there was no rehabilitation, one could only assume that the child would still be in a great deal of danger.

The judge heard the case, listening intently to both sides until he had heard enough. He ordered that the child remain in state custody until the family complied with the case plan. He berated the parents for not showing up during scheduled visits with Brice and for showing little interest in his emotional welfare. The parents said nothing. The judge set a motion to review the case again in six months.

When Shy left the courthouse she was met by Brice's entire family. Walking past them, she ignored the curses and threats, and while feeling significantly frightened, she tried not to show it. She scanned her peripheral for stray deputies going to or leaving work and found none.

Just as she got to her car, she heard "Hey, bitch!" and turned as Brice's grandmother wielded a cola bottle at her, smashing out the back glass of her car. Jumping inside with shards of broken glass covering the entire back seat and part of the front, Shy couldn't lock the doors fast enough. The family was furious and just brazen enough to tear her limb from limb in broad daylight. As she started the engine, six of the family members surrounded the car, screaming at her, challenging her to get back out. Revving the motor, she put the car in gear, and dared them to stand in the way. Brice's dad and another guy were standing in front of the car and had to jump out of the way before she plowed over them.

This wasn't the first time angry families had threatened her life. It came with the job. She drove down Slidell Street feeling foolish that she hadn't had an officer escort her to her car after a heated court battle. The metallic taste of adrenaline from the consumption of both fear and fury filled the back of her mouth and throat.

She saw a deputy that she thought she knew getting into his cruiser at the local J-Mart. Swerving the car at the last minute, she caught the very end of the parking lot with such a squall that it caught the deputy's attention. She pulled up beside him, and he approached with a stern expression until he realized who it was.

"Shy? Are you all right? What happened?" The deputy was checking out her broken window. His name was Percy Wright, a kind man who gave out more warnings than tickets. He and Shy had worked numerous child abuse cases together, and Shy had a great deal of respect for him. While he might have been gentle with your average speeder, he plowed over child abuse perpetrators with the vengeance of a grizzly bear, never showing the slightest bit of mercy. Shy admired his valor and advocacy for children. They had even become friends on a professional level. Seeing his kind face after nearly being bludgeoned to death almost reduced her to tears.

"Percy, I just left the courthouse and was threatened by a family. I put a little boy in foster care several months ago …" She was talking so fast that the deputy asked her to slow down. She nodded, took a breath, and continued, "We had the first hearing today, and the judge ordered that the boy stay in foster care based on my recommendation. The boy's grandmother threw a bottle at me, and it smashed out the window."

"Do you know the lady's name?"

"Yes, it's Downy, uh, Martha I think. She testified today."

"Think they're still at the courthouse?"

"I don't know. Maybe. I just left there."

"You gonna be at DHS?"

"Yes."

He was walking back to his car and hollered over his shoulder, "I'll call you in a bit."

She yelled back, "Thank you, Percy." He waved at her as he hopped in his car and sped out of the parking lot with his lights on and his sirens blaring. She knew he was doing her a professional courtesy and was grateful.

When she got back to the office Bill asked her if she was okay.

"No, but I don't want to talk about it." He left her alone.

Percy called about two hours later. It seemed that some of the family members were still conglomerated around the courthouse parking lot when he pulled in. He said that the whole bunch of them was going to be arrested if someone didn't confess to breaking the social worker's window. Grandma confessed when she thought some of her precious babies were going to be thrown in jail. She agreed to pay for the window and give Shy a written apology if she wouldn't press charges.

"I think I can deal with that." Shy said.

"Well, I told her that you were going to give the estimate to me, and I would take it to her and collect the money. That way you don't have put yourself in danger again with those weirdo's."

"I wonder if she'll really pay for it."

"Oh, she'll pay. She was pretty scared when I left."

"I don't know how to thank you, Percy. I just couldn't let her get away with it. What message would that be sending. No telling how many times I'll see that family in court again."

"And next time you'll have an officer walk you to your car?"

"No doubt about that."

For the rest of the afternoon Shy had half a dozen people ask her what happened to her car, and she was tired of explaining the story. At four o'clock she began winding everything down and getting ready to go home. The secretary rang through.

"Ms. Sauze, you have a call on line two. Officer Wright."

She picked up the phone and pushed line two. "Percy?"

"Shy, hey, I need to see you for just a second. Can you swing by here? Won't take long."

"Uh," she looked at her watch, "Sure, I'll be there in about fifteen minutes."

She gathered her things and left her unfinished charting on her desk. It was company policy to lock the charts in the file cabinet to prevent a possible breach of confidentiality. She'd just lock the office so the cleaning lady, or anyone else for that matter, wouldn't feel tempted to look through them.

Shy didn't tell Bill she was leaving, afraid he might think of a reason to keep her there longer. She was anxious to find out what Percy wanted and wished she had asked him on the phone. She assumed that he needed her to sign some legal documents about her car.

It only took her five minutes to get from DHS to the courthouse. She felt a bit hesitant as she pulled into the parking lot of her recent assault and walked from her car to the front entrance as quickly as she could. When she opened the door to the courthouse she immediately recognized Ms. Downy and stiffened. Percy stepped out into the hallway when he heard the front door open. He thought it was probably Shy and didn't want her to feel threatened.

"Miss Sauze," he said in a professional tone, "Ms. Downy has something she'd like to tell you."

The woman stood up and walked toward her. She looked every bit of sixty-five and not nearly as dangerous without the rest of the clan. She had a large crease burrowed into her forehead that deepened when she began to speak.

"I had no business throwing that bottle." Her voice was frail, quite opposite of the "Bitch!" that was directed at Shy in the parking lot. "I'm so sorry. I should have been mad at my son and his wife. I haven't seen my grandson in three months because of them." She looked down briefly and then back at Shy. "I let it out on you. I'm sorry, and I'd like to make amends." She handed Shy a check for three times the amount it would cost to fix her window.

"Ms. Downy, I'm sure the window's not going to cost this much."

"Please, just take it with my apologies." She turned and looked at the officer, nodded, and walked passed Shy to the door. Shy felt a slight bit of empathy emerge for the old woman.

"Ms. Downy, the family gets visitation every Thursday after school. Would you like to come? I bet Brice would love to see you."

The old lady teared up a bit. "Honey, I didn't know I could come." Shy nodded. The lady stiffened and made a stern face. "Well, you bet I'll be there."

Shy hoped that she would. Brice had been stood up by his parents so many times that his little spirit had become fragile. After the woman left the building Shy turned to Percy with a bewildered expression. "Percy, I don't know how to thank you."

"Hey, for all the times I've called you out in the middle of the night, this was the least I could do."

She smiled at him, noticing for the first time the dark circles that had begun to form under his eyes. She had been so consumed in the excitement of her broken window that she had forgotten to ask him how his daughter was. Knowing all that Percy and his family had been going through made her broken window seem petty by comparison.

"Percy, how's Clare?"

He shrugged and smiled at her, worry lines had begun to etch deeply about his eyes and forehead. He said, "She's going to be all right." He didn't sound convinced.

Clare was Percy's only child. She was fifteen and had been diagnosed with cancer a year-and-a-half ago. It was reported by the *Maburn Daily* that Tills had taken up a generous donation that enabled Clare to have a bone marrow transplant this last June. Shy had heard that the girl had recently become ill again, and that her physicians were concerned that her body was rejecting the transplant.

"Is there anything I can do?"

"Yes," he said, "pray for her."

Ms. Downy held true to her promise. She was fifteen minutes early for Brice's visit on Thursday. She had a sack of coloring books, crayons, and candy. The foster parents had errands to run in Maburn so they were kind enough to bring him to DHS instead of Shy having to run out and get him.

"Well, hi there, Brice." Shy put her hands on her knees and bent over slightly so that she could give Brice better eye contact. "I heard you started soccer practice this week. How do you like it?"

He nodded. His blue eyes glowed in the florescent lights of the office. "I like it okay. I bet Mom and Dad aren't here, are they?"

She shook her head but spoke quickly before he had a chance to start crying. "But you do have a visitor. I bet you're really going to be surprised."

This distracted him enough to keep from crying, but his pitiful little expression never changed. She stood up and held out her hand. "Come on, let's go see who it is."

As she opened the door to the family room, Brice's face filled with glee. "Nana!" He wiggled away from Shy and ran to his

Cries of the Orchids

grandmother, nearly bowling the old woman over. Shy closed the door and let them be alone. After about twenty minutes, plenty of time for the initial excitement to have worn off, Shy went into the observation room. It contained a two-way mirror so that workers could monitor the interaction between the family members and, in cases where the perpetrator was visiting with the child, ensure that the child was safe. Ms. Downy had gotten violent with her two days ago, and Shy just wanted to make sure that the woman wouldn't try to walk out with Brice or say anything that would upset him further.

She pushed the button that employed the tiny microphones in the family room. It was a wonderful tool for interviewing a child that had been abused. A staff member or a video camera could be a witness to the child's testimony without the child having to repeat the horrible story over and over. She could immediately hear Brice's voice.

"Nana, why didn't Mom and Dad come?"

She hugged him and said, "I don't know, honey. Sometimes they don't think right, and they make bad decisions. But I know they love you." Brice started to cry, and she pulled him onto her lap, arms wrapped tightly around him and cried with him. Shy was so moved to see that someone cared so deeply about this little boy. He needed this so badly.

"And do you know what?" Ms. Downy continued, rocking him slowly and patting him on the bottom, "Your social worker told me I could come to your visits." He didn't look up, just kept his face buried in her neck.

Shy heard a muffled, "All of my visits?"

"Yes, sir. And Nana will be here every Thursday until you come home."

"But when do I get to go home?"

"When Mom and Dad get help and start thinking better. We have to know that you're safe, baby. Nana needs to know that her little Brice will never get hurt again."

"But can't I go home with you?"

Shy watched the woman's eyes roll upwards and fill with tears again. "I wish you could, baby. Nana would just love that."

When the foster parents came to get Brice, he hung on to his grandmother and started screaming, "NO! PLEASE, NANA! I WANT TO GO WITH YOU!" Ms. Downy had considerable pain in her eyes and looked to Shy for help. Shy walked over to Brice and knelt down beside him.

"Brice, Nana will be back next week. And don't forget about soccer practice. You don't want to miss that, do you?"

Brice turned on her, kicking and hitting, screaming at the top of his lungs. Shy was holding up her hands to defend herself when Ms. Downy grabbed the boy by the arm. She had to holler to get his attention.

"Now, I won't have it! You will not behave this way! Tell her you're sorry, right now."

Brice was crying so hard that he was snubbing. "I'm sorry." He starting sobbing again, and Ms. Downy held him tightly.

"Now you listen to me," she patted the back of his head, "stop that crying and listen." She pulled him away so that she could look him in the eyes. "Nana knows it's not fair. It's not fair at all. But me and you, we're going to be strong and get through this! You hear me?" The boy nodded, still crying. He wiped his runny nose on the sleeve of his shirt.

"Now, you hold your head up. You're a Downy! We Downy's can make it through anything." He held his head up, still snubbing. She kissed him sweetly and gave him the same expression that she gave Shy in the police department, stiff with furrowed forehead, as if preparing for battle.

"Now, Nana will see you next week. I don't want to hear that you acted out, now. You're going to be strong."

He nodded and said, "I love you, Nana."

"I love you, too. Now you go with your social worker, and I'll be here waiting on you when you come next week." She waved her hand toward him as if she were shooing him. "Go on, now."

Brice took Shy by the hand. They walked to the door, and he turned for one last look at his grandmother. She pointed to her head and lifted it high, and he held his head up, too.

When the door was shut behind them, Ms. Downy put her head in her hands and sobbed.

Chapter Seven

The rain barely sprinkled atop the fresh new morning. It was the perfect day for staying in bed and reading a good book, and Shy begrudged her work schedule. As she headed out the door, she tried to shield her fresh hairdo with her briefcase. It was useless. Hopping quickly into the car to prevent any further damage, she threw her briefcase into the back seat and took a long, deep breath.

She could see through the drops on the windshield that the tiny white flowers scattered about the grass were beginning to open up again. She thought it strange how they closed up each night and reopened at the first sign of daylight. It was as if the day's stresses were just too much for them and after a good night's rest they thought they might give the world another chance. Shy could relate.

The rain spattered on the windshield as Shy made her way down the winding country road to Mattie's. She loved the rain and could hardly think of anything better than waking up on a rainy Saturday morning and snuggling back up in her warm bed. She would spend the rest of the day curled up with a book and an unscented candle burning on the end table beside her. There was a light fragrance in the air that came just before the rain. It was serene and almost hypnotic.

She adjusted the channels of the radio until she found Edwin McCain singing *I'll Be*, a song befitting her mood. The song was soothing and romantic. It reminded her of a wedding she had attended where this very song played as the bride walked down the aisle. She'd never been to a wedding where the chapel was decorated so beautifully. But it wasn't the pomp and circumstance that allured Shy. It was the way the groom looked at the bride, and the way he touched her face when he kissed her. Shy yearned to be loved like that.

She was once involved with a nice man she'd met in her hometown six years ago. She was only twenty and had fallen hopelessly in love with him. After three years of dating he'd begun to hint of marriage. She remembered the butterflies swarming so heavily within her that she thought her stomach might explode.

When it became imminent that he was going to ask her to marry him, Shy felt it important, albeit painful, to tell him she was unable to have children. He held her and told her that he loved her and nothing mattered except that they should be together forever. But the proposal never came.

Three months later he told her that his job was sending him to Tulsa for specialized training. He sent her letters regularly for the first couple of months. Two weeks before he was due to come home, he sent her a final letter saying that he'd accepted a permanent position in Tulsa that he couldn't afford to pass up. He told her that it would be unfair of him to allow her not to see other people. He ended by saying that he loved her and wished her the best. She never heard from him again.

She turned the radio off and decided to make a conscious effort to think on other things. Noticing that her car was veering slightly to the left, she made a mental note to have the tires checked when she got back into town. The raindrops plopped thickly against the windshield, forcing her to move the wipers to the highest speed.

She was thankful that Ford's auto repair was able to fix her window last Friday. No telling what kind of damage the rain would have done to her back seat. After she paid the man, she still had five hundred dollars left of the money Brice's grandmother had given her. Ms. Downy didn't look like the type of person that could dole out such large sums of money. Shy wondered how she came up with it. She took four hundred dollars to the bank and opened an account in Brice's name and kept the other hundred for her trouble.

Cries of the Orchids

Mattie's house was getting very close, and Shy found herself praying that Mattie had come through this time. She just couldn't bear the idea of Jake going into the hard, cold foster care system. The rain had now transformed into a soft mist that left her only needing a periodic swoosh of her windshield wipers. For some reason the controls on her wipers would only adjust to very fast or somewhat fast. So every time she needed the windshield cleared during a light mist, she had to do it manually. She'd drive a bit then click the wipers. Drive a bit more and click the wipers.

As she pulled into Mattie's driveway she found herself praying once again that the house was clean. If her theory proved untrue, she could only assume that Mattie would never keep her home clean enough as to not pose a danger to Jake. She would have no choice but to take Jake into custody.

She put the car in park and sighed heavily. *Come on, Mattie, show me you can do this.* She looked up and saw Mattie's oversized head peering through the window. Shy got out of the car and tried, in vain, to protect her hair from the wet particles of rain. Walking up to the tiny porch, she knocked on the door. Mattie's voice came booming through the thin walls of the house.

"Miss Shy, you can't come in yet!"

Shy looked at her watch and then pulled the collar of her coat up around her neck. Mattie's tiny porch was hardly enough to protect anyone from the elements. She waited about twenty seconds more and then knocked on the door again.

"Okay, I'm comin'." Mattie's voice sounded cheerful. It was a good sign. Mattie opened the door with an impish grin on her face. Her eyes fashioned the jubilance of a five-year-old on Christmas morning.

"Come on in," she said.

"Mattie, you look very excited about something." Shy couldn't help smiling. Mattie had such energy about her. It was easy to get caught up in it. Shy stepped from the porch into the living room. She immediately detected the sterile scent of bleach and Lysol. The living room was in perfect order. Not one single thing was out of place. Mattie stood to the side of Shy. Her hands were on her hips as she waited anxiously for a response.

"Oh my goodness, Mattie! Look at this place. It's spotless." Mattie squealed and began bouncing up and down and clapping her hands together. The weight of her made the floor beneath them vibrate. She smiled so big that her mouth exposed a missing molar on the left lower side of her jaw.

"You want to see the rest?" she asked.

"I'd love to."

Mattie took Shy by the hand and rushed her to the back bedroom. Mattie's bed was made. The top of her dresser was nicely organized. The floor was clean and her clothes were neatly hung in her tiny closet. Mattie showed her the bathroom. It too was spotless.

Mattie suddenly slowed down as if she were moving in slow motion in front of Jake's room. She whispered, "I wanna show you Jake's room, but we have ta be very quiet cuz he's sleepin'."

Shy whispered, "All right, I'll be quiet."

Mattie took her by the hand again and tiptoed into Jake's room. The room was as neat as a pin. His toys were piled in one corner of the room. His hygiene supplies were stacked neatly beside a chair in another corner. His playpen was in the third corner, but it was empty.

Shy kept her voice at a whisper, "Where's Jake?"

"Over here." Mattie made her way over to Jake's closet. In spite of how softly she tried to walk, the weight of Mattie's body made the floor creek and groan in opposition. A stained red blanket lay on the floor of the closet. Jake was fast asleep. Mattie was beaming.

"It's a cave, and I made it for him." She'd become so excited about her invention that she forgot to whisper. Jake moved around a bit but didn't wake up. Mattie recoiled and then held one finger up to her lips as if she needed to remind Shy that they had to be quiet. Shy held her index finger up to her lips to show Mattie that she understood. Mattie moved over to where Shy was standing and put her mouth up to Shy's ear.

"He likes to sleep in there. Do you like it?"

Because Mattie had torn one of the sliding doors off, half of the closet was exposed at all times. There was nothing in the floor that could harm the baby, and Shy couldn't think of a reason why Jake couldn't take a nap in "the new cave" every once in awhile.

While Shy felt confident that Jake could care less about where he slept, Mattie often projected her childhood stuff onto her baby and wanted to give him everything she would have thought was fun when she was a child. She couldn't afford many toys, but she could sure tear off a door and make a cave.

"I think it's great as long as you keep the baby monitor with you, so you'll know when he wakes up. Otherwise, when he's a bit older he could crawl out of there and get into something. You also want to be sure that there is nothing on the floor that he could put in his mouth and choke on." Shy thought for a moment and added, "It might be a good idea to let him sleep in the playpen and only let him play in the cave when you're watching him."

"Yes, ma'am, but I don't want to wake him up, right now. Hey, you want to see the kitchen?"

"I sure do, but let's get the monitor in case Jake wakes up."

Mattie grabbed the monitor. She put one beside Jake and clipped the other to her waistline. Shy followed Mattie from Jake's room through the living room to the partitioned doors of the kitchen. Mattie paused, gleaming at Shy, "Are you ready?" Shy nodded and forced her eyes to widen as if she were anticipating a big surprise. Mattie flung open the doors and let out a big, "TAA-DAA!"

The kitchen was every bit as clean as Shy had seen it last week. Everything was in its place. There weren't even dishes in the drainer. Mattie walked over to the table and held her hand out to exhibit a lopsided, very strange looking cake with bright pink frosting. Mattie stood motionless beside the cake with her hand extended toward it. She resembled a large, homely version of a *Price Is Right* model.

"Oh, Mattie, it's beautiful. I didn't know you could bake."

Shy moved a little closer. She'd never seen the likes of such a cake. It was bumpy as if several pieces were connected together to mold a conglomerate of, well ... she didn't know. The pink icing, she assumed, was from a Betty Crocker can. It was spread thickly over the cake. "Miss Shy" was scratched into its surface.

"Mattie, I do believe that this is one of the nicest things anyone has ever done for me."

Mattie beamed with pride. "Do you want a piece?"

"I sure do. And guess what, I brought the Sprites this time." She pulled out the Sprites that she'd put in her oversized purse. "But I think we're going to need some ice. They've been in here since this morning."

"Okay, I'll get the glasses," Mattie grinned as she walked hurriedly to the cupboard that housed her glasses. When she opened the cabinet, two roaches scurried across the inside of the door. Mattie slammed it shut and looked at Shy who quickly made another comment about how beautiful the cake was, pretending she'd not seen the insects. Opening the cabinet door again, slowly this time, Mattie saw that the roaches were gone. She got out two glasses, filled them with ice, and took them to the table.

"And now for the cake," she gleamed, walking to the cabinet that was up and to the left of the sink. When she opened the cabinet door, roaches scrambled in every direction. They ranged from tiny, baby roaches to the kind you could harness and gallop across the room. Shy thought there were at least twenty. They were on the cabinet door, on the dishes and crawling up the shelves. Mattie tried to shut the cabinet door but five of them had fallen onto the kitchen counter.

Mattie turned and looked at Shy. Try as she might, Shy was sure her facial expression revealed her repulsion of roaches. Mattie looked down at the floor, and her eyes began to water. Shy immediately went into rescue mode. "Oh, I just hate when that happens to me. I'm glad I'm not the only one who's had to deal with those rascals."

Mattie looked up at her, tears flowed from her eyes. Shy felt such compassion for her, as she knew how hard Mattie had tried to make this day special. She walked toward Mattie, her voice soft and tender. "Mattie, there's no reason to cry. Roaches can show up in the cleanest of homes. We just need to get some foggers. That will take care of them."

"You think?"

"Yeah, that's what I use."

"Do they really come in your house?"

"Oh, my goodness, all the time," she lied. "They come from the outside and try to find a warm place to stay." Shy continued with a fabricated story, "One time my mom and dad came over to my house for dinner. My mom was sitting on the couch and one of those real big roaches, some people call them water bugs," Shy said with exaggerated expressions, "it fell off the wall into my mom's hair. Can you believe it?"

Mattie's eyes widened to the size of silver dollars. "What'd she do?"

"She screamed and jumped around until my dad got it out of her hair. Isn't that awful? I was so embarrassed!" Both women began to laugh.

"Hey, I'm dying to try a piece of that cake," Shy said with enthusiasm.

Mattie got the plates, two forks, and a knife and washed all of them with soap. She cut a large piece for Shy and a smaller piece for herself.

"So, who taught you how to bake a cake?" Shy asked.

"I learned it myself. The last time I went to the store I seen this purdy, pink icing. And I made the cake part with a secret recipe I made up myself."

"A secret recipe, huh?" She eyed the cake suspiciously and forked at a small piece. A lump the size of a golf ball fell off. She was afraid to put even a small morsel of the cake in her mouth but refusing to eat it after Mattie worked so hard was not an option. She put a small bite in her mouth. It actually wasn't as bad as she thought it would be.

"Mattie, this is really good." Shy hated lying, but in this case she didn't see the harm in stretching the truth. "Want to share your secret recipe?"

Mattie's eyes glowed with excitement. "You won't tell?"

"Cross my heart."

"Okay, you take five cans of those big biscuits and mash them all together and cook it." Mattie looked at her wide-eyed. Her body was wiggling about with excitement. "And then you take a can o' that pink frostin' and get a knife and just spread it on there!"

"What a novel idea." Shy smiled, feeling relieved that she had only eaten biscuits and frosting.

"You wanna know how I put your name on it?" Mattie beamed.

"I was just wondering that."

"Well, I just took that knife and used it to put all those letters on there. Just like a pencil."

"I can't tell you how much I love it, Mattie. Thank you so much."

A crackling noise came over the monitor attached to Mattie's hip. It sounded as if Jake were waking up. This was confirmed with the baby's whimper as Mattie got up to get him. She was just at the front of the hallway when someone knocked at the door, causing Mattie to spin around in surprise. "Company? I got company!" She looked back toward Jake's room and then at Shy as if pondering what to do first, answer the door or tend to Jake.

Shy came to her rescue, "Mattie, I'll get the door. You go ahead and get Jake."

Mattie nodded and whispered with restrained excitement, "Never had company. Who do you suppose it is?"

Shy whispered back, "I got it. Go ahead and get Jake." She grinned at Mattie's enthusiasm about having a visitor. Mattie nodded and stomped heavily down the hallway. Shy walked to the door, curious herself at who might be on the other side of the door. Perhaps it was someone selling vacuum cleaners or maybe a preacher trying to build his congregation. Shy could only guess. She opened the door slightly and peered through the sliver of an opening to the person on the other side of the door.

"Hello, Miss Sauze." Ben Crossno stood looking at her through the two and a half inch crack.

When Shy recognized the deputy, she opened the door all the way, an expression of concern on her face. "Is something wrong, officer?"

"Oh, no, I'm sorry if I startled you. Sheriff Tills sent me out to patrol this area and get used to all the nooks and crannies on this end of the county. I thought I recognized your car and thought I'd stop by and say 'hi.'"

"Oh," she looked puzzled, "Ben, is it?"

"Yes 'um."

"How did you know what my car looked like?"

"I saw you leave the restaurant. The yellow bumper sticker that says 'Normal People Make Me Crazy' kind of gave you away," he said as Shy laughed. Mattie walked in carrying Jake. His eyes were red and a bit swollen from sleeping hard.

Mattie saw the uniformed deputy and got very upset, "Why's the police here?"

"It's okay, Mattie. This is, uh, my friend, Ben Crossno. He just stopped to visit for a minute."

Mattie eyed the two of them suspiciously, "Are ya'll boyfriend and girlfriend?"

Shy answered "no" immediately, but not before her cheeks flushed. Ben got tickled. Mattie continued with her blatant honesty. "Well, I thank he sure is cute, Miss Shy."

Ben didn't seem to be embarrassed. He turned to Mattie, "I wonder what it would take to get a girl like Miss Sauze to go out with me."

Mattie was puzzled. "Who's Miss Sauze?"

Shy rubbed her temple and flushed again. "Uh, me, Mattie. Remember, that's my last name."

Mattie looked like a gleeful little girl who romanticized love. She looked to Shy for any hints of how she should answer Ben's question. Shy was looking down at the floor with a disconcerted expression on her face.

"Well," Mattie said, her southern drawl turning the word into two syllables, "I think you should just say something like 'will you go out with me, Miss Shy?'" Mattie looked at Shy for approval.

Shy looked up and smiled, "I think I should be getting back to the office."

"But what about the Sprikes?" Mattie asked.

"I'll tell you what, lets hold off on the Sprites until next week. I really should hurry back."

Mattie seemed disappointed. She turned to go get Shy's cake and wrap it up for her. Ben felt apprehensive about what he had just done. "I hope I haven't interrupted anything."

"No, really, I just, uh, I have to go on back to work. I've got a lot to do this afternoon."

Mattie returned with the entire cake wrapped in foil.

"Oh, Mattie, you didn't have to give me the whole cake."

"But I made it for you."

Shy felt a bit guilty about not spending more time with Mattie, particularly since Mattie had done so well cleaning her house and took the time to bake her a special cake.

"You were so sweet to make me this cake. I tell ya what, what do you say next week I bake you a cake? And I'll come a bit earlier so that we can visit longer. You think you might like that?"

The disappointment immediately lifted from Mattie's face. "Oh, yes, ma'am. Can you make one that's purple?"

"You want me to make a purple cake? I'm not sure I know how, but I'll try."

"Okay. It's a deal." Mattie gave Shy a big hug.

Shy noticed that Mattie smelled clean and fresh. She also noticed that Mattie was wearing clothes with no stains. She felt relieved and happy about Mattie's compliance to the case plan. Shy patted Jake on the back.

"I'm very proud of you, Mattie. You've done good work. You're house looks beautiful." Mattie looked much like a child who'd just gotten a gold star from her teacher.

Shy walked outside. Ben was still standing on the porch. "Mr. Crossno, it's nice to see you again."

"Well?" His blue eyes made her heart swoon. He was a tall man of just over six foot. He had a nice tan and a lovely smile. His facial features were Romanesque and strong. Bulging muscles rolled out from his short sleeve uniform. His dark, careless hair was cut neatly above his ears. Shy thought Ben was probably one of the most handsome men she'd ever seen.

"Well, what?" She smiled but was careful not to appear flirtatious or misleading. He smiled back.

"I guess you're going to make this difficult for me," Ben said.

"Mr. Crossno--"

"Please, call me Ben."

Cries of the Orchids

"Okay, Ben. I'm extremely flattered, and I'm sure you could have any girl you wanted. The truth is, I'm just not interested in becoming involved with anyone."

"I only wanted to share a dinner with you. I wasn't planning on asking you to marry me until next week."

They both laughed, but Shy cut it short when she saw that her left front tire was completely void of air. "Oh, no."

Ben turned his eyes to look at what had upset her. "Uh, oh. Well, let's just fix it. Go ahead and pop your trunk, and I'll get the spare."

"Problem," she said under hunched shoulders.

"What's that?"

"You're looking at the spare."

"You had a full size tire as a spare?"

"Yes," she looked down at the flattened tire with frustration, "I bought the car from an elderly couple a year ago. I had a blow out on I30 about three months ago. A trucker saw it and pulled over to help. He put the spare on this wheel right here. I've been meaning to buy another to put in the trunk but kept forgetting. She felt stupid as she explained the story. "What should I do?"

He inspected the flat tire carefully and found a three-inch nail wedged to the inner side of the tire. A quarter of an inch rip surrounded it.

"Well, I tell you what," he looked at his watch, "My shift is over in about three hours. How about I take you back to work. I'll take the tire and run it by the service station. Hopefully they can plug it."

"So, you think they may be able to fix it?"

"Maybe, why don't I go ahead and take it off."

"I'd be extremely grateful."

Ben dug inside the trunk of the car and found the jack and a crowbar. Meanwhile, Shy walked back to the house and asked Mattie if it would be okay to keep the car in her yard for a few hours.

Ben loaded the flat tire in the trunk of the patrol car and took Shy back to work. She was relieved that Ben had stopped by Mattie's. The nearest store was nine miles away, and Shy would have been in quite a fix. She remembered how hard the car was veering when she was on the small, country road heading to Mattie's and now she knew why. *A stupid nail*. She was grateful that Ben showed up when he did.

At the office, she scanned through her open cases for those that needed home visits. In every open child protective service case, she had to drop by unannounced a minimum of one time per week. In very serious cases, she'd drop by every day until the family's in-home therapist felt like it was safe for the social worker to start tapering off.

Shy had three families that she needed to see this afternoon. She asked Bill if she could borrow his car to make her rounds. The first family was a single mother who had two daughters, one seven and one thirteen years old. Three months ago the teenage girl called DHS after her mother slapped her across the face. Shy met the girl at school and found her to be a manipulative little brat who didn't get what she wanted at home. Apparently the girl wanted to go out on a date with a nineteen-year-old boy. When mom said, "absolutely not" the girl became hostile and defiant. She called her mother an assortment of choice names, and the mother slapped her in the face.

Shy thought the girl deserved a good smack in the face. She went to the home that same day and visited with the girl's mother who confirmed her daughter's story. She told Shy that her daughter was getting out of control, and she didn't know what to do.

The mother worked a full-time job as a secretary at her younger daughter's school. Her salary qualified her to be in the category of the working poor. She barely made it from paycheck to paycheck, and yet her salary fell just above the poverty line. She qualified for nothing. She and her girls needed therapy desperately, but her insurance didn't cover psychiatric care, and she certainly couldn't afford seventy dollars a week for therapy sessions.

Shy normally wouldn't have opened a case for this family. It was obvious, after talking to each member of the family, that the mother was not an abusive parent. She was, however, at a loss as to what to do with her unruly teenage daughter. Per mom's request, Shy opened the case so the family would qualify for free family therapy.

Over the next three months, the mother noted a slight improvement in her daughter's oppositional behavior. The girl continued to be disrespectful to her mother but no longer swore at her. The mother said that she and her daughter were beginning to talk and that, overall, she felt things were better.

The other two cases she had to see were kids in foster care. She visited the kids and their families. All were well and reported zero problems. One of the kids had recently attended a dental checkup and was told he needed braces. Shy jotted down a note to apply for a special fund to cover the expenses. Back at the office, she spent about forty minutes jotting down case notes.

Bill dropped by her office. "Hey, how'd it go?"

"Everyone's fine. Here are your keys. Thank you for letting me drive your car." Shy handed Bill the keys and added, "Oh, I almost forgot, Donnie needs braces. Can you sign this special order?"

"Sure," he scribbled his signature, "just make sure and attach a copy of the dentist's recommendation. Do you need a ride out to Mattie's to get your car?"

Shy looked at the clock hanging on the wall behind her. It was four thirty-five. "No, but thank you. Officer Crossno said he'd pick me up at five. Are you on your way out?"

Bill tried to hide the pangs of jealousy that burned his lungs and threatened to choke him. "Yeah, I'm gone. I've got call tonight. See you in the morning."

"See ya." Her voice sounded unusually chipper for the end of a long Monday. Bill couldn't help wondering if Ben Crossno had anything to do with it.

At five minutes 'til, Shy looked out the window and saw Ben waiting for her in the black and white patrol car. She grabbed her purse and briefcase and told everyone "good-bye" as she headed out onto the parking lot.

"Well, hi there." Ben was grinning at her behind his sunglasses.

"Hi, yourself," she said smiling. Shy walked past his open window around the front of the car to the passenger side. She opened the door and backed in, sitting first and then moving her legs in gracefully, careful not to inadvertently show anything she didn't want shown. As she shut the door and fastened her seatbelt, Shy was suddenly aware of how vulnerable she felt. She hardly knew Ben, and yet she felt indebted to him for all he'd done for her today.

"I called the tire shop," he said, "they were able to take the nail out and plug it."

"What's the damage?"

"Probably about four bucks."

"Really, and you think it'll be all right? I mean, you don't think I need a new tire?"

"I think it'll make it quite a bit further. Still got quite a bit of tread left on it. I would suggest you go ahead and get you a spare, though."

She smiled, "Yes, sir."

They pulled into the service station. Ben loaded up the mended tire while Shy selected an efficient spare. Once all was loaded up, they headed back out to Mattie's to retrieve her car. Mattie was thrilled to see Shy twice in one day. As Shy went inside, Ben stayed out and put the tire back on her car.

Mattie was bouncing Jake on her knee. "Did ya eat the cake I made?"

Shy felt guilty as she'd forgotten all about the cake. Wondering if she left it in the patrol car, she stretched the truth a bit, "No, Mattie, I thought it would be just perfect after dinner tonight with a cup of coffee."

It worked. Mattie grinned, "Yeah, that would be good."

Jake was trying desperately to get Shy's attention. He stretched his arms, kicked his feet and babbled. When none of this worked, he let out a large squeal.

"I'm sorry, Jakey, were you talking to me?" The eye contact with Shy made him cackle. He had one large dimple on his left cheek, and his mouth was open so wide it exposed a tooth drowning in baby drool on his lower gum.

"Oh, my goodness, did you make a tooth?"

"He did!" Mattie exclaimed proudly.

Shy walked over to the baby. "Come here, you." She picked him up and held him high over her head. A string of drool oozed from his mouth and trickled onto her cheek.

"Hey," she chuckled, "are you spittin' on me?" Mattie gave her a clean cloth out of the laundry basket beside the couch. Shy adjusted the baby to her right hip and took the cloth from Mattie.

"It's okay, Mattie. If baby drool is the worst thing that ever happens to me, I'll be in good shape." She wiped her cheek and caught a glimpse of Ben out the window. He'd already put the new tire on and was lowering the car back down. He'd taken his shirt off and his shoulders and forehead glistened with sweat. Mattie saw Shy watching Ben.

"You think he's gonna be your boyfriend someday?"

"Mattie," Shy smiled at her shaking her head.

"He's awful cute, and you shore are purdy."

"You know, Mattie, I can always count on you to lift my spirits. Thanks for the sweet compliment, but I'm not looking for a boyfriend."

"You're not?" Mattie looked at her in disbelief, "Why?"

"Oh, it's a long story, I guess. Speaking of boyfriends," she tried to change the subject, "how come you've never told me about Jake's dad?"

Mattie's expression turned dark. She turned away from Shy.

"Mattie?"

"He wasn't my boyfriend."

Shy's stomach was beginning to knot up as she watched Mattie struggle with a skeleton from her past. "Mattie, did someone hurt you?"

Mattie nodded but didn't say anything. Shy was looking at her in disbelief. She'd always assumed that Mattie had gotten involved with someone in Louisiana, and it had been too difficult to talk about. It had never occurred to her that Mattie might have been raped.

"Mattie," Shy sat down beside Mattie and held her hand in concern, "do you want to talk about it?"

Tears began to swell in Mattie's eyes. "That man hurt me real bad. And I ain't ever done nothin' to him. I didn't even know 'um."

"Oh, Mattie, I'm so sorry." Shy put her arms around Mattie and felt furious that someone had done this to her. "No one deserves to be hurt like that Mattie. It wasn't your fault."

Mattie pulled away from her and forced a smile. "I don't like to think about that anymore, Miss Shy. And anyways, I'm okay now. I got Jake, and I wouldn't have him if that man hadn't done that to me." Mattie took Jake from Shy and smiled at him.

"Mattie, you're such a strong woman." Shy wanted to explore whether or not Mattie would be receptive to therapy, but now wasn't the time. Mattie was finished talking about the past, and Shy didn't want to push. "Are you sure you're okay, Mattie?"

"I promise." Mattie started talking to Jake, and he squealed back at her.

Mattie wasn't okay, and Shy knew it. She made a mental note to look into getting Mattie set up with an in home therapist if Mattie would be willing to see one. She knew that Ben would soon be done with the car. And she didn't want to leave Mattie after drudging up something so horrible.

Ben knocked on the door, and Shy got up to answer. Ben was drenched. Even his hair was wet. He'd put his shirt back on but left it unbuttoned. Muscles rippled down his chest and stomach.

"I think you're all fixed," he said.

"Thank you so much, Ben, for everything."

"Anytime."

They stood in awkward silence for about five seconds. Shy turned to Mattie. She seemed to be fine, but Shy was still concerned about her. "Mattie, do you need me to stay here with you for a little while?"

Mattie took a break from playing with Jake and looked at her. "Well, are you wantin' to spend the night? Cuz, I ain't got no extra blankets. You'll have to go to your house and get some extras. Or …" Mattie was smiling like a nine year old before a slumber party, "we could stay at your house tonight."

Shy turned to Ben, "Could you give us just a minute." She shut the door and squatted down beside Mattie.

"Mattie, I wasn't talking about spending the night."

Mattie looked disappointed. Shy continued, "We were talking about some things that were pretty upsetting earlier. I don't want to leave you unless I know you're okay."

"I told you I'm okay," Mattie said frankly, "but you can still spend the night."

"Mattie, I can't spend the night." Shy was about to get frustrated when she realized that Mattie was probably just avoiding the deeper issue.

"I just want you to promise me that if you ever need to talk you'll find some way to get a hold of me."

"Yes, ma'am."

"Day or night?"

"I promise."

Shy smiled at her, feeling much more secure about Mattie's emotional status. "Now, don't you forget about our picnic next week." Shy walked to the door.

"I won't. Wave bye-bye, Jake." Mattie took Jake's chubby, drawn up fist and waved it in the air.

"Bye-bye, Jake" Shy looked at Mattie one more time for evidence of emotional upset. She seemed to be all right. She smiled at both of them and shut the door behind her.

Outside, Shy turned to Ben, "I can't thank you enough."

"It was my pleasure. Feel free to call if you need anything. I'm in the directory." Shy opened the car door and stepped in. Ben got inside the patrol car and turned the ignition on. Shy sighed heavily and stepped back out of the car. She walked toward Ben as he unrolled the window.

"How about tomorrow night?"

"You're not asking me out on a date, are you?" he teased.

She chuckled, "Don't worry. I won't ask you to marry me until next week." As the words came out, she immediately regretted saying them and added, "I'm just trying to offer you a 'thank you' dinner."

"I'm in. Where would you like to go?"

"How about we meet at the French Cottage at seven?"

"I'll see you then."

Chapter Eight

Kayline looked at the small gold clock perched at the end of the desk. It was four fifteen, only forty five minutes to go. She thought five o'clock would never come. It had been a particularly long Monday. After completing three autopsy reports, she assisted Collins on two procedures. Exhausted, she had started a document on one of the procedures that she'd assisted Collins with this morning and was busily typing away on an old electric typewriter she'd borrowed from accounting.

Technical support called her this morning and said that her computer would be delivered at ten in the morning. Hallelujah. After three and a half months with no computer, she'd realized how much she'd taken it for granted and considered bronzing it in gold as soon as it was delivered. She typed the last sentence of the document just as Collins entered the office, briefcase in hand.

"I've completed the procedures on B7 through B12. Transport will be here in the morning."

"So quickly? But we just got them last week." She couldn't believe it. How could he be done? She noticed his eyebrow raise as if he thought she were questioning his ability and recovered quickly, "You are so fast. When did you get finished with them?" The eyebrow came down.

"Early this morning."

Kayline felt her innards tighten. She knew what was coming next. He finished this morning but would casually wait until four thirty in the freakin' afternoon to dump the reports on her. She wanted to scream but held out on the notion that he might just let her do them in the morning.

"The Watson family?"

"That's right. Labs showed smoke inhalation and carbon monoxide poisoning on all five. Write them up and have them on my desk first thing in the morning."

Her heart sank into her abdomen. It would take her at least four hours to complete all five reports on the old typewriter. "Dr. Collins, would it be possible to wait until tomorrow to do them? My computer will be here then, and I--"

"That's unacceptable. As I recall telling you, transport will be here first thing in the morning to remove the bodies. I want to review your work before they go out." Without saying another word, he grabbed his hat from the coat rack and walked out the door.

Kayline fought the urge to chase after him and claw him in the face. The anger swelled so strongly that she thought she might explode. This was the third time he'd dumped his work on her in the last two weeks. And waiting until four thirty to dump five reports on her was reprehensible.

She stormed into his office and grabbed the first thing that caught her eye. It was a miniature crystal golf bag ornament with tiny clubs. The golf bag had a gold rim. She picked it up and hurled it at the wall, smashing it into tiny bits, immediately regretting it. Fear replaced the intense anger. *How could she have done that?* She quickly got on her knees and started picking up the tiny shards of glass. Her mind was spinning as she tried to think of an alibi. Maybe he wouldn't even know it was missing.

The last thing she needed was to lose her job. She'd worked hard to get where she was, and she probably couldn't get the pay or benefits anywhere else. She scooped the last of the pieces up and wrapped them in several paper towels. As an extra precaution, she went to the ladies' restroom down the hall and threw the remains in the trash. *There,* Kayline thought, amazed at how much better she felt. She smiled a little and sighed heavily, trying to let go of any remaining hostility.

Back in the office, Kayline rubbed her temples and tried to concentrate on what needed to be done first. She was looking at the old typewriter, hating it for all the extra work it made her do, when a thought hit her. Why couldn't she just take the charts home with her. Since Collins said all the family members died the same way, she could type one report then plug in the subsequent names. She would have five reports completed in a third of the time.

Kayline looked at her watch. It was five o'clock. If she left now, she could have them all done by six thirty. It was against policy to take charts out of the building, but she could slip them back in the morning, and no one would be the wiser. She perked up and wondered why she didn't think of this sooner.

Kayline went to Collins' file cabinet where he stored his autopsy reviews and thumbed through the charts until she found the W's. As she looked through the section twice, she found the Watson charts were missing. Perhaps they were misfiled, she thought, as she tried to think of where the charts might be. Kayline began rummaging through the V's but found nothing. She started on the X's and found one of the Watson charts third from the back. But where were the other four?

Kayline returned to her desk and opened the chart, trying to remember if the cause of death was smoke inhalation, carbon monoxide poisoning or both. As she thumbed through the chart, she became confused and frustrated. The chart was incomplete. All it contained was a face sheet with the demographics of the deceased and reports from the coroner and sheriff of Hot Spring County. In fact, this was the very same report that she read two weeks ago. Collins' notes weren't in it, no labs, no nothing.

Kayline punched in the extension for the lab. She should be able to get the information over the phone. "Ernie, hi, it's Kayline.

"Hi, lady, you're here awfully late." Ernie was a kind man who had helped her out of more than one fix with Collins.

"Yeah, he did it to me again," she huffed.

"I figured that," he said with a quiet laugh, "how can I help?"

"Could you please pull up the labs on the Watson family?"

"Sure. Hold on a sec." Kayline was grateful for her rapport with the lab. She rarely made a fuss with anyone, and it came in handy during times like these. As she waited for Ernie to boot up the lab results, Kayline made one last check around Collins' desk. She found nothing in his out box and only blank charting papers filed in his desk drawer. She pulled on the drawer to the right side of his desk, but it was locked.

Ernie came back on the line. "Kayline, when were the samples sent in?"

"I don't know. He said that transport would be here in the morning. There were five autopsies. I guess some of the samples would have been turned in last week at the latest."

"Could they have been keyed under another name? Maybe the drawer numbers?"

"Don't tell me that you're not finding them." Kayline put a hand to her temple and rubbed hard. "I don't know the drawer numbers, because I can't find the charts. I guess I can go down to the morgue."

"Well, let me do some digging around here, and I'll call you back. What was the case head's first name?"

"Uh, hold on." Kayline went back to the file on her desk and flipped it open. She walked back to the phone in Collins' office and held it to her ear. "The case head is Carol Watson."

"Okay, I'll call you back."

Kayline sat at her desk with her head in her hands. She didn't want to page Collins. He would be angry with her for not remembering cause of death when he just told her. That he didn't even leave her the damn charts was inconsequential.

Kayline waited twenty minutes before dialing Ernie again. "Did you find anything?"

"I'm still digging. Why don't you go on down to the morgue and get the drawer numbers."

Kayline hung up the phone with a gnawing in her stomach. She doubted that the labs could be pulled up under the drawer numbers alone. With grave hesitation, she picked up the phone and punched in Collins' beeper number. After waiting another twenty minutes, she dialed the number again, begrudging the idea that Collins' pager would now be going off twice, irritating him further. She hated herself for allowing him to intimidate her.

Cries of the Orchids

As the minutes continued to roll by, Kayline sat at her desk, rehashing yet another wasted hour of her life. Intimidation was soon replaced by hostility and resentment, which reddened the surface beneath her cheeks. Collins dumped five reports on her thirty minutes before time to leave with an incomplete chart for statistical data, and he won't even return his damn pages. She felt the hair on her neck prickle.

At five forty five she looked at the chart to see if she might be able to glean most of the report information from it. Thankfully, it contained most of the data: names, ages, birthdays, etc. Kayline knew Collins wouldn't be happy, but if she had to, she could draw up the reports and attach his procedural notes to them in the morning.

Thinking about the procedural notes gave her another idea. Collins said that the cause of death was the same for all five bodies. She could go to the morgue and get a lung sample from one of the cadavers and then take the sample to Ernie. She could type up all five reports at home and simply plug in the lab results as soon as Ernie faxed them. Kayline relaxed a bit as she collected her things and headed to the morgue. The hard part would be getting Ernie to fax the information to her home. While it was against state policy for information to leave the building, she thought she might be able to talk Ernie in to it.

Kayline took the stairs to the second floor. In all of her years working at the crime lab she'd never quite adjusted to the stale, formaldehyde-tainted smell of the morgue. The first time she'd sat in on a procedure she had to leave the room twice. She threw up once but had the dry heaves well into the evening every time she thought about it. Though the smell was little more than a nuisance now, she still found herself a bit queasy at times.

As Kayline opened the door to the morgue, the chill of the room swept over her. The air was damp and musty. The first thing she did was garb herself with a baby blue, paper lab smock, mask, and latex gloves. After checking the placement list, she turned to assess the stainless steel drawers in front of her. The Watsons were placed in B11 through B15 from youngest to oldest.

Kayline knew that the youngest child was an infant and would be more difficult to obtain a sample. She decided to go with

B12 and reached into a large drawer of sterile utensils, pulling out a small scalpel and clamp. She laid the utensils over a draped rolling table.

Kayline moved herself and the table to B12. As she reached for the handle of the drawer, she braced herself for its contents. It was always difficult to see a child cadaver, especially one that was severely burned. She took in a deep breath of sterile air and pulled hard to an inevitably ghastly sight that stirred both fear and sadness, in spite of the professional courage she had conjured up.

The stench of charred, human flesh nearly gagged her, and she tried to hold her breath as she rushed for the vapor rub in her purse. Kayline stood by the door and rubbed the ointment under her nose and on the inside of her mask. She allowed a good three minutes to let the strong, menthol odor satiate her sense of smell before returning to the corpse.

The child could have been no more than three years old. Kayline knew by reading the chart that the child was a female; however, there was no evidence of that by looking. The girl's hair had been completely burned off along with her nose and upper lip. A tiny row of teeth jutted out of the mouth area just under the opening that used to be the child's nose. There were only three fingers remaining between both hands, and her feet were little more than fused stumps without toes.

Fingers and toes, Kayline thought sadly, picturing the mother counting each digit, as all mothers do upon the birth of a baby. She was immediately overcome with an odd sense of solace that the mother died too. What agony the mother would have endured, looking at her little one, recounting fingers and toes. Kayline didn't remember the child's name from the chart, and she was glad for that. A name might encourage visions of pretty pink dresses, baby dolls, and butterflies. This cadaver was "B12." It was best that way.

Once she was somewhat adjusted to the horror and odor, she fine tuned her mind, a process she'd learned long ago, to focus only on the job at hand. She gently positioned the child so that she could get the best view of the chest area and noticed small tufts of burned fabric between the girl's legs and under her arms. The rest of the clothing was obviously burned off. Kayline grabbed the scalpel from the table beside her and focused on the chest cavity. She was not able to see where Collins had cut. She looked closer, scanning every inch of the area for tiny sutures. Nothing.

Son of a bitch, she thought in a fit of rage. *He hadn't even done the autopsy. How typical of Collins. To him, it was an obvious cause of death. And no doubt they all inhaled toxic fumes before dying. Why not just skip the damn autopsy!*

Kayline was livid. She checked the other four bodies. Not one single cut had been made on any of them. Now she understood why there were no charts or lab results. *The nerve of him! Let's just drop the fictitious reports of the untouched bodies on Kayline at the last minute.* She ranted and raved and threw out a few choice curse words all in the name of John Collins until she was able to calm down enough to formulate a plan.

Unable to think of any reason why the cause of death wouldn't be the same for all of them, Kayline decided to take a lung sample from two of them just to be sure. She selected B12 and B15. It certainly wouldn't be a full workup, but at least it would give her enough information to accurately complete her reports. Obviously when Hot Spring County doesn't see an autopsy report the proverbial shit will hit the fan. Collins could stew in his own juices for all she cared.

Kayline re-opened B12, this time so angry with Collins that her emotions about the dead child didn't consume her. She placed the scalpel at the sight of the chest area and pressed firmly. Bits of crusted skin flaked off, landing on the white paper that the child lay on. After making a five-inch cut, she placed a clamp between the charred folds of skin and exposed a tiny blackened lung.

She obtained a quarter size sample and put it in a tiny sample container, labeling it B12. After removing the clamp, she began the process of suturing the cut, not really knowing why. There was certainly no possible hope of an open casket funeral. Nonetheless, it was policy and she felt bound to it.

She went through the same process with the mother of the child, AKA B15. She was surprised to find that part of the chest and upper abdomen were not as extensively burned as the rest of the body. Kayline assumed that she must have been holding something as she died- perhaps the infant. Because of this, obtaining a lung sample was a bit easier. The flesh over the sternum was still soft, and she was able to cut into the chest cavity with less effort. She packaged the sample, labeled it 'B15', and sutured the cut.

Closing the drawer, she rolled the table toward the cabinet. After placing the scalpel and the clamp in the sterilization fluid beside the sink, Kayline took off her gloves, smock, and mask and threw them in the trash. She looked at her watch. It was fifteen after six. Grabbing her purse, briefcase, and the samples, she rushed down to the lab.

Ernie was sitting behind the counter tinkering away at the computer. He was a large man with a pale, round face, and his white lab coat didn't help matters. His dark brown hair with silver gray sprouts spattered behind a receding hairline. He looked up as Kayline walked through the door.

"Ernie, I need a big favor."

"Anything for you," he grinned widely, exposing a silver cap on one of his back molars.

"I was wondering if you could run these for me."

He took the sample cups and eyed them carefully. "Shouldn't be a problem. I'll have the report sent to you in the morning."

"Actually," she displayed her best 'please' expression, "I was wondering if you could do it now."

"Wow. What's the hurry?"

"Collins put these five reports on me at four thirty this afternoon. He wants them on his desk first thing in the morning."

"Sounds about right. Are these samples on the family you called about earlier?"

"Yeah, I'd like to be asleep by midnight. So what do you think? Can you run them for me? I'd really appreciate it."

He relented, "Sure. I can't think of anything better I have to do tonight. Where should I fax the results?"

"Ernie, I know it's against policy, but I really need them faxed to my house. Collins gave me permission to do that since my computer is out." It was a justifiable lie.

"Oh, well, all right. Here's a pen. Write down your fax number."

She jotted down her number and said, "Thanks, Ernie, I owe you one."

The parking lot was beginning to darken and the florescent lights were on. She walked hurriedly to her vehicle, careful to scan the parking lot, as she was still a bit paranoid from being followed the other night. She still wondered if it had been Malcom in the crème sedan. Who else could it have been? She shrugged it off. This was not the time for a spell of consternation. She was on a mission, which would hopefully end with a two-hour rerun of her favorite show.

At home, she threw her purse on the recliner in front of the television. She took her briefcase upstairs, turned on the computer, and pulled out the Watson chart. Moving the mouse, she clicked on 'open files' and then 'new document'. Looking at her watch, she saw that she had forty-five minutes until her favorite show came on. She'd broken record time before, and she could do it again.

In no time at all she was clicking away. She had done so many of these reports she'd almost had the meat of the report completed in ten minutes. In twenty minutes she had the entire "ghost" document completed. Now, all she had to do was wait on Ernie's fax, plug in the results, and print each document.

Kayline went downstairs to get a drink, feeling a bit of a hop in her step now that she could see the light at the end of the tunnel. She filled a glass with ice cubes and coke. The fizz had just begun to simmer in the glass when she heard the fax machine buzz into action. She left her drink and ran upstairs.

Kayline snatched the fax from the machine. The first page was the standard face sheet telling her that four pages were coming with a note from Ernie saying, "Don't stay up too late." Patiently, she waited for the machine to finish ticking and humming out the second sheet. She pulled it from the scanner's mouth and read it carefully until she found the information she was looking for. It showed the statistical figures and percentages that ultimately showed both carbon monoxide poisoning and smoke inhalation as the cause of death for B15.

She scrolled down to the appropriate place and typed in the information, and then she scrolled back up to the top of the page and typed in "Carol Watson," her birthday, and social security number. After this, Kayline maneuvered the mouse to the printer icon and clicked on it. Within seconds she heard the chirping of the printer. She leaned back in her chair and took in a deep breath. Within minutes she would be finished with a job that should have taken four hours to complete on the old typewriter.

The third sheet came out of the fax. It had basically the same figures. When the first report completed printing, she scrolled back to the top of the screen. She deleted "Carol Watson" and replaced it with "Emily Watson." Emily, she thought sadly, wishing that she could have completed the reports without ever knowing the little girl's name.

Kayline deleted Carol's date of birth and social security number, and then she replaced them with Emily's demographics. She clicked on the printer icon and waited for the printer to resume. She looked at her watch. It was seven forty five. At the rate she was going, she would only miss the first few minutes of *Ally McBeal*.

The fax spat out the fourth page, which would list any chemicals in the lung sample that deviated from smoke and carbon monoxide, breaking them down into precise percentages of saturation. This page was particularly useful in determining what chemical or narcotics were used with drug addicts or in cases of suicide by overdose. It was unlikely she would find anything on this page other than pollutants but, who knows? Maybe one of the kids was on medication or maybe mom had a drink. She snatched the third page and then the final page. Taking both pages, she headed downstairs to get her drink.

By the time she returned upstairs the second report would be complete. Two down and three to go! Downstairs, she clicked on the television and went to the kitchen. She grabbed the coke can and filled up the glass where the soda had fizzled down. Laying the pages in front of her, she took a swallow of her soda and started scanning the percentages. There was a small percentage of nicotine in B15. Other than that, the statistics were unremarkable.

Just as she was turning to look at B12's report, something caught her eye. It was at the bottom of the fourth page, second row. It showed a seventy percent saturation of chloroform. *Chloroform?*

Kayline looked over the column of chemicals again, thinking that she wasn't seeing it correctly. With another sheet of paper she formed a straight line from percentage to chemical. Her hands began to tremble. She looked at the other report- seventy-nine percent saturation of the same chemical. Her heart was beginning to race. She grabbed the phone on the other side of the counter and dialed the lab. *Ernie, please be there,* she pleaded, her thoughts racing uncontrollably from one possible explanation to another. But they all led to more questions. Why hadn't Collins performed the autopsies? Why was there nothing in the Watson chart? *Why weren't the labs keyed into the system?* Beads of sweat began to form at her hairline.

"Hi," she tried to make her voice sound normal but suspected that she still sounded shaken, "would Ernie still happen to be there? Oh…okay…um, this is Kayline from Collins' office. Would you happen to have his home number?" She waited with impatience as the woman explained that she couldn't give out an employee's home number. "I understand the policy about not giving out home numbers, but this is an emergency."

Kayline felt agitation mingle with panic. "Okay, I'll tell you what, I'm going to page Collins and have him give you a call." She hoped the bluff would work. No one at the crime lab with any sense would want to deal with Collins. Kayline scurried for a pen as the woman rattled off Ernie's home number. She found one in the drawer beside the oven and wrote the number on her hand.

"No, I won't tell him you gave out the number." She hung up the phone before the woman could say "goodbye."

Ernie's wife answered the phone and told Kayline that Ernie had called ten minutes earlier to tell her he was leaving work. She said he would be home any minute, and she'd have him call as soon as he walked in the door. The phone rang five minutes later.

"Kayline, my wife said that you called. Everything okay?"

"Hi, Ernie. Yeah, everything's fine." She hoped she sounded convincing. "Listen…I was wondering if any chemicals could combine during a house fire and mimic another chemical."

"You talking about chloroform?"

"Yeah, I was just thinking, you know, that maybe other chemicals could combine during a fire, like fabrics, foam, or cleaning supplies?"

"No, the lab has a pretty sophisticated system that differentiates between all that stuff. Pretty sad, huh?"

"What?" Kayline asked, still trying to absorb what she'd just heard.

"Looks like B12 and B15 were murdered. One of them was a little kid, huh? Hey, you know something else? I never did find anything on this family. Not even a hard copy. Wonder what happened."

"I don't know," Kayline's heart pounded.

"You sure you're okay?"

"Yeah, I'm fine. Just a little tired." Ernie didn't need to know what she knew. She wasn't sure what kind of a mess she'd gotten herself into, and she didn't want to jeopardize anyone else. "Well, I'm going to go so that I can finish up those reports. Thank you for running them for me."

"Anytime. See you in the morning."

Kayline hung up the phone and leaned with her back against the wall. Her legs were shaking as she slowly slid to the floor, tucking her knees to her chest. The lab reports lay on the floor in front of her feet. Ernie's words were pounding inside her skull. *Looks like B12 and B15 were murdered.*

Chapter Nine

Shy left work to freshen up a bit. She felt a little queasy and wondered if she were making a mistake. Calling the restaurant, she left word for Ben that she was running an hour behind and wondered if he would wait for her or see this as a sign that she didn't want to see him. Shy felt a strong physical attraction to him and decided to make a conscious effort to keep an emotional distance.

She changed into a long, sleek black dress that had gold buttons all the way up the neck and selected a pair of small, gold, hoop earrings and a thin gold chain. Applying a touch of makeup, she softened it with a dust of powder. When she checked the time, she saw that it was already eight o'clock.

Pulling her hair up into a classy French twist, she clipped it so that it all held together. Fine wisps of hair fell softly around her face. She checked herself out in the mirror, aware of the effort she was putting into making herself look extra special.

On the way to the restaurant, she felt almost dizzy. She told herself that she was only hungry and that she wasn't feeling this way because she was meeting Ben. Her feet were a bit sore from walking in high heels all day, so she decided to valet park to prevent extra walking.

Inside the restaurant, she scanned the bar and dining area. She didn't see Ben. He probably got tired of waiting. The hostess greeted her. She asked for a table for two just in case he happened to show up later. The hostess took her to a quaint little table in a secluded area.

The restaurant was tastefully decorated with antique novelties. A stunning mural spread across the entire wall beside Shy's table. It was a painting of a beautiful green meadow with purple orchids against a bright sky of magentas, blues, and oranges. A shadow of a great oak stood solemnly at the top of a solitary hill. Its dark branches mingled with the different hues of fuchsia and orange. It was signed by Sophia Leone. Shy wondered if this was a relative of the owners. The waitress came to get her drink order.

"Tell me, did one of the owners paint this mural?"

"Actually, it was the owner's daughter."

"It's stunning."

"Yes, it's quite beautiful, isn't it?"

Shy sat gazing at the portrait. "It's hard for me to take my eyes off of it."

"You will be surprised to know that the owner's daughter was only in the seventh grade when she painted it."

"You're kidding me."

"No, I was here when she finished it. She's got quite a talent, doesn't she?"

"I'll say." At that moment Shy noticed Ben walking through the front entrance. She waved at him to catch his attention. He looked particularly stunning in a dark blue suit with a pinstriped shirt and silk, maroon tie with dark blue accents. As Ben settled into the seat beside her, Shy got a whiff of his cologne and it made her stomach flutter.

"Thought I wasn't going to see you tonight," he said.

"I'm sorry. I was running late. I didn't get your phone number this afternoon, so I called the restaurant and left a message for you. Did you get it?"

"Yes, they gave it to me. I had some errands to run anyway. No problem. You look beautiful."

She said, "Thanks," but looked away, feeling awkward, as if she were back in high school with braces on her teeth and a big, glaring pimple on her nose. Thankfully, it didn't take long before the conversation started rolling and the awkwardness disappeared. After about thirty minutes, Shy felt completely comfortable with Ben. He was very easy to talk with and had a wonderful sense of humor.

They talked for an hour before the food arrived. Shy had ordered grilled salmon covered with chestnuts and a buttery herb sauce. Ben ordered a rib-eye steak. The aroma of both dinners intermingled into a delicious blend that caused Shy's stomach to rumble with anticipation. She picked up her fork; ready to cram as much into her mouth as she possibly could while still being somewhat polite.

She cut off a small piece of fish and stuck it in her mouth quickly. As she was about to consume a second piece, she noticed that Ben's eyes were closed, his head slightly bowed. She had forgotten to pray. Feeling flushed, she quickly put her fork down and bowed her head, wondering if this was how other people felt when she prayed in front of them.

It only took about twenty minutes for both of them to devour the dinners. The waitress brought Shy another glass of wine and Ben a cup of coffee. The restaurant became sparse as people finished their meals and left the building. It was nine forty-five and the restaurant would close in fifteen minutes.

Ben gave the waitress his credit card. She returned quickly with a slip for him to sign and returned the card to him. They could hear the humming of a vacuum cleaner running in the private dining area across the room.

"I guess we'd better go before they lock us in," Ben said.

Shy stood up and grabbed her purse. Ben took her gently behind the arm and escorted her out of the building. They waited for her car, chattering the entire time. Shy didn't feel the least bit tired. On the contrary, she felt exhilarated and vibrant.

"So, what time do you have to be at work tomorrow?" she asked.

"I'm off for the next three days. The sheriff's office has us on a four-day-on, three-day-off schedule."

"Lucky you."

"What time do you have to be in tomorrow?"

"Nine."

He grinned at her flirtatiously. "Isn't it past your bed time? Or would you like to stay out a bit later?"

She was glad he asked. "I think my mom will let me stay out a bit longer." She was smiling at him. "So, where would you like to go?"

"You've been here longer than me," he said, "why don't you pick?"

She thought for a moment and then grinned at him. "Follow me."

She drove to her apartment. Pulling into the space beside her, Ben unrolled his window, "Is this your place?"

"Yeah, I wanted to come by here and change. Do you mind?"

"Not at all," he said, slipping out of his jeep.

They went inside. Shy offered Ben something to drink and then ran upstairs to change clothes. She grabbed a white tank top and a pair of blue jean cut-offs. Hanging her dress up neatly, she hurriedly put on a pair of socks and tennis shoes and went back down stairs.

"Wow. I feel over-dressed," Ben said.

"Do you want to go home and change?"

"I think I'll be just fine." They got into Ben's jeep. Shy guided him to the interstate. They took the Social Hill exit and drove twenty miles until they saw a sign that read Lenox Marcus with an arrow pointing left. The paved road turned to gravel and then to dirt. Groves of pine trees intermingled with oaks on either side of the tiny road, accentuating the darkness of the night. They drove ten more minutes before the trees opened up to a camping area with picnic tables and barbeque grills surrounded by black water that shimmered from the moon.

"Where in the world are we?" he asked.

"This is my secret place. I come out here a lot when I need to be alone. There's rarely ever anyone here. Well, except for this one family. They've come here every year since I can remember, the Wetheringtons."

"Every year?"

"Yep, and all summer long."

"Where are they now?"

"I don't know. They didn't come last summer either. I used to love watching the four little girls running about or screaming while their dad threw them in the water. And the mother, she always had something cooking. It always smelled good here when I came to study. I used to think those little girls were the luckiest kids alive. And I'll bet they didn't even know it."

"Man, this place is beautiful. How did you find it?"

"I was out driving one day. I'd had a particularly bad child abuse case and needed to clear my head. This is where I ended up. I've been coming here ever since."

"Well, I can certainly see why."

"Let's get out."

The air was heavy and thick. They were the only people on the point with the only sounds being the crickets and frogs as they chirped in unison with the gentle, hypnotic lapping of the water against the land. Ben looked around in awe at everything the moonlight would allow him to see. "I'm glad I didn't pick the place to go. I sure couldn't have competed with this."

"Yeah, seems like when my life is chaotic I can come here, and everything seems to picce back together."

Ben began to feel uncomfortable as his oxford shirt began sticking to his skin. Shy was talking about how beautiful the moon was but stopped when Ben began unbuttoning his shirt. Noticing how abruptly she stopped talking, Ben dropped his hands to his side, "I'm sorry. Would it offend you if I took my shirt off? It's kind of hot out here."

"Oh, of course not. Go ahead."

The fact was she wanted more than anything to see his bare chest again. She couldn't remember a time when she felt more physically attracted to a man. And it didn't help that he was so charming. After he took his shirt off, she took several inconspicuous glances of his rippling chest. The moon gave just enough light so that she was able to look for longer periods of time without it being obvious. He wasn't particularly hairy, and she found that appealing.

Shy took Ben on a hiking trail. The trees shaded the moon and sometimes it was difficult to see. They laughed as they groped through the darkness. Taking a shortcut to a small man-made bridge that crossed over a tiny creek, they sat on it and talked for hours, covering everything from jobs, past jobs, childhood, and other significant relationships, all the while taking in the sweet scent of summer.

"You know that woman, what was her name, Mattie?"

"Yes," she nodded.

"You were so good with her."

"Thank you," she smiled, "It's been a long journey. I care a great deal for her and her baby."

"It was obvious. You don't fit the profile of other social workers I've worked with."

"What do you mean?"

"I don't know," he shrugged, "A lot of social workers that I've worked with don't seem to care about the clients. They're just doing their jobs."

"Yeah, I can see how people can get burned out. It's very emotional sometimes. And what about you? You don't fit the profile of the Hot Spring County Sheriff's Office."

"What's that supposed to mean?"

Shy cut her eyes at Ben. "Sheriff Tills? Puh-leeze."

Ben laughed, "Yeah, he's uh, a little different, isn't he?"

"He's a racist. I don't know that that makes him different. I just don't think a racist should be in any position of power."

"What makes you think he's racist?"

"Oh, it's kind of personal. Something he did to a childhood friend of mine. Basically, Tills tormented his family. It was a long time ago. Who knows, maybe Tills has changed, but I'm not going to run out and vote for him any time soon."

"Your friend is black?"

Shy cocked her eyebrows defensively, "My best friend," putting emphasis on the word "best." She continued with, "And yes, he's black. Do you have a problem with that?" Her voice was harsh.

"I'm sorry; I didn't mean to offend you. It just wasn't something I expected from someone living in rural Arkansas. It tells me a lot about you."

"What's that supposed to mean?" Shy continued to have an air of hostility in her tone.

"Educated, open minded, tolerant, unafraid to go against the grain," he teased with, "horrible things like that." Shy softened and grinned at him. Ben continued with, "So, you were going to tell me why people call you Shy."

She laughed; feeling a bit embarrassed to repeat the story. "Well, when I was two and a half my parents took me to a family reunion. At one point, they looked up, and I was running around completely naked. I had taken off all my clothes and my diaper. They were so embarrassed. From that day forward, the entire family called me 'Shy'. I was seven years old before I knew that my real name was Sharon. Can you believe that?" They were both laughing.

"So, are your parents still living in Arkansas?" he asked.

"No, my mom moved to Texas about six years ago."

"And your dad?"

"He died when I was twelve. In a fire."

"I'm sorry."

"Yeah, it was hard. I miss him a lot." It was a major understatement. But Ben didn't have to know all of her secrets.

When Shy was twelve she decided to light some candles that were embedded in a beautiful Christmas arrangement placed in the center of the dining room table. Her father was asleep on the couch, and her mother had gone to visit a friend who was in the hospital. She didn't have permission to light the candles. She only wanted to see what the centerpiece looked like when it was lit.

Laying her ham sandwich down on the table, she found a lighter in the kitchen drawer. There were five candles in all. Green garland was entwined around the glass globes that held each candle. Rich burgundy and gold ribbon mingled around and about the garland with pinecones and tiny wrapped presents accentuating each bend and loop of the ribbon.

One candle was loose and leaned against the garland. Shy lit the candle and let the wax drip down into the globe. After about five large drops of wax, she held the candle firmly in the globe until the wax cooled. When she let go, the candle stood straight up in its container.

Shy lit the other candles and then turned out the dining room light. She stood back and gazed at the centerpiece with delight, as the family dog leaned against her knees. "Look, Ruff!" she said in awe as the metallic gold lining on the burgundy fabric glittered with each flicker of candlelight, further magnified by the reflection from the glass globes. It was beautiful. So beautiful, in fact, that she wanted her nine year old sister, Shea, to see it.

She ran upstairs to get her sister but immediately became distracted by fury when she saw Shea wearing her favorite red sweater. An argument ensued, and Shy forgot all about the candles burning downstairs.

Twenty minutes later, after tearing the sweater from Shea's body, Shy was startled to hear her father hollering downstairs. Shy had never in all of her twelve years, heard fear in her father's voice, until then. He was screaming for the girls to get out of the house. Shy had a sinking feeling as she remembered the burning candles that she had neglected.

She hurriedly followed her sister down the stairs and was horrified to see that her worst fear had become reality. The dining area was completely consumed with flames. The drapes that hung over the bay window were ablaze by the fire as it channeled up to the ceiling. She remembered her father grabbing her arm and screaming, "Outside! NOW!" Shy and her topless little sister stood out on the lawn and watched the fire burst through the bay window. Her dad was yelling for the neighbors to call the fire department. Nelson's dad had already called and was running across the street in a vain effort to help. Glorie was in her bathrobe. She draped a blanket around Shea and convinced her to go to their house and wait for their mother to get home. Shy wouldn't leave the scene. She watched the fire inch its way about the house, slowly destroying her home. Nelson stood beside her and held her hand.

All Shy could think about was how much trouble she was going to be in when they found out how the fire got started. She didn't know what happened. Was it the candle she rigged? Did it not hold? Or maybe Ruff? Did he jump on the table for the remainder of her ham sandwich? It didn't really matter how it happened. She didn't have permission to light the candles. She was watching her home burn down, and it was all her fault. It was then that she realized that Ruff wasn't outside with them.

She started screaming, "Dad, Ruff is still in there!" Her dad looked at the flames as if pondering the decision to go back in. Nelson's dad told him not to, but he did it anyway. Ruff was family, and Shy was grateful that her daddy was so brave. She just couldn't bear knowing that Ruff might die because of her stupidity.

She remembered Nelson draping his arm around her. She sank her head into his chest and cried, "Pray that Daddy finds him, Nelson."

Nelson squeezed his best friend and said, "Don't worry, he will."

It never dawned on Shy that her dad might not make it back out. She had always considered him to be a superhuman of sorts. He was the strongest, smartest man in the world. She never considered the fact that he could actually die. Not her dad.

Fire trucks with blaring sirens surrounded the house as firemen scrambled across the lawn pulling hoses behind them. Nelson's father grabbed onto one of the firemen and pointed to the front door, "A man's still in there!" Several firemen rushed to the front of the house, spraying gallons of water futilely over the blazing inferno. And as the flames devoured every inch of her home, Shy stood silently, holding onto the hope that her dad would walk through the flames with Ruff. He never did.

"So, you have no family here?" Ben asked.

She shook her head, "Nope. I have a sister, but she lives in Virginia with her husband."

At one point, Ben reached over and put his hand on top of hers, slowly moving his fingers up to the corners of hers and then all the way back up to her fingertips. It was sensual and erotic. Shy felt her lower abdomen quiver.

They talked until two o'clock in the morning. Shy couldn't believe how fast the time flew. As much as she didn't want to, she had to get home and get some sleep if she wanted to be halfway productive tomorrow. They drove home without one moment of dead-air time. Shy felt like she could talk to him non-stop for another three hours. Conversation with Ben was natural and easy, as if Shy had known him forever.

Back at her apartment she was reluctant to get out of the jeep. She didn't want him to go.

"Shy, I can't remember when I've had a better evening."

"Me either. I've had a wonderful time."

"I'd really like to kiss you."

She looked down and felt the blood rush to her cheeks. She wanted him to kiss her. She'd wanted him to kiss her at the lake. Shy looked at him, his blue eyes searing hers. Her heart was pounding so hard that she feared he might hear it. She heard herself say, "I think I'd like that."

He leaned over, took her right hand and pulled her gently to him, wrapping her arm around his waist so that she moved closer. With her chest to his, he held her to him, touching her cheek gently with his free hand. He stared into her eyes for what seemed like an eternity, making her feel flushed and vulnerable.

"I think you're beautiful," he said as he touched his lips to hers, moving his head slightly, tracing her lips without actually kissing her. It was sensual and made her hunger for more. He clasped her upper lip gently between his as he moved his hand from her cheek to the back of her head, intermingling his fingers with her hair. She felt his tongue move between her lips. The kiss was so passionate that Shy thought she would melt into him.

It had been so long since a man had held her that she'd forgotten what emotions it could arouse inside of her, fear being among them. She suddenly felt scared, unable to ward off the swell of familiarity she had shared with someone years ago, and the pain she felt when he left her. She pulled away from Ben, feeling nervous and flustered.

"Um," she ran her fingers through her hair nervously and then smiled at him, careful not to keep eye contact for more than two seconds. "I guess I'd better get inside."

"Okay," he said pulling his hand from her cheek. "I'd really like to see you again."

She fidgeted with the hem of her shorts. "I'd like that." He gave her a quick kiss on the cheek and waited until she got safely inside before turning on the ignition.

Shy hopped into the bathtub and soaked for about thirty minutes, reflecting on the days events, wanting to relive the last several hours over and over. She got out of the tub, dried off quickly, and threw on her favorite cotton nightgown. After making sure the door was locked and all the lights were out, she climbed into bed and pulled the covers tightly around her neck. She was tired and fell asleep quickly.

That night, she dreamed of a vast green meadow with a beautiful sea of purple orchids. She stood in the middle of them, holding an infant child whose face was blurred. She didn't know who the child was, but she had immense love for it. The sky was a beautiful shade of aqua green and blue. She saw herself standing there, smiling lovingly at the infant, when all of a sudden the sky turned dark.

Black clouds surrounded the air above her. The beautiful orchids turned demonic and developed sharp, yellow teeth. They screeched, leaping viciously and snapping at her. She knew they wanted to devour the infant and would kill her to get to it. There was nowhere to run. They were all around her as far as she could see.

Out of nowhere, a solitary white cloud descended from the darkness. From the ground she could see that Ben was standing on top of it. She tried to cry out to him, but she had no voice. And for some strange reason she didn't need it. The cloud moved closer and enveloped her and the baby, lifting them out of harm's way.

The demonic orchids screamed in anger, eventually turning on each other. They were biting, eating, and drawing blood from one another. Shy didn't want to watch the grizzly sight, but she knew she had to. It was part of the journey.

Chapter Ten

Kayline sat up all night. It was now four o'clock in the morning. She didn't know exactly what was going on, but one thing she knew for sure, a woman and her four babies were brutally murdered and her boss was involved in a coverup. *But why?* She was scared. Eight hours of processing what she should do with the information had only yielded two bloody fingertips from biting her nails to the quick.

She paced the floor nervously, aware that she had just an hour-and-a-half till dawn. At eight Collins would be expecting the reports. Kayline finally decided to pack her clothes and leave. She didn't know where she would go. Calling her parents or her friends was not an option for fear of putting them in danger. Collins was a powerful man and there was no telling who else might be involved. Kayline remembered the disproportionate number of files in Hot Spring County and Saline as opposed to the rest of the state. How many other families had been murdered?

Kayline also remembered a number of times when she wasn't able to boot up labs from the computer. Collins had always told her to contact him and not the lab should that ever happen. He had always been able to pull them up when she couldn't. She never knew why until now. There were no labs. He made them up.

Looking around her apartment, she knew it was too dangerous to stay there. She grabbed a large suitcase out of the closet and began filling it, throwing in as much as the suitcase could hold. *What else? What else!* She repeated the question compulsively and held the palm of her hand to her forehead. *Money!* She grabbed her purse. If she could find her ATM card she would leave right now. She'd withdraw $500.00 and go as far as it would take her.

She got frustrated when she couldn't locate the card immediately and dumped the contents of her purse on the floor, finding the card in the zipped side pocket of her wallet. She hurriedly grabbed at the items and started shoving them back into her purse. The crumpled napkin with Malcom's phone number caught her eye. She held it up. *Did he know something?* Did he know she would be in trouble? He referred to himself as a, "Mr. Fix It." Was he trying to tell her something- that someday she might need him? She grabbed the phone and then put it back down, remembering the crème colored sedan leaving the parking lot at the restaurant. What if it *had been* Malcom? That would mean he was following her. Why?

Remembering Malcom's kind eyes, Kayline decided she had no one else to turn to. She picked the phone back up and punched in the numbers before she had a chance to chicken out. A groggy voice answered the phone.

"Malcom? It's me, Kayline. I'm in trouble. I don't know what to do." Malcom told her not to say anything else over the phone. He said he'd be there in thirty minutes.

She paced some more realizing that she hung up the phone without giving him her address. He sounded like he already knew. How could he have known her address? She tried to redirect her thoughts and decided to grab another suitcase and pack some more of her belongings.

She wrote a quick note to her parents, telling them she loved them and only saying enough to keep them from worrying about her while she was gone. Writing that she would call as soon as she could, Kayline addressed the letter quickly and put a stamp on it. As she stepped outside, she looked around cautiously, fearful of the darkness that surrounded her. Affixing the letter to the mailbox beside the door, she jumped back inside and locked it.

All she had to do now was wait. She curled up in a blanket on the sofa. With nothing else to distract her thoughts, she allowed her mind to race. What if Malcom is part of the whole thing? But her

Cries of the Orchids

heart told her she could trust him. It had to have been someone else following her that night.

Hearing the muffled purr of a car pulling up, Kayline looked out of her living room window to the parking lot outside. Terror rose in her throat as she recognized the crème colored sedan. She was frozen with fear, unable to move, unable to breathe. She saw Malcom get out of the car. He looked up and saw her standing in the window and waved. She temporarily broke away from the fear, convincing herself that Malcom could be trusted. Rushing to the door, she unlatched it before she could freeze up again.

Malcom by-passed the pleasantries. "Are you okay, hon?" Kayline looked into Malcom's kind eyes, and she wanted to cry. He waited for her to nod and continued, "Lets hurry. We've got to get out of here."

They headed for the car and Malcom opened the trunk for her. She loaded her suitcases, and they both got into the car. She told him the whole story as he drove.

"What did you do with the reports?"

"I put them in one of the suitcases. I deleted the documents on the computer."

"Good girl."

"Malcom, what's going on?"

"I can't tell you that."

"So, you know what's going on?"

"Yes, 'um, we were concerned that you would get into this predicament."

"We who?"

"Can't tell you that."

"Is that why you were following me the other night?"

"Yes, 'um."

"Well, is there anything you can tell me?" She asked in fear and frustration.

"Yes. I can tell you that in two hours you will have a brand new identity."

"A new identity? Why?"

He looked at her. His face was solemn and serious. "Miss Hathcock, welcome to the wonderful world of witness protection."

Chapter Eleven

Collins checked his watch again. It was fifteen after eight, and he was more than agitated. Not so much that Kayline was late, but that she'd blatantly disobeyed him. He was explicitly clear about having the reports on his desk by eight o'clock, not five after and certainly not fifteen. That anyone would dare not follow his instructions implicitly was grounds for immediate termination.

He liked the fact that he could intimidate folks just by looking at them. Most of the employees at the crime lab did dances around him and that was all the better. In fact, he had yet to find an intellectual equal and often found himself unnerved by the stupidity of most everyone around him. Collins was his own god and expected everyone to cower in his presence.

A year and a half ago a young intern dared to question his decision to use staples rather than stitches to sew a wound. The boy's argument was that stitches would be less profound for the family during the funeral. Collins stared at the intern coldly and said nothing. The other staff members held their breath. No one questions Dr. John Collins. The intern never came back. Word was that Collins called the kid's supervisor and had him transferred.

Collins picked up the phone and called the switchboard, "Denise, this is Collins. Any word from Ms. Hathcock this morning? Nothing? Thank you."

Collins looked at his list of today's objectives. He had two procedures. He got Kayline to do the Watson reports for him and because of that he'd be done by noon today. He considered calling her but didn't want to give the impression that he needed her. Collins needed no one.

On his computer, he inserted the disc he made of the fabricated autopsy procedures and labs. After uploading the files into the main drive, he printed them up, and put them in a manila envelope to send to Tills. Collins stepped out of his office and plopped the envelope on Kayline's desk to mail. He checked his watch again. It was eight thirty-five. Warding off further agitation, he left the office and headed downstairs to begin his first procedure.

At the morgue, Collins attired himself in the usual garb and draped a blue sterile sheet over the portable table. He reached into the utensil drawer to collect the necessary instruments and placed them strategically on the table. Moving the table to drawer C2, something unusual caught his attention through his peripheral vision, making him turn back toward the cabinet.

It was the sterilization fluid. Something was in it. Odd, he thought. He hadn't done a procedure in several days. The instruments should have all been cleaned. He moved closer to the fluid and saw the tiny scalpel and clamp. Collins felt his nerves ignite and burn about the muscles in his neck and shoulders. It had been at least three weeks since he had used instruments of that size. He rushed to B11, pulled out the drawer, and was relieved to find no evidence that the body had been disturbed in anyway. He opened B12 and through close examination, was able to see a small cut with tiny sutures on the wall of the chest cavity. "Dammit!" he yelled with both fear and fury, pushing the drawer with such force that the tiny cadaver slammed to the front of it with a thud. Pulling each consecutive drawer out fiercely, he saw nothing until he found the jagged cut with sutures on B15's chest.

Collins shoved the portable table, propelling it across the room. Various instruments clanked about the floor in different directions. A lab tech in the hallway heard the noise and opened the door asking, "Is everything okay?" Collins glared at her. She turned quickly and walked out of the room without waiting for a response.

Perspiration began to form on the doctor's forehead. His fists were clenched so tightly that his knuckles were drained of color. He paced the floor and tried to collect his thoughts. Obviously, Kayline knew that he hadn't done the autopsies. *What else did she know?*

Collins wiped the sweat from his forehead and dialed housekeeping. He cleared his throat and tried to sound collected, "Yeah, I had a little accident up in the morgue. I need someone here ASAP to clean this mess up." He hung up the phone and went to the lab. The lab clerk was busily filing papers. When she saw Collins, she immediately stood up. "Hi, Doctor Collins," she said, fidgeting nervously with a button on her smock.

"Who was working last night?" he demanded.

"Umm, I'm not sure."

"Well, find out," he said through clenched teeth.

"Yes, sir." She rushed to the back. After five minutes she and Ernie returned.

"I was working yesterday evening, Doctor. How can I help you?"

Collins tried to appear cool. "Did you run a sample last night?"

"Yes, sir. I ran two. Do you need me to make another copy?"

"What do you mean 'another copy'?"

"Oh, I faxed them to Kayline last night. Did she not give them to you?" Ernie was clearing his throat.

"No, she's not here, yet," he said, trying to restrain the fierce tension in his neck and shoulders. "You faxed them to the office?"

"No, sir, she wanted to do some work at home on her computer."

Collins' face turned pale with a dark red hue setting deep below the surface of his cheeks. He was unable to conceal his fury. His left eye began to twitch nervously.

"You okay, Doc? I mean it won't be a problem to pull a copy off the computer."

Collins looked crazed, and this made Ernie even more anxious. Glaring, Collins spoke in a low, seething tone one might expect from the antichrist, "What is the policy, Mr.....?"

"Ernie, sir, Ernie Cobb." Ernie began to feel heat pop up in kernels around his collar.

Collins put both hands on the counter in front of the lab tech and continued with teeth clenched. "What is the policy, Mr. Cobb, about faxing privileged information outside of this lab?" He asked in a slow, patronizing manner.

"Sir, I realize it's against policy. I just thought, since you told Kayline she could do work on her personal computer, it would be all right."

Collins' face became distorted into the likes of a demented animal. Ernie tensed and felt his stomach shudder.

"Consider yourself terminated, Mr. Cobb. I'll have a letter faxed to your supervisor this afternoon." Collins turned and walked out of the lab. Ernie stood there, dumbfounded by what had just occurred as his colleague put a sympathetic hand on his shoulder.

Collins loosened his tie but continued to choke on his own fear. Back in the office he pulled up the Watson's real lab results on the computer. He scanned through it until he saw what Kayline must have seen the night before. The saturation percentage of Chloroform was seventy-five percent on one and seventy-nine percent on the other, lethal doses. Collins deleted both files, leaving only the statistics he'd conjured up on the fabricated files.

He sat back and ran his fingers through his hair nervously. Now what to do with Kayline? He had to get those reports from her. His lungs burned, and he felt as though he might suffocate. He grabbed the phone and dialed Jack Kult's number saying, "Jack, I've got trouble, man, big trouble. Can't tell you over the phone. Yeah, I'll be there in twenty minutes."

He called transportation. A young voice answered, "Transportation, this is Joe."

Collins skipped the pleasantries, "Yeah, it's Collins. Any way you can move B11 through 15 out by nine o'clock?"

"Hmmmm," came the young voice, "afraid not. We're booked until 2:00."

Collins clenched his fists. Let me speak with the supervisor."

"I am the supervisor, sir."

"Then let me talk to *your* supervisor," Collins said with as much venom to make small droplets of spit spew from his mouth.

Cries of the Orchids

"Mrs. Tannenbaum is not here, sir. Would you like her voicemail?"

Collins pulled in every fiber of his central nervous system to gain composure. He'd fire the boy on the spot if he didn't need him to move the bodies. Besides, the Board may get suspicious if he went on a firing spree. He drew in a deep breath and tried another approach. "Well, Joe, I really need you to make this happen. It's getting crowded in here, and I'm expecting three more this morning." As he said this, Collins moved to his computer to manipulate the data in case Joe should happen to verify the information. He pulled up the morgue census as Joe replied with another annoying "Hmmmm" and told Collins he would see what he could do and call back.

"Thank you," Collins said calmly and slammed the phone down. He found several files from cases he'd done three and four years ago and began plugging in names to the current census until it appeared that every drawer in the morgue was filled. Pulling up the window containing upcoming deliveries, Collins found that there were none scheduled until Thursday. He falsified the data so that it appeared that three corpses were being delivered that afternoon at one o'clock.

Joe called back within twenty minutes. He would have the Watson family moved out by 9:15a.m. Grabbing his keys and briefcase, Collins headed out the door.

Chapter Twelve

Shy was heading out to her first case of the morning. A single mother of two came to DHS supportive services for her and her children. According to the intake the woman's name was Traci Barett. She had two children, Piersen, age seven, and Hannah, age three. The inquiry said that Traci divorced her husband, a lawyer from Little Rock, after seven years of domestic violence. Apparently, on one occasion, she was beaten so badly she was put into the hospital for three weeks.

With only a high school education, she was scared to leave, afraid she wouldn't be able to support her children. Eight months ago, after her husband smacked her across the face for making mashed potatoes instead of baked potatoes, she loaded up the children and moved into a shelter for battered women and children.

Shy was currently on Route Seven. She squinted her eyes to see the number on the mailbox. It said fifty-four. The Barett residence should be the next driveway. A mile and a half later she saw box number fifty-five. A small white-framed home stood just in front of a small grove of trees. Shy could see the top of what must have been an enormous home behind the grove. The driveway had white gravel and forked off ahead. Part of the driveway led to the tiny white house and then it branched off, disappearing into the grove of trees, probably to the mansion behind the little house.

Shy pulled up beside the house and put her car in park. She walked around to the front of the house and knocked on the door. The fall air was starting to turn crisp. She snuggled up in her jacket and waited as the door opened to a three-inch crack. A young boy's freckled face peered through the opening.

"Hi, is your mom home?"

"I can't talk to strangers."

"Oh, I see. That's a very good rule."

The child's mother came up behind the boy, opened the door all the way and said, "I'm sorry. Hi, I'm Traci. You must be Ms. Sauze."

"Please don't apologize." She looked toward the child, "I think that not talking to strangers is very important." She held out her hand, "Please call me Shy."

Traci shook Shy's hand and politely asked, "Please, won't you come in?"

Shy walked into the house. The living room was modestly furnished and tastefully decorated. A three-year-old with bright blonde curls sat in the corner. She had a towel and was laying it neatly on the floor, smoothing out the wrinkles. Taking a small rag doll, she placed it in the middle of the towel and then covered it gently.

"Come on in to the kitchen. Can I get you a cup of coffee?" Traci asked.

"I'd love some."

An elderly man sat at the table with a steamy cup of coffee in front of him.

"Shy, this is Carl Border. He's our landlord, but we see him as part of the family." She put a hand on his shoulder and kissed him on the forehead. He smiled and nodded in Shy's direction.

"Nice to meet you, Mr. Border," Shy said.

Blonde curls bounced past her. The little girl, holding the rag doll swaddled in the towel said, "PaPa wock da baby."

Mr. Border took the baby from her. "You want PaPa to rock the baby?" He crackled a slow, deep laugh and stood up slowly, cradling the doll in one hand and taking the little girl's hand with the other.

"Come on, young'un. Let's go to the living room and rock the baby in there. This lady and Mama need to talk."

Traci turned to Shy with a look of admiration, "He bought her that doll. She won't play with anything else."

"How nice to have someone like him for a landlord."

"I'll say. His wife died two years ago from cancer. They never had children. I guess he just kind of adopted us. He's been such a blessing."

"Does he live in the house behind you?"

"You mean the palace?" Traci chuckled.

"It is awfully big," Shy smiled.

"Yes, that's his house, but he spends most of his time down here with the kids. And when he's not here, the kids are over there with him. They really need him, considering that their dad has stopped seeing them.

"He never sees them?" Shy asked.

"Last time he saw them was Christmas."

"Gee, I'm so sorry. Poor kids."

Traci smiled sweetly, "I guess that's a story in and of itself." The two women talked for over an hour with intermittent distractions of Mr. Border and the kids laughing in the next room. Shy assisted Traci with the completion of Medicaid and food stamp forms.

"Do you think you might need the housing authority to help you out with rent and utilities?"

"It would sure help. My husband pulled some strings with the judge. I only get five hundred a month in child support for both kids."

"You're kidding."

"Afraid not. That's the only income I have."

"What a courageous step you made getting away from him. So many battered women are too afraid to leave their abusive husbands."

"Yes, thank you. It took many prayers."

Shy gave Traci the phone number and address to the housing authority and collected her paperwork. "Okay, I think this is all I need. I'll get these forms processed for you immediately, and hopefully you'll be getting some relief pretty soon."

Traci thanked Shy and guided her through the living room to the door. Mr. Border was reading a book and moved stiffly from the chair. He walked over to her and extended a hand. "Nice to meet you," he said.

"Nice to meet you, too, Mr. Border." She shook his hand. The little girl had begun to bounce up and down. She was holding the book that Mr. Border had been reading to the kids. Innocence abounding, she said, "Papa, wead da book."

Mr. Border began to laugh and looked at the little one adoringly. "I'm coming, young 'un." He turned to Shy and said, "Sorry 'bout all the noise in here. Sometimes we get a little rowdy."

"I think they're lucky to have you," she smiled.

"Thank you," he replied bashfully. Moving back toward the recliner, Mr. Border sat down while both children scrambled for a knee to sit on.

It was ten thirty before she got back to DHS. At eleven, the secretary buzzed her office announcing, "Miss Sauze, you have a visitor."

Shy always preferred that clients make appointments. She looked at her watch and rolled her head in frustration. "Please ask them to have a seat. I'll be with them shortly."

The secretary relayed the message and came back over the telephone speaker. "Uh, Miss Sauze, he said 'no' that he wouldn't have a seat and for you to get your scrawny rear end out here."

"What? Who is it?"

Shy could hear the secretary ask the man for his name. She returned, reluctantly. "Miss Sauze, uh, he said he's Batman." The secretary lowered her voice. "It's a black man. I think he's got problems. You want me to get Bill?"

"No," Shy smiled and rolled away from her desk, "I'm coming."

She walked down the hall to the waiting area and opened the door. Nelson was leaning over the desk, staring at the secretary like a crazed psycho. He was saying, "Did you hear that? Well, did you hear that? But did you hear that?" The uptight secretary had a bewildered look on her face. She kept shaking her head 'no' but Nelson just kept repeating the question. Shy wanted to burst out laughing.

"Nelson!" He turned around and looked at Shy, then stuffed his hands in the pockets of his red jacket and tucked his head in pretend shame. Shy stifled the laughter and pointed toward her office. "Get in here!" Walking toward her like a puppy with his tail tucked between his legs, Shy closed the door to the waiting room, and smacked him on the arm. "You've got to stop doing stuff like that! I think you scared her." They both began to laugh.

By now, the secretary had called Bill, and he was nearly running down the corridor. When he saw Nelson, he stopped and rolled his eyes. "Joan just called me. Was that you in there acting like an idiot?"

Nelson grinned and held his hand out. He stated, "Guilty as charged."

Bill shook Nelson's hand, smiled, and said, "Good to see you, man." Bill and Nelson met each other every month at the supervisor's staff meetings. Bill had a great deal of respect for Nelson and some of his ideas to increase productivity. But the respect was not mutual. Nelson was the first person Shy called when she nearly resigned several years ago over Bill's "dead baby" comment. He was appalled, and he really hadn't had a lot of respect for Bill since then. Nelson was always polite to Bill, but he could only tolerate him in doses. Seeing him once a month during the supervisor's meetings was more than enough for him.

"Guess I'll go do some damage control with Joan," Bill said with a smile, and then added, "I'll be right back."

Shy gave Nelson a big hug. "What are you doing here, anyway?"

He hugged her back and whispered, "I'll tell you later. Let's go eat before Bill invites himself to come along."

Shy looked at him, nodded, and whispered, "I'll grab my purse." They ran out the back door before Bill had a chance to come back.

As they were pulling out of the parking lot Nelson said, "Don't look back. Bill is standing at the entrance trying to wave us down."

"How do you know?"

"Saw him in the rearview mirror."

"Oh, Nelson. I feel sorry for him. You want to go back and get him?"

Nelson shot her a look through the corner of his eyes. "Now, what do you think?"

She smiled, "Okay." She knew Nelson didn't care much for Bill and there was no sense in arguing.

"So, do they still have that little Chinese restaurant here?"

"Yep, still here."

"Good. Let's go there. That okay with you?"

"Sounds great to me. But I gotta warn you, Tills has been hanging out there a lot lately."

"Oh, boy. My favorite person." Nelson said this with a great deal of sarcasm. Nelson and Tills had quite a history. Tills, who was a deputy during Nelson's childhood, was one of the major players in trying to get the Jackson family to move from Maburn. He harassed them, pulling them over almost every time they left the driveway.

Nelson remembered that one time, after about three hundred dollars worth of conjured speeding tickets, Tills looked at Nelson's dad, Frank, and growled, "Ain't you learned your lesson yet, nigger?"

If being the only black kid in the Maburn school district wasn't hard enough, Nelson had to watch his dad being humiliated by the likes of a stupid jackass with a gun. It got to the point where the Jacksons didn't go anywhere if they knew Tills was on duty. Not even to church. Nelson's dad would sneak out and go to work, but that was it.

After several missed Sundays, someone from Nelson's church, a friend of a judge who was friends with the Sheriff of Hot Spring County, made a few phone calls. No one was quite sure what happened, but most of the harassment from Tills mysteriously stopped.

After Nelson's dad died in 1988, Glorie and the kids moved to Saline to be closer to her family and the church. But, not before she and her family had started a trend in Maburn. Now, a third of Maburn's population was black.

"Do you want to go somewhere else?" Shy offered.

Nelson grinned at her asking, "And miss the opportunity to see my favorite sheriff?"

"Well, let's just hope we don't see him."

Cries of the Orchids

Nelson pulled into the only vacant spot in the parking lot. Shy was famished, so the smell of chicken fried rice and steamed vegetables made her stomach growl.

"Wow, we picked a busy time to come. I don't ever think I've seen it this crowded in here," Shy said. They inched around people until they found a vacant table in the corner of the room. Wasting no time, they looked at menus and ordered chicken fried rice and iced tea when the waitress came by. "Sure thing." It was the same waitress Shy had seen when she was there with Bill a couple of months ago. She smacked on pink bubble gum and prissed off to get the drink order.

"So, tell me. What are you doing in Maburn, today?" Shy asked.

"I had an investigation just outside of the city limits. Thought I'd swing by here and have lunch with my best friend."

"And I'm so glad. So what…they got you doing investigations again?"

"Yeah, until the freeze is over," he said. Shy rolled her eyes and nodded like she understood.

"I really don't mind helping out. We've got some good caseworkers in Saline. I sure don't want them to burn out and leave me."

"No doubt," she sighed.

Nelson's expression tensed. "Did you hear that another family died in Saline?"

Shy put her drink down, looked at him sympathetically, and asked, "One of your cases?" He nodded.

"What happened?" she asked.

"They think one of the kids turned on a gas burner on the stove. They all perished from breathing the fumes. A mom and her three kids. I guess we can thank God no one lit a match. I heard that the gas must have been burning for days before anyone realized it. Could have blown up their house and the families' on either side of them." Shy was shaking her head back and forth, thinking of the wasted lives. He looked at her seriously. "Don't you think it's odd?"

"What?"

"All of these families dying. Did you know that another family died in Dallas County two weeks ago?"

"No."

"I heard about it on the news."

"Please spare me the details. I don't want to hear any more." Shy's forehead was creased, and she looked genuinely sad.

Nelson felt a little guilty. "Sorry, baby girl. I just thought it was odd. Anyway," he changed the subject, "what's up with you and Ben? You still seeing him?" Shy smiled but said nothing.

"Uh-oh, what happened?" Nelson asked, as the waitress came and quietly placed the teas in front of them.

Shy paused briefly and then said, "Nothing. I mean everything. I mean…..I don't know!" She smiled and then looked down.

He reached over the table, held her hand and said, "Sounds like the love bug to me!" She grinned bitterly.

"Oh, I get it," he said.

"What?"

"That pathetic smile of yours. We're back to the baby issue again, aren't we?"

"Afraid so," she sighed heavily.

"Does he know?"

"Of course not. I mean, we just started dating."

"You like him?" Nelson asked.

"I like him a lot," she nodded.

"Then you should probably dump him now."

"What do you mean?"

"Possible rejection. That's what you're afraid of right? I mean, you could fall in love with the guy, and he might leave you when he finds out you can't have kids. Ain't that what it's about?"

"Don't be absurd, Nelson. It's way too early to even consider anything like that."

"Exactly, and that's why you should dump him now. I mean, if you're going to do it anyway, may as well be now, before things get too serious."

Shy became irritated, "I don't appreciate your making light of this Nelson. I happen to like Ben a lot. He's a great guy, and a decision like that wouldn't be easy."

Nelson flopped his head around in exaggerated frustration. "First of all, don't be coppin' attitude with me." Jabbing at his chest, he said, "Cuz, uh, you don't want none of this. Know what I'm sayin?" After getting a giggle out of her, he continued, "It *is* an easy decision, baby girl. It's the *easiest* decision for *you*. You say you care about this man and that he's a great guy. You've been known to dump guys like that or not get involved with them at all because of your fear."

"No, that's not true. When I've ended relationships or not gotten involved, it was because I knew the man deserved more, okay. I cared enough to know they should have been with a woman who could have children."

"Don't play me, girl. You can't bullshit a bullshitter. It's all about *you,* not them. If it had anything to do with the man, you'd give him the opportunity to decide what's best for him. You wouldn't be makin' his mind up for him. But look, if it makes you feel better to deceive yourself, go on. I'm listening." He stared at her wide-eyed.

She started to speak out in protest, but knew that Nelson was right. Her mind raced with so many emotions that she could find nothing left to say on the subject. She needed to think. "You know," she said, "you're the only consistent thing in my life." She intertwined her fingers into his, "I miss you, my friend."

"I miss you, too, friend."

The waitress came back with two steamy hot plates of chicken fried rice askng, "Anything else?" They both shook their heads, and she turned and walked away.

"I'm starving," she said, leaning over her plate.

"Me, too. Hey, you know what? If you don't call Mama soon, you're gonna be in a mess of trouble." Stuffing an oversized spoonful of rice into his mouth, Nelson nodded his head vigorously for emphasis.

"Uh oh, is she mad at me?"

With wide, overstated eyes and arched eyebrows, Nelson said, "Everytime I see her I hear, 'Ain't heard from my baby girl in more than a month! You reckon' she doin' alright?' Baby girl this and baby girl that. I'm pretty tired of hearin' it."

She smiled, "I'll call her today. I promise."

After twenty minutes, they'd cleaned their plates and the waitress was clearing the table. She returned and filled their tea glasses.

"I tried to call you last weekend. Where were you?" Shy asked.

"I was helping Rhonda move to her new apartment," he said. Shy rolled her eyes.

"What?" he asked defensively.

"I really don't like that girl, Nelson."

"Why?"

"She's just not your type."

"And you, I guess, know what my type is?"

She smiled at him and shrugged her shoulders. Nelson said, "You're not happy with any of the girls I go out with."

"Hey, that's not true! I really liked Claire."

"Oh, no," he sighed, "here we go again! Claire and I have been broken up for two years, friend. How many times do I have to tell you and Mama? It's over!"

"Well, we just want what's best for you, and Rhonda isn't it."

Nelson rolled his eyes and shook his head back and forth. There was no point in arguing with Shy. She was probably right anyway. His only recourse was, "Girl, don't *even* make me start talkin' 'bout the guys you date."

"What guys?"

"Hmmph. That's exactly what I'm talkin' about!" he loudly exclaimed.

Shy laughed and looked about the room with embarrassment to see if anyone was listening. She hadn't noticed that Tills was sitting across the room. He was staring at them. He didn't know that Nelson was Frank Jackson's son, the man he'd harassed years ago. Nelson was grown up now. Tills' expression revealed that he couldn't believe Shy was having lunch with a *nigger*.

"You know the man we were talking about earlier?" Shy asked, "The one that likes to come here and eat?" Nelson nodded, knowing exactly who she was talking about. "He's here but don't look," Shy had an impish grin on her face. "Want to have some fun?"

Nelson nodded and Shy continued. "Okay, lean over here."

Nelson leaned over toward Shy, and she gave him a quick kiss on the lips. They left money on the table and stood up to leave. Shy wrapped Nelson's arm around her waist, and they walked to the door. Just for dramatic effect, she looked at Tills and gave him a wink as they walked out. Tills just looked the other way in clear disgust.

"You're such a brat!" Nelson laughed as they got in the car. "You better be careful, girl. You know he doesn't like black people. No telling what he thinks about the white people who date us."

"I'm not scared of Tills," she spouted.

"Don't start getting sassy. I'm just saying there's consequences. I just want you to be careful around that man. He's not someone you want to be playing games with. You hear me?"

"Yes, sir," she said.

Nelson took Shy back to the office and gave her a big hug. "Don't forget to call Mama."

"I won't."

"I love you, baby girl."

"I love you, too, Nelson. I'll call you tomorrow." She got out of the car and shut the door as he yelled, "You can't."

She reopened the door. "Why?"

"I'll be at Rhonda's." He smiled, showing all of his teeth. She rolled her eyes and slammed the door. Nelson started laughing and waved to her as he drove away.

Inside the building, Shy immediately picked up the phone and dialed Glorie's number. She heard Glorie's throaty "Hello?" after two rings.

"Glorie, it's me." Shy knew what would come next. She waited for Glorie to say, "Oh, it's my baby girl." And then Glorie would go on and on about how much she loved her and missed her, and then she would scold Shy for not calling sooner. Then she would ask Shy if she was getting enough to eat, etcetera, etcetera, etcetera.

Glorie had been calling Shy her "baby girl" since Shy was seven. It used to irritate her, because she thought she was too big to be called "baby" anything. And then Nelson would start calling her that just to irritate her further. She would chase him around the big oak tree in the middle of the yard as he yelled "Baby girl. Baby girl." Now Shy thought the name was endearing.

"Yeah, I've missed you, too. Yes, ma'am." Shy couldn't help but smile. Here it comes. "I know. I've been so busy. Yes, ma'am. I know it's no excuse. I'm going to try to get over there real soon. Maybe next week? Okay. Fried chicken would be great. Yes, I've been eating well." Glorie always worried that Shy was too thin. "No, I promise. I've been eating plenty." Pausing a moment, Glorie then staggered around the "have you found a new boyfriend, yet?" question. Ten minutes later, Shy was off the phone, promising herself that she would keep in better contact with Glorie. She stuck a note on the calendar to remind her of dinner next week at the Jackson home.

Shy went home and took a bath. Changing into a pair of shorts and a t-shirt, she was going to Ben's house at seven and couldn't wait to see him. With pepperoni pizza in hand, she knocked on his door at a quarter 'til seven. Ben was dressed in athletic shorts with a white Nike t-shirt. Just seeing him made her heart pulsate erratically. Ben had rented a comedy, and they sat on the couch, munching on crisp pepperoni smothered in gooey mozzarella. Ben had a difficult time keeping his hands off of her, and she didn't mind at all.

The movie lasted three hours, but they hardly watched any of it. Ben had pizza sauce on his face. When Shy brought this to his attention he kissed her hard and long, smearing the sauce onto her face. This started another episode of tickling, cuddling, kissing and holding. She loved being near him in any capacity. The television erupted in a loud display of static and snow when the tape ran out.

Ben turned the power off to the VCR and went into the kitchen to get two wine glasses and a bottle of Chablis.

"Oh, that looks really good," Shy said.

"Yeah, it does, doesn't it?"

They drank the wine as Ben began clicking through the channels, not that it mattered, for he knew they wouldn't be watching television. He settled on the channel seven news. A red-headed reporter looked solemn as she said, "And on other news this evening, two people lost their lives this morning in Hot Spring County."

Ben perked up, putting both feet on the floor, and leaned forward. He hit the volume. "They were traveling north on highway seven over Caprin Dam," the reporter continued, "when the driver lost control of the vehicle, causing it to break through the guard rail and plummet into the Versod River."

On the screen, a crème-colored sedan was being fished out of the lake by a large crane. Two body bags were being loaded into an ambulance. "The accident occurred around five o'clock this morning. The bodies have not yet been identified, but sources at the Hot Spring County Sheriff's office suspect that the driver of the car may have been intoxicated. We're going live on the scene now with Sheriff Tills, Shannon Ford reporting. Shannon?"

A cute little blonde reporter with an equally bleak expression appeared on the screen with Sheriff Tills standing beside her. By this time, it was dark outside, but you could still see the car in the background. It had been hoisted up into the air by the crane and was now dangling twelve feet in the air with mud and moss hanging from it.

"Thank you, Sherry. We're coming to you live, on the scene, with Hot Spring County's Sheriff Tills." Tills stood motionless but smug. The television made his huge belly look twice as large. Shy wrinkled her nose at the sight of him. The reporter asked, "Sheriff, it is rumored that this accident may have been the result of a drunk driver. Do you have any comments about that?"

Tills moved his hand to his hip and shifted to his other leg. "Well, several opened beer cans were recovered from inside the vehicle. We suspect intoxication, but an autopsy will have to confirm that. It's just another hard lesson on why folks shouldn't drink and drive." Ben changed the channel and sat there with a shocked look on his face.

"How awful. Did you have to work that wreck?" Shy asked.

"Uh, no, I didn't even know it had happened."

"But, you worked all day. You didn't even hear about it?"

"Well, uh, I didn't start until seven, and I hit the ground running." He was shocked by what he'd just seen but tried not to show it. "I really didn't stay in the courthouse much either, so I didn't hear anything about it."

"Oh."

For the next hour or so, Ben seemed distracted and distant. Shy asked him if he was okay, and he said that he was just tired. She wondered if there wasn't more to it but didn't want to push. At midnight she kissed him goodnight and got up to leave, feeling fragmented and concerned that Ben's withdrawal meant that he wasn't interested in her. Before she made it to the door, she was whisked around by him. He looked at her intensely and kissed her hard but gently. She left his home feeling like an awkward teenager and looking desperately forward to seeing him again.

Chapter Thirteen

Shy sat at her desk with a mountain of charts in front of her. It was two o'clock in the afternoon, and she'd already managed to visit three homes, begin services for a family with no food or electricity, and start an investigation on a child taken to the emergency room with a broken arm.

Mattie had really proven herself over the last two months, and Shy was extremely pleased that she was able to close the case. The amount of time she invested with Mattie over the months put her way behind on other cases. Bill even had to chip in a time or two with her caseload.

Shy contacted an agency located just outside of Maburn that provided independent living services and social events for mentally retarded adults. The agency also provided free on sight daycare, as well as transportation. Mattie desperately needed adult companionship and finding this agency was a dream come true. And who knows, they may even help Mattie get a job. She was certainly capable if trained well and supervised closely. Mattie had also agreed to counseling. An in-home therapist was due to begin sessions with her in two weeks.

After today the case would be closed, and Shy's workload would be much less demanding. If Mattie could gain social support and make new friends, she would be less dependent on Shy to meet her social needs. Shy kept telling herself that this was a good thing and that she was being selfish to feel sad that the case was closing.

Shy telephoned the Chicken Hut and ordered a bucket of chicken, mashed potatoes and gravy, coleslaw and biscuits. She and Mattie planned the picnic for today at four-thirty. She had an hour to document today's notes before Brice had his visitation with Ms. Downy. When she was finished, she put the folders in their appropriate places and neatened her desk just in time to hear a light tap on the door.

It was Ms. Downy. She carried her usual bag of goodies for Brice and showed Shy the new jacket she had bought for him. "I just figured he might need this at night if he goes anywhere."

In spite of her first impression of Ms. Downy, Shy was starting to like her a great deal. She was good with Brice, and it was obvious that she adored him. Shy talked with Bill about the possibility of Ms. Downy getting custody of Brice. Bill told her that it might be possible after about six months of parenting classes and counseling. Shy told Ms. Downy about this, and she agreed to go. She was very excited about the prospect of getting Brice and expressed a lot of gratitude toward Shy.

Brice showed up fifteen minutes later. Shy no longer felt it necessary to monitor the visit through the two-way mirror. After eight weeks of getting to know Ms. Downy, Shy had chalked the bottle throwing to an isolated moment triggered by stress and grief.

Brice was doing much better emotionally. He still cried when he had to leave his grandmother, but he always knew she would be back the next week. The poor little boy didn't feel completely abandoned anymore. At least he knew that his grandmother loved him.

Shy stopped by the local Minute Mart and bought two Sprites. She bought the dinner and put it in her trunk so there would be enough room for Mattie, Jake, the car seat, and all of their things. Bits of purple frosting were still enmeshed in the carpet from the cake she made Mattie several weeks ago. The cake was ugly, but Mattie loved it. It was still warm the day Shy took it out there. The frosting melted and oozed off of the plate in spite of the tin foil she had wrapped around it. *What a mess.* Shy thought she would never get the stains out of her carpet.

It was the first week of October, and the temperature was beginning to cool off quite a bit. She was thankful. A hundred-

and-two-degree heat coupled with Arkansas' humidity sapped her energy. She was so ready for the crisp air of fall. Driving down the little country road to Mattie's, she noticed that some of the leaves were beginning to transform into a glorious orange.

Mattie and Jake were ready and waiting when Shy pulled into the drive. Shy helped Mattie load the car seat, Jake, and the diaper bag. In fifteen minutes they were off to the big, celebratory picnic. "So, Mattie, how does it feel to have your case closed?"

"It feels real good, uh huh! 'Cause that means I done good, right?"

"That's what it means. And I'm very proud of you."

"I know it."

Shy was tickled at Mattie's enthusiasm. She drove to the city park, and Mattie was becoming more and more excited with every passing mile. "You know, me and Christina used to watch Andy Griffin. You know that show?" Shy nodded and smiled at the mispronunciation of the name.

Mattie continued, "Well, you know Aunt Bea used to make a picnic, sometimes even for the people in jail."

Shy chuckled a bit, "I remember that she use to do that. All the time, huh? I think you're excited about this picnic."

"Everybody's excited when they go on a picnic. Even Jake was excited. He can't talk, but when I told him we was goin' on a picnic he kicked his legs real hard and laughed. And he's also excited that his birthday is next week."

"Oh, that's right. Jakey turns one next week." Shy said this in baby talk as if Jake could understand.

Pulling into the park, Shy turned the ignition off as Mattie barreled out of the car and stood at the trunk bouncing up and down as if she were an oversized five-year-old. When she saw the chicken dinner her eyebrows lowered.

"What's wrong, Mattie?"

"Where's the picnic?"

"What do you mean?" Shy asked.

"Aunt Bea always put the picnic in a basket with white and red checker cloth."

"Oh, I see." Shy paused for effect and then added, "Well, what do you think we should do?"

"I don't know," Mattie said with despair.

"We have quite a dilemma, huh?" Shy asked, "you reckon we can still have a picnic without a basket and checkered cloth?"

"Well," Mattie was deep in thought. Her index finger scratched at her temple, "There's no picnic rules, is there?"

"I'm not aware of any picnic rules, except that you have to have food, and you have to have fun."

"Yeah, that's what I think, too. And, Jake's never seen Andy Griffin, so he won't know the difference. And, I like chicken a bunch."

"Guess what else I brought?" Shy asked.

"What?"

Shy pulled a Sprite out of the brown paper sack. Mattie was gleeful and pulled both hands up to her mouth. Her smile spread colossally, and exposed a row of stained, crooked teeth.

"Why don't you go ahead and get Jake out. We've got some celebrating to do."

"Yes ma'am!" Mattie clapped her hands and ran to the side of the car.

They wiped off a picnic table and loaded it with chicken and all the fixings. Shy got the sack of paper plates, towels, and plastic forks. She loaded her camera with a new roll of film and took pictures throughout the lunch. They had a wonderful time, laughing and talking. Jake ate some mashed potatoes with his fingers. Within fifteen minutes, he had it all over his face and in his hair.

After nearly two hours, they cleaned up the mess and loaded the vehicle to go home. Mattie asked Shy if she could stop by "Wal-Mart's" so she could get diapers for Jake. Shy re-routed for Wal-Mart. She wanted to drop the film off anyway.

Back at Mattie's house, Shy reiterated how proud she was of her for keeping her house clean. She told Mattie that as soon as she got the pictures developed she would come back out and give them to her. Mattie gave Shy a big bear hug and a kiss on the cheek. Realizing that the case was now closed, Shy cried all the way home and tried to remind herself that she would see them again.

That evening she and Ben went to the state fair. They'd spent five days out of seven together for the last three months. Being with Ben was natural. It was as if their souls were created to be together, and Shy was beginning to forget what life was like before him. After several hours at the fair, they returned to Ben's house and talked over a glass of wine.

At eleven o'clock, Shy looked at her watch and said, "I guess I had better go on home. I have a busy day tomorrow."

"Please don't go. Stay here with me tonight."

"Ben, I can't."

"Please, we won't do anything," he whined, "I just want to hold you while I sleep."

"Ben, I can't."

"Why?"

She settled into her chair and looked at him sweetly. "It's not that I don't want to. The fact is I can't think of anything I want to do more. It's just that, well, there are just some things that need to wait for a deeper, more committed relationship."

"Like marriage?" he asked.

"Yes," she said, "like marriage."

"I love you, Shy. I've never loved anyone like this before."

"I love you, too, Ben."

"And you know what?" He moved his chair up to hers and turned her around so that they were face to face. "Someday, you're going to be my wife. Do you know that?"

She didn't know what to say. She wanted to melt into him, but the emotional tension was so great that she chose to ease it with humor. "You think you want me to be your wife after knowing me for only three months?" She started laughing and teasing with him saying, "You know I turn evil after the thirteenth week. You might want to hold that thought for a while!"

"Laugh if you want. But it's true. You're going to be my wife someday." He didn't want her to think that he was only saying this to get her to spend the night with him. He meant what he said and if he had to wait, that was okay. He picked up a pillow from the sofa, threw it at her and said, "Now, get out of my house."

Heartily, she exclaimed, "Hey! Stop!"

He stood up, scooped her from the couch, and slung her over his shoulder yelling, "I said get out!" He grabbed her purse from the living room chair as he headed for the door. Shy started choking on her own spit from being held upside down while laughing. He opened the door, sat her down outside, and strapped the purse around her neck awkwardly. Shy coughed but kept laughing. He held her face with both hands, and all laughing ceased. Looking at her intensely, he said, "All I know is that I love you, Shy. I love you with everything in my heart." He kissed her and said, "Someday, you'll be the mother of my children."

Ben paused for dramatic effect; then, teasing again he said, "Now, leave!" He turned around, walked toward the house, and yelled for all of the neighbors to hear, "And you can stop making sexual advances towards me until you give me a ring and a date!" He went back in the house and slammed the door, leaving her standing alone.

Normally, Shy would have been humored, albeit embarrassed by Ben's behavior. Instead, she stood there, speechless. *Children?* For a moment she had forgotten her secret. There was no more laughing or entertaining the fairy tale. Her stomach turned sour, and she rushed to get in her car to leave.

She cried all the way home. As much as she wanted a life with Ben, she knew it could never work. She would never be able to produce a child for him. And, if she eventually summoned the courage to tell him, he would leave her- maybe not immediately but eventually. And why wouldn't he? Who would want to marry a woman who wasn't whole?

That night, she tried to sleep but felt restless. Her body could not relax. She decided to resolve the situation by telling Ben that things were moving too fast, and that she wanted to date other people. Just thinking about it was painful. She loved him desperately, and she knew that lying to him was selfish. It would hurt Ben more than if she came out and told him the truth. However, she didn't think she could bear his knowing her secret; and, she couldn't bear being rejected again.

Chapter Fourteen

Collins was back at work from a two-week vacation. The last case was just a little too close. No doubt Kayline had figured out the scheme in which he was involved. She may not have known the particulars, but he had no doubt that she had enough information to incriminate him.

When he first saw the scalpel in the sterilization fluid, he nearly wet his pants. He knew she'd been in there, and he knew she'd gotten a lung sample from two of the cadavers. Ultimately, she had learned enough to establish reasonable doubt against him.

Kult really salvaged his backside. After Collins' near heart attack in the morgue, he met with Kult and told him the entire story. Kult put his mind at ease, telling Collins that everyone who had a strong possibility of becoming privy to the details of the plan was being "observed" by one of his people. This included Kayline, as well as some of the deputies in Hot Spring and Saline Counties. If at any point they hinted of knowing anything about the program, they were "taken care of." Kayline had been taken care of. Kult explained that he had her phones tapped, both at the office and at home. He was alerted the moment she called Ernie and asked him to run a sample.

"You never told me anything about this."

"Calm down, buddy. I just didn't want you to be involved in axing your own assistant if the need arose. Are you sorry I did it?"

He wasn't. Kult continued to reassure him that no stone had been left unturned. His people were good. All was well.

"What about Ernie in the lab?"

"I've got a guy on him now. So far, he hasn't put two and two together. Seems pretty oblivious. I don't think he'll be a problem."

"And the guy that was with Kayline. Who was that?"

Kult explained that the man's name was Alex P. Malcom, a retired federal agent turned alcoholic. He eventually got fired from the Bureau when he was unable to put the booze down following the death of his wife. Eventually he sobered up and went out on his own as a private investigator. He got his nose involved where he shouldn't have.

"And how do you know all this?"

"He did a little job for me two years ago when I thought the wife was out foolin' around. He did really good work, and I got to know him pretty good. But I misjudged his character and thought I could hire him as one of my 'observation guys.' He told me he wanted no part of it."

"Hell, Kult. What all did you tell him?"

"Would you put a little bit of trust in me, man? We're airtight. We've got a lot of powerful people supporting us. No one can touch us." He took a deep breath and dropped his tone. "Look, why don't you go take yourself a little vacation. I know this close call has shaken you up. I'll stay here and man the fort. We won't have any more cases for a while. I'll make sure of that. Everything's cool, man."

Collins was beginning to believe him but still had a few more questions. "Anything left on her computer?"

"I had a guy sneak in and look for evidence. Nothing was found. He programmed a virus into her computer. Her system is permanently shut down. So far there's nothing that will come back to us. The only thing Bug found was a letter to her parents. He destroyed it."

"Bug? Who's Bug?"

"He works for us," Kult changed the subject before Collins could ask more questions about Bug, "Are the bodies buried?"

"Tomorrow."

"Good deal."

And that was it. Collins tried to work two more weeks but was paranoid and frazzled that the rug would be pulled out from underneath him at any moment. What if an eyewitness saw something that Kult didn't know about? What if the plan was found out? It was all getting too risky. How many people did Kult have involved in this deal? By the end of the second week he had worked himself into a frenzy and decided to take Kult up on his offer. He made plans to run off to Mexico for a brief sabbatical. He just needed a breather from the paranoia.

After covering everything with administration, he had one of the assistant medical examiners pick up the slack for him. They thought he needed some time off to work through Kayline's death-that he was really taking it hard.

After two long weeks of basking on the beaches of Cozumel, he was a new man. He had phoned Kult twice during the vacation.

"Everything's quiet, man. Just enjoy the sun. Wish I was there." The confidence in Kult's voice reassured him. Maybe everything *was* cool.

When he returned home he felt much better and slipped easily back into his routine. A month passed by without any alarm or concern about Kayline or the way she died. He later replaced her with a beautiful dark-haired vixen in her mid twenties and often fantasized about the day he would seduce her.

It was early December before he heard from Kult about another case. "We're meeting on the fifteenth to discuss funding for Maburn." Kult and Collins were always careful to use codes when they were on the phone. What this meant was that Tills had another case.

Collins was hesitant. "Jack, are you sure?"

"You're not getting squirmy on me, are you?"

"Not squirmy, just concerned. Actually, I have two concerns. One is that we haven't let the dust settle from, uh, my vacation."

"You've had almost two months," Jack was beginning to sound impatient, "what's the other concern?"

"Well, I think that Maburn may be getting too much recognition in our meetings. Maybe we should discuss funding for another town."

"We'll talk about it at the meeting. I'll expect you there. Seven o'clock at Wilson's house."

Collins hung up the phone and immediately began feeling queasy. He no longer felt confident in Kult and wanted out in spite of his endearment to the extra income. Walking around with a fat wallet sure had its perks, but it was no longer worth the consequences.

He wondered what would happen if he told the group that he wanted out. Would they "put a man" on him? He was in so deeply now that he couldn't see a way out.

December fifteenth came soon enough. The group met at Mayor Chris Wilson's home in Benton. All the members from Maburn were there as were the regulars from Saline County. There were a couple of new guys sitting near the pool table talking, laughing and chumming it up. He heard one of them exclaim, "Hell, it's about time we came up with a plan! This nation's going to hell in a hand basket."

Sheriff Tills stood in the corner by the Christmas tree guzzling a beer and talking with the sheriff from Saline County. The Maburn County Coroner, a guy named John Haysen, stood with them but couldn't get a word in for Tills' bellowing. There were five other members from other various offices across Hot Spring and Saline Counties. So far, none of these five had been given any cases. The group was still training them on how to have successful applications without getting caught. This entailed getting special grants from the federal government to set up programs where mothers on public assistance can move toward independence, thus reducing the tax dollars spent on state funded programs.

Subsidies for education, employment assistance, daycare, housing, medical assistance, and food programs were all managed by a committee established within each county by the mayor of the largest town within the county or by another designated official. As it was set up, a few dollars were actually dribbled down to structure a few minimal programs. The bulk of the money, however, was routed to an overseas account and subsequently dispersed among the members. The trick was getting all of the key players in an airtight position and managing the books in such a manner that it didn't arouse suspicion. Kult prided himself in the extraordinary planning and preparation in his town- the substandard programs that appeared to be working fabulously, the strong reduction in families needing support and thus the continued need for such programs and their future funding, and the loyalty of the committee members whom he gathered after scrupulous research- all resulting in his future legacy. He would be deemed the man who had the answers.

When the meeting came to order, Kult introduced the two new members. One was a man named Chris Newton, a senator from Pulaski County. The other guy was the mayor of Aldridge, Texas. He was an old time friend of Mayor Wilson's and wanted to look at piloting the program in various counties of Texas. The two new members were sworn in. Collins found his breath thickening with increased uneasiness.

As chairperson of the plan committee, Kult spoke first, giving an account of the Watson family and the problems that occurred. Collins jumped in when necessary. The group discussed preventative measures for maintaining the integrity and secrecy of the plan. Tills occasionally blurted out some self-important nonsense that the group generally ignored.

Collins agreed that not having done an autopsy on the bodies was careless and that it wouldn't happen again. He also explained that he was able to pull up the computer file and change the incriminating evidence. A member from Saline County expressed concern about lab workers who may have seen the results.

Collins explained that, by in large, the folks in the lab were too busy to actually look at the results from lab reports. They just ran them, keyed them into the computer, and stuck them in his box. They did so many each day that they couldn't possibly keep up with all the names and statistics. Kult chimed in that the situation in the lab was being carefully monitored and that, so far, there was no reason for alarm. Then, turning his attention to Tills' he ruled, "No more chloroform. Too risky." Tills let out a burp and nodded simultaneously.

Kult looked up from writing, "Let's talk about the new business."

Tills, of course, spoke up first. At the risk of anyone not thinking he was as important as he knew he was, he always made sure to have new business. "I've got a couple of good ones in mind for the program. Kult and I have already discussed one of them a bit." Kult affirmed with a nod.

Someone in the group said, "Let's hear it."

"Wait," Collins said cautiously, "I'm wondering if it wouldn't be a good idea to let the next couple of cases come from somewhere other than Hot Spring County. Perhaps Saline?" As chairperson of the committee and plan developer, Collins was well aware that Kult received a sizeable return from each City or County receiving the federal grant. His greatest financial compensation, however, came from the participation of his own town.

"No," Kult interrupted, "I understand we may have a leak there." He looked at the Saline County Sheriff who nodded.

"Care to elaborate?" Collins asked incredulously.

As Kult eyed Collins, the Saline County Sheriff gave the specifics saying, "I've been informed that a social worker in Saline is asking a lot of questions. Preventative measures are in place, I assure you."

"Now, with all of that said," Kult turned away from Collins' gaze, looked at one of the new members and stated, "Collins raises a good question. It's important to distribute the cases according to the size of the county for two reasons. One, of course, is to reduce suspicion. The other is to provide an appropriate ratio of success. In other words, one family that has been removed from public assistance in a small county could be equal to twenty in a larger county. The grants provided to the state are based on percentages of success, or families removed from the system, rather than the actual number. However," he continued with his gaze returning to Collins, "we've only had one case in Hot Spring County in a nine-month-span, and it's my belief that another case would be appropriate at this time. Tills, please continue."

Moisture trickled under Collins' armpit as Tills addressed the group. "The first is a retarded woman with a kid. The state is spending a fortune on the both of them."

Haysen spoke up, "What are they getting now?"

Kult answered, "I put a man on this as soon as Tills brought it to me. Apparently the family is getting Supplemental Security Income, Food Stamps, Housing, Medicaid and Support Services from DHS. We paid for the labor, delivery and after care of the baby, and we'll likely end up paying for two or three more kids. In addition to this, we learned that the woman spent most of her life in foster care. According to the latest statistics, and I'm happy to provide you with the articles, a child of a mother raised in foster care is three times more likely to end up in foster care than a child whose mother wasn't raised in the system. From this we can glean that it's highly likely that one or more of her kids will end up in foster care. "Anyone care to guess the cost of one year of foster care?"

He waited. When no one answered he replied, "Twenty-five thousand a year." That's in a regular foster home. If they're in a therapeutic foster home, the cost is almost forty thousand a year." Several men whistled at the high figures.

"I've done the math," Kult said. He handed a stack of papers to Haysen, who began passing them out to each member. "And I'm supplying each of you with a copy of all the services this woman has been provided through the government and the approximate cost of each program. As you can see, to date, this woman has cost our government approximately two hundred and sixty nine thousand dollars, and she wasn't even raised in a therapeutic foster home."

Kult continued, "Now, since Mom's retarded, she will likely be on government assistance the rest of her life. And, considering the likelihood that some or all of her prospective children will end up in state custody- most likely therapeutic care, because it's the latest craze among social workers- I don't have to tell you folks this one family has the potential to cost us millions, depending on the number of kids she has." Several of the men looked at each other, shaking their heads in disgust.

Collins tried to play devil's advocate in hopes of prolonging or maybe even terminating the plan. But, after the staggering figures were presented, he didn't have much luck. He wasn't concerned about the retarded girl or the baby. Honestly, he felt that it would be for the good of all to have them dead. What he did care about was the good of his own hide.

Tills bellowed forth, "Basically the girl's a menace to society. She's a leech to our state income and there's absolutely nothing productive about her life. I mean, we're looking at what's best for our state and having some retard suckin' on all our resources ain't it."

Two members hollered, "Amen." They took a vote, and the "aye's" won out.

Kult passed the motion and warned Tills to also get the baby saying, "If you only get the girl, her bastard kid will be put in foster care. That'll be a big chunk taken out of the returns. Take your time, and do it right."

"Yes, sir."

"And what's the name again?"

"Johnson," Tills' expression looked cold and calculating, "Mattie Johnson."

Chapter Fifteen

Shy spent the morning visiting with Traci Barett, making sure that she received the Medicaid cards for Hannah and Piersen and that all of the other services were in place. The women sat at the kitchen table drinking coffee and watching Mr. Border and Hannah through the window. Traci smiled and shook her head adoringly, "They're supposed to be collecting leaves."

Hannah was neck deep in a pile of leaves that Mr. Border had raked up. Every now and then she would yell, "Watch PaPa!" and jump up, throwing leaves high over her head. Mr. Border had her Raggedy Ann doll tucked under his arm so that he could clap for Hannah every time she threw leaves in the air. The doll was dressed in a diaper that went up to its neck. Traci chuckled, "If she's not redressing the doll ten times a day, she's got poor Carl babysitting it."

"She's so cute," Shy laughed, and then added, "Actually, they both are." Traci agreed with a nod.

"How's Piersen adjusting in school?"

"So far so good. He's making good grades and has a lot of friends. I guess I can't ask for any more than that."

Shy smiled at her and said, "Well, Traci, it sounds like you've got everything under control."

"I couldn't have done it without your help. I'm so grateful. Hopefully, I won't need welfare for long. I'm going back to school next semester."

"Really? That's wonderful. What are you going for?"

"I'd like to be a physical therapy assistant. I just have a few more hours to go. Maybe I can be done by this time next year."

"Oh, Traci, that would be great. I didn't know you had been to college."

"Yes, I went before I married the kids' dad."

"Well, good for you. I wish all my cases were this easy." As the women finished their coffee, Shy explained how the Medicaid cards should be used to cover medical expenses including prescription medication for the children. She also explained that, unfortunately, Arkansas did not have a Medicaid program to cover adults without disabilities. Therefore, Traci would not be covered by the program. Traci expressed gratitude for whatever help she could get saying, "At least my children are covered."

On the way back to the office, Shy had time to think about Ben. She had not seen him or spoken to him in a week, having "chickened out" on her plan to tell him things were moving too fast. She just couldn't do it. He kept leaving messages on her machine asking her what he had done to upset her, telling her that he loved her, and begging her to return his calls. Shy missed him badly. She finally turned her machine off. He deserved more than what she was able to give him. Pulling into the parking lot of DHS, she wiped the mascara that stained her cheeks and touched up her make up. She spent the rest of the day documenting in charts and preparing an affidavit for court. Finding it difficult to concentrate, she was glad to see four-thirty come.

The day was bright with crisp winds blowing about the trees. Early winter was Shy's favorite time of the year, and she was ready to get out in it. She ran a few errands and headed to the grocery store. The local market was busier than usual. Several of the aisles had numerous carts in them with people scanning over the items of their shopping lists. It took her thirty minutes to wind her way through the maze of people, collect a few munchies, and get through the check out line.

She sat the groceries in the floorboard of the back seat and started the car. The sky had evolved into a beautiful display of pink, purple, and blue that reminded her of the mural she'd seen at the French Cottage the night of her first date with Ben. She sighed heavily and decided to make one more stop at Wal-Mart to see if the pictures of the picnic with Mattie had been developed. It had been a week since she dropped the film off, and she thought they would surely be ready by now. She hoped that at least one of them would be nice enough to frame. Mattie had so few pictures of herself and Jake.

As she entered the store, she found herself hoping desperately that no one would recognize her. She was tired of keeping her feelings at bay, having done enough of that at work today. Now all she wanted to do was get Mattie's pictures and return to her home where she could soak in her own misery.

The photo clerk rummaged through an organized crate of alphabetically-ordered pictures until she reached the S's. "Here we are. Sharon Sauze?"

"Yes, ma'am."

"Would you like to go ahead and look at them?"

"Sure." Shy opened the package of pictures. She eyed each of them intently until she came across one in particular that touched her heart. It was a picture of Mattie's backside as she held the baby high in the air. The angle caught the perfect expression of Jake's gleeful, wide eyes. He was laughing so hard that his solitary tooth stood out as if it were a pearl against a dark backdrop. The picture was so vivid she could almost hear Jake's squeal. She turned the picture around so that the clerk could see it.

"Could you turn this into an eight by ten?"

"Sure, just let me get the negative and mark it." The clerk took the negatives and held them over a light attached to the counter. She made a small note on an envelope and stuck that particular negative inside saying, "Should be ready in about four days."

"Thank you." Shy paid for the other pictures and tucked them in her purse. She would give them to Mattie the next time she was out that way.

It was nearly six o'clock. A dark gray mask was beginning to settle over dusk. As Shy left the building, she noticed a black and white police unit with yellow pinstripes pull into the handicap lane right next to the door. At first she thought it was Ben and her heart skipped a beat. It was Percy. He hung his head out the window, "Hi there, Shy. What are you doing?"

She smiled, putting her best face forward. "Hi, Percy. Since when did you become handicapped?"

He looked down in an attempt to show shame. "Caught red-handed," he grinned. Shy thought Percy looked much better than the last time she had seen him. He looked rested and seemed almost peppy.

"How is Clare doing?" Shy asked.

"She's doing great. Even going back to school. It was touch and go for a while there, you know. She's such a fighter."

"She must take after her daddy."

Percy smiled at her. "Had our doctor's appointment last Friday. Her white blood count is back to normal. Can you believe it? Looks like her body is taking the transplant."

"Oh, Percy, that's wonderful. God can do miracles, can't He? And I can't think of anyone more deserving of a miracle than you."

Percy looked away from her, and she thought she saw a subtle shift in his mood. When he looked back at her he said, "No, I'm not deserving of a miracle, but Clare," tears began to fill his eyes, "now she deserves one. I had to do everything I could, you know," he looked away briefly, "to save her."

Shy reached out and touched his arm gently. "Of course, you did. That's the kind of dad you are."

Percy sniffed back a couple of tears and then forced his affection to brighten. "Enough about me. What's been goin' on with you?"

Shy took the hint and changed the subject. "Nothing remarkable, I guess, since the Watsons."

Percy's expression deepened again as he nodded and looked away. Shy felt like an insensitive idiot for mentioning the Watsons. Percy didn't need to hear about children dying. Changing the subject again as quickly as possible, she asked, "Anything new at the sheriff's office?"

He shook his head, "Naw, not really. Well, except for Crossno. Ain't none of my business, but the boy sure has been hangin' his jaw

Cries of the Orchids

lately. Seems sad all the time. Reckon that may have anything to do with you?"

Her heart ached. She nodded at Percy, "Perhaps."

"Well, you even look sad yourself, if you don't mind me saying."

"I guess I am," she said with a weak grin.

"Well, if I haven't learned anything else over the last couple of years, I've learned that life is too short for foolishness."

Shy nodded as Percy's dispatch radio gave out a loud grainy noise followed by a female dispatcher, "We have a DOA at thirteen fourteen Military. Possible suicide. All units respond."

Percy grimaced as if he knew it was coming. He leaned into his shoulder and clicked his CB, "Roger that." He looked at her with sad eyes and put the car in reverse.

"Wait!" Shy yelled, clutching the driver's side window to prevent Percy from leaving. Mattie lived on that road. "What was the address?"

"Uh, I can't--"

"Tell me the address, Percy!"

"Shy don't go out there."

"I'm following you."

"You can't follow me, Shy."

"DAMN IT, PERCY, JUST GO!"

She threw her purse onto the passenger's seat, turned on the ignition and spun out of the parking lot behind the blue lights. The dispatcher had said DOA. Shy knew that meant "dead on arrival." She breathed heavily, trying to force her lungs out of her throat. She tried to remember Mattie's address. *What were the numbers on her mailbox?* She kept trying to tell herself it wasn't Mattie. *Mattie wouldn't commit suicide. She loved Jake too much.*

Percy was ahead of her, driving seventy-five miles an hour down the twisting country road. Dust showered Shy's car, turning her hood into a fine mist of brown sheath. She willed him to pull off the road and stop at a house she didn't recognize. As they sped further down the road, Shy's heart became rampant. "Please, God, don't let it be Mattie or the baby! Please, God!"

Mattie's small house was only two blocks away. *Please go past it! Please go past it! It's not her! It can't be her!* The tiny house grew closer. Three patrol cars consumed the tiny yard. Flashing blue lights illuminated the sky. Yellow tape reading "crime scene" formed a barrier on the front porch.

Shy felt a guttural scream emerge from her core, "Mattie!" She didn't know how she got the car parked. All she knew was that she was suddenly on the porch fighting with the yellow tape, screaming out Mattie's name. She felt strong arms around her, holding her, trying to console her. "You can't go in there, Shy." It was Ben. "She's gone, honey." He tried to console her. "She's gone."

"No!" She scratched and clawed at Ben, until she was finally able to break free and tear through the yellow tape.

"Shy, wait!" Ben yelled at her, but she couldn't hear him. She was already in the door. Mattie was lying on the floor. A pool of blood spread under her head and out onto the linoleum floor. Her eyes were open and transfixed. A gun was laying six inches from her right hand. Shy collapsed to her knees. Pain swelled up so strong and raw that she thought she might implode. With tears flowing from her eyes, she whimpered, "Oh, Mattie." Taking her hand and gently closing Mattie's eyes, Shy could hear Sheriff Tills and another man talking in the kitchen. They were whispering and unaware of her presence.

"Where's the baby, damn it?" Tills said.

"He wasn't in the room with the playpen. Do you think she might have left him with someone?"

"Naw, no family. Shit! Keep looking. Maybe she stuffed him under a cabinet or something. She was a retard; no tellin' what she did with him!"

Shy stood up and walked to the entrance of the kitchen. She looked at the men and asked, "Where's the baby?" Her eyes were wide and near crazed, resembling a mother grizzly ready to attack. The men were startled and nervously eyed each other, wondering how she had gotten past the police barricade.

Tills was the first to speak, "Miss, Sauze, now, hon, I realize you bein' the social worker and all ..." Tills, while pulling his belt up and over his waistline said, "Hate you had to see this, sugar." He was shaking his head back and forth slowly, as if to convey compassion saying, "It's a shame when someone takes their own life. I'm sure you know you did everything you could." Tills was rambling and stumbling over his words. "Now, uh, we can't have you in here and about the crime scene."

Shy stared at him with cold, angry eyes, "Where's the baby?"

"Well, now just calm down." Tills had moved toward her and now had her gently by the arm. She jerked away from him with such force that he stumbled backward into the wall. He gathered his bearings and tried to catch her, yelling at her frantically, "Miss Sauze, this is a crime scene! I'm gonna have to ask you to step outside or be arrested!"

She ignored him as she ran down the hallway to Jake's room. She looked at the bundled blankets in the playpen and moved toward them slowly, afraid she wouldn't see his tiny head sticking out of them. When she didn't see Jake immediately, she foraged through the blankets frantically. The playpen was empty. She prayed, *Please, God, let me find him!*

Tills was now standing behind her, trying to reason with her. "Miss Sauze, we're still investigating the where 'bouts of the baby." Since he didn't want a big upset with this case, having Shy there was too risky. They had to find that baby before she did.

Speaking to her in a gentle voice, he said, "Now, I know you're upset, but we really need to get you outside and away from the crime scene."

He put a gentle hand on her shoulder, but she shrugged away and looked at him with swells of tears in her eyes. "I have to find him Sheriff, don't you understand that! I won't leave until I find him!" Tills put more authority in his voice as he became desperate to get Shy out. He told her that he was going to get a couple of his deputies to have her removed. When she ignored him, Tills stomped out of the room to follow through with the threat.

Shy closed her eyes and uttered a silent prayer when she suddenly remembered the cave Mattie had made for Jake in the closet. Her heart beat faster as she moved toward it. *God, please let him be in there!* The exposed portion of the closet where Mattie had torn the door off revealed nothing. She closed her eyes tightly as she slid the door to the other side, praying again that he would be in there. When she opened her eyes she saw Jake curled up and asleep on the ragged red blanket with his bottle lying beside him. Shy crumpled to her knees beside him and started sobbing. As she gathered him up into her arms, Sheriff Tills and his deputies entered the room.

"I found him," she said to Tills in joyous relief, kissing Jake on the forehead and wiping her tears.

Tills was speechless. He fidgeted from one leg to the other, remembering what Kult said about killing both the mother and the baby. "Well, uh, look at that. Glad we found him. You can, uh, just leave him in the playpen and uh …"

Shy had already stood up and was walking toward the door. She looked at him through red, swollen eyes. "I'll be taking him with me."

As she tried to move past Tills, he grabbed her arm sternly, "You can't, uh, just let us----" Shy jerked away and scowled at him with cold, hard eyes. "I can, Sheriff, and I will. This baby is now in state custody, and if you should find the need to interview him as to his mother's death," she said with venomous sarcasm, "you can find him at the hospital."

Shy walked past him, holding Jake's head to her chest as she moved past Mattie's inert body in the living room. Walking through the door of Mattie's home for the last time, she began to sob again. Ben saw her walk down the stairs of the tiny porch. He ran to her, desperate to reach out and comfort her, but Shy walked passed him without giving him eye contact.

The sheriff and the coroner just stood and looked at one another as Shy pulled out of the driveway with Jake. The coroner dropped his head and chewed on the side of his lip. Tills said a few curse words and threw his head back in disbelief. The mayor was not going to be happy.

Chapter Sixteen

Shy took Jake to the hospital for an examination. She was sure he was fine, but she didn't want to take any chances. Out in the waiting room, she called Bill and cried hysterically as she told him the story. Bill told her that he was on his way.

After thirty minutes the nurse told Shy she could come on back. Jake was sitting in a steel hospital crib. When he saw Shy he grabbed the rails and pulled himself up. With a gleeful expression, he bounced up and down yelling, "Ty!" When Shy walked over to him, he let go of the rail with one hand to reach for her. He lost his balance, and Shy grabbed him before he fell. "Uh-oh," she said, "I got you."

"Uh-oh!" Jake parroted, as she held him close and kissed him. *What would become of this baby? How could he ever know how much his mommy loved him?* Jake continued to babble, innocently oblivious that his world had been ripped away from him.

It took Bill almost forty-five minutes to get there. Shy saw him walk through the door. He looked at her empathically and said, "Rough night, huh, kiddo."

"Oh, Bill," she cried, her neck wet with tears, "it was awful! It was just so awful!"

He wrapped his arms around both Shy and Jake as she sobbed on his shoulder. Jake grinned and tried to play with Bill's bottom lip. Bill nibbled at him and made the baby squeal with bliss. Shy's eyesight was blurred from tears. She could see a man and a woman standing behind Bill just outside the door. Swiping at the tears to clear her vision, she realized that she recognized the couple. She'd placed a foster child with them almost a year ago. She was confused. *What were they doing here?* And then reality set in- they were here for the baby. Shy started shaking her head and moving backward, clutching Jake firmly. "No, Bill. No! He's not going into foster care." Bill walked toward her, and she started to cry harder. "NO! Bill, don't do this."

"Shy," his voice was soft and gentle, "you know you can't keep this baby."

"But I can," she wept. "He doesn't know these people. He doesn't have anyone."

"Shy, listen to me. They're good people. You know they are. They'll take good care of Jake."

Jake heard his name and yelled, "Dake!"

"Bill, please. I'll quit my job. There won't be a conflict of interest. Please." She begged so profoundly that even Bill was moved to tears.

"Honey, give me the baby."

"No, Bill." She put her back to him and held Jake toward the wall. "Please don't do this!"

Bill had to physically remove Jake from her arms, and as he did, Shy crumpled to her knees. He handed the baby to his new foster parents and urged them to leave quickly. Jake immediately started crying when handed to the strangers. He could be heard all the way down the hallway crying, "Mama! No! Mama!....Ty!...Ty!...."

Bill walked over to Shy who was now sitting on the floor with her knees up to her chest. She was crying quietly with her face in her hands. Bill tried to console her, but she shook her head and told him to leave. He didn't. He just stood to the side and gave her some space.

She sobbed quietly as she silently asked herself unanswerable questions: *Why did Mattie kill herself? Was it because she was lonely? Was it because I wasn't visiting as often? Why?* Shy felt a strong arm swoop under her knees and behind her back, lifting her into the air. It was Ben. Neither of them said a word. She laid her head on his shoulder and wept. Ben walked passed Bill without saying a word, and Bill hated him for carrying Shy away from him.

Cries of the Orchids

Taking Shy to his apartment, Ben layed her on his couch with a heavy blanket wrapped around her. He went into the kitchen momentarily and came back out with some hot tea and lemon. Putting both cups on the sofa table, he kneeled down beside her.

Shy leaned up on one arm, looking him squarely in the face, and said, "I can't have any children, Ben."

Ben thought she was delirious from the shock of today's events. Saying nothing, he just continued stroking her cheek. She pulled herself to a sitting position and spoke a bit louder asking, "Did you hear me? I said I can't have children. I will *never* be able to have children."

Ben sighed, feeling confusion, he asked, "Honey, is that why you've been avoiding me and not returning my calls?" She nodded miserably.

"Oh, Shy," he said, moving up to the couch beside her and hugging her tightly, "I love you so much. Don't you know that?"

"You said you wanted me to be the mother of your children."

"Or dog," he said abruptly, "kids or a dog. That's what I meant to say," he said with a grin, "now, if you tell me you're allergic to dogs then you're definitely out of the picture."

Shy laughed over Ben's absurdity and then started crying again as her thoughts returned to Mattie and Jake. Ben reached out and held her. "Ben, why'd she do it?" Saying nothing, he just held her and listened.

"What about Jake? How could she leave him? Ben, I saw them every week. She loved that baby. She wouldn't have left him." Her sobs grew louder. He rocked her back and forth gently, holding the nape of her neck as she lay against his chest.

"She wouldn't have left him." She repeated this intermittently between the sobs and cried until she fell asleep from exhaustion. Ben lay awake all night holding her, rocking her, and thinking.

Chapter Seventeen

Shy returned to work after a day-and-a-half of hard grieving. Bill told her she could take more time off, but she thought she would do better if she kept her mind busy. Bill wouldn't allow her to see Jake in his new foster home. He felt it would make it more difficult for the baby to adjust. Shy could hardly make it from one hour to the next without feeling the pangs of grief and sorrow. She wanted so badly to hold Jake and let him know she was there. Shy begged Bill to let her foster parent him, but he was resolute about that being a major disregard of state policy. She said again that she would quit her job, go through foster parent training, anything. Bill said that even if she did take the measures to become a foster parent, it would be unlikely that the state would place an infant with a single woman who had no income.

She felt helpless. He wouldn't even allow her to call the foster parents to check on him. At one point, when she began to cry again, Bill held her shoulders firmly, looked her squarely in the eyes, and stated, "Honey, for your sake and the baby's, let him go."

Mattie's body was still at the crime lab. Shy was told that it would probably be another three days before it would be sent to Wilkins' Funeral Home in Maburn. She made a quick phone call to the funeral home to see if there was anything they needed. They said they would call her if they thought of anything.

She had lunch with Ben, though she really couldn't force much on her stomach. Ben wanted to see her tonight, but she felt like being alone. The rest of the afternoon was fairly quiet. She made a few home visits while trying to make a reasonable effort to conceal her agony. After that, she finished up some three-day-old paperwork. Bill took on all the new investigations to keep her workload light for the next couple of weeks.

Shy left work around five o'clock and bought a hamburger on the way home. By nine o'clock she was in her bathrobe, the burger still tightly wrapped on the kitchen counter. She sat on the couch and called Ben to invite him for an early morning run and breakfast. She thought if she let all of her emotions pour out through physical exertion first thing in the morning, the rest of her day would go a bit better. She needed to be strong so that she could be halfway productive at work. Maybe a good run in the morning would help.

Sleep was restless. She kept thinking about Mattie with her child like innocence and how Mattie always seemed so happy. *Why would she kill herself?* It was almost inconceivable. She almost gave her life for Jake last winter. Why would she leave him now to grow up in the foster care system she hated? It didn't make sense.

It took her more than an hour to drift off to sleep, and even then she stirred to the infant cries of a baby far removed from the only world he knew. She would reach out and call to him but couldn't see him. And, her dreams found her once again in the field of demonic flowers. They were snapping at her feet with their sharp yellow teeth. She could see the infant far in the distance, surrounded by the flowers, crying and reaching out to her. But every time she drew near the child, he would disappear. At three in the morning, Shy awoke in a cold sweat. With her heart pounding painfully in her chest, she was unable to go back to sleep.

Ben was there shortly before five. Shy was putting on her tennis shoes when she heard the doorbell ring. She finished tying her laces and ran downstairs to open the door.

"Good morning."

"Hi," he put his arms around her waist and kissed her on the nose, "how are you feeling today?"

"Better, I think," she smiled weakly. Dark circles lined the skin below her eyes.

"How'd you sleep last night?" he asked.

"Not too good."

Cries of the Orchids

"I was afraid of that."

The morning was still black, only lit by the dim orange hue of the streetlights. They headed out into the darkness with a light jog, ran ten blocks; and then turned back with a sprint. By the time they reached Shy's apartment, they were both out of breath.

In between heavy breaths, Shy said she would put on some coffee. Ben stood by the kitchen table as she filled the cylinder with water and put six scoops of coffee grounds in the filtered percolator.

"I think I'm getting old," Ben said as he wiped his sweaty brow on his shirt.

"I thought I saw a couple of gray hairs the other night," she teased.

"Watch it."

She kissed him on the forehead and told him she was going to run upstairs and take a quick shower.

"I'll start breakfast," he said.

"Thanks. You know where everything is. I'll be back down in a bit."

Shy went upstairs and opened her closet. She found a pair of khaki slacks and a short sleeve stretchy black blouse. Her black heels were on the top shelf of her closet, and she had to stand on the tip of her toes to reach them. Laying everything on the bed neatly, grabbing her bathrobe and a towel, she was looking forward to a quick shower. Afterwards, she dressed quickly and headed downstairs to the aroma of coffee and scrambled eggs.

Ben heard her and hollered, "So, what are you in the mood for?"

She walked up behind him and wrapped her arms around his waist, intertwining her fingers just over his belly button. She laid her head on his back and repeated, "What am I in the mood for?"

Ben turned around and raised his voice dramatically, "Okay, are you just trying to get in my pants? Because you know that I take offense to that!"

"Oh, Ben. Stop," she laughed.

"You may get whatever you want from the other guys, but you don't get none of this until I have a ring and a date, little sister."

Shy popped him on the arm saying, "Would you hush?"

He kissed her on the forehead, "How about eggs and toast?"

"Sounds great," she said. "I'll pour some coffee."

Ben continued to scramble the eggs as Shy grabbed two cups from the cupboard. Within five minutes the breakfast was finished, and she and Ben were sitting on the couch with their cups and plates on the coffee table in front of them.

The morning news had just begun. The same bubbly blonde appeared on the T.V. screen. Shy never could understand the type of person who could actually work at this hour and look good at the same time. The woman's usually happy expression was solemn. Frown lines formed around her mouth.

Shy's lack of food since Mattie's death had summoned a ravenous appetite. She spooned in a large amount of eggs- so much, in fact, that she cut her eyes to see if Ben had seen both of her cheek's puffed out as if she were a hamster with pouches full of seeds. He, thankfully, had his eyes fixed on the morning news. She turned her eyes to the television. The chirpy reporter's expression had turned solemn when she said, "Another house fire claims the lives of a Hot Spring County family this morning on Camen Road. The home, a rental, owned by Mr. Carl Border of Glen Rosen...."

Shy choked on the eggs which began a coughing spasm that projected pieces of egg all over the coffee table and carpet. Ben began patting her back saying, "Honey, you okay?"

She held a hand up and nodded but continued to cough. She heard the newscaster conclude with "No survivors." When Shy was finally able to talk, she exclaimed, "Ben, I know those people!"

"What?"

"Yes. I just saw them the other day. Traci Barett and her two kids. And Mr. Border, did the reporter say if he died too?"

"I didn't hear. Who's Mr. Border?"

"Ben, I've gotta go." She put her plate on the coffee table.

Ben grabbed her arm, "Wait! Where are you going?"

"I'm going out there."

"What? Why? What do you hope to accomplish?"

"I don't know. I need to check on Mr. Border," she said.

"Shy, don't go."

"I've got to." She rustled around for her keys and purse. Grabbing her briefcase, she rushed out the door.

"Shy, wait a minute." It was too late. He rushed to the door, but she was already in her car. He put his head in his hands and rubbed his scalp. *She was getting too curious. What if she stumbled onto the truth?* He decided to put a call in to his boss. Shy was becoming too great of a risk.

Rays of light were just beginning to seep through the blackened morning air. The chill of a new day cast an eerie fog among the trees. The density was further thickened by the smoke rolling from the house-fire down the road. A car up ahead, either going or coming from work, drove slowly by the site, rubber-necking to get a glimpse of the burned house through the heavy haze. Shy pulled up behind the car, and it accelerated, going about its business. Pulling into the driveway, she could see the shadow of a frail old man standing by the skeletal remains of the Barett's home. Getting out of her car, she closed the door gently, as if she were afraid of awakening the old man from his slumber. The morning held an eerie chill that made her teeth chatter slightly.

Mr. Border stood leaning on his cane with a glazed, fixated expression that stared off toward the remains but at nothing in particular. Shy was afraid the old man might be in shock. She took in a deep breath and moved toward him slowly. "Mr. Border?" she said softly as her stomach twisted and turned violently. He looked at her. His eyes had been rubbed and burned with tears to the extent that she was sure he would have mild scabs surrounding the soft folds of tissue in the corner of his eyes.

"Mr. Border, have you been here all night?" she asked, her voice filled with genuine concern. He looked away from her and looked back at the house. Smoke moved from the remains in a ghostly manner toward the fog, intermingling and moving together as if lovers, reforming and shaping until they became one.

A badly burned composition of yarn, fabric, and stuffing resembling the remains of a pretty Raggedy Ann doll was cradled in the crook of his arm.

"Mr. Border," Shy said softly. He stared off while his hand and cane trembled in unison. "Mr. Border, why don't you come with me. Let's get away from here for awhile."

Tears stained his weathered cheeks. He shook his head. "I should have had that wiring checked." He said bleakly, "I knew I should have had it checked." His voice quivered, as he took the sleeve of his flannel shirt and rubbed it across his eyes. He held the burned doll up to his face. "I gave her this, you know." He began to sob into the doll. Not the normal cries of someone in pain but the deep, primal pain of grief that can only be felt in one's darkest hour. Shy knew it well. All too recently it threatened to rip her heart out and leave her lifeless. She was unable to restrain her own tears from falling. She reached for him, but he pulled away and began the slow walk toward the medium of trees that separated his home from the rental. Shy watched his walking carefully as if every step was painful. She hurt for him in the same way she hurt for Jake.

Mr. Border stopped and leaned on his cane. He stood for what seemed like forever without saying a word, as if he were trying to find the courage to say what was on his mind. "Why didn't she wake up?" His voice was barely audible. He turned to Shy. "I can't understand why she didn't wake up." His voice was shaky and pleading as if somehow the answer to this question might bring them back. Shy stood silently, helpless to help him. Mr. Border squinted his eyes and shook his head angrily. "She would have heard the alarms." The tears came again, flowing uncontrollably as he said, "I just put them in two weeks ago. Why didn't she hear the fire alarms?" His voice became a scream, searing through the valley, "Why didn't she hear the damn alarms!"

Shy walked to him, trying once again to console him, but he waved her away and began walking toward the grove of trees. Embers from the burned remains of the house continued to emit smoke. The smell was a morbid reminder of lives lost only hours before. Shy could still hear the fragile sobs of Mr. Border as his shadow became lost within the trees in front of his home. Her body felt lethargic. Her stomach was queasy.

Shy was halfway home when she realized that she'd actually gotten in her car and driven away from the scene. She felt foggy and numb, as if she'd taken a half a dozen painkillers. A woman and her four babies were incinerated in a house fire just weeks ago and now another family dies tragically in the same way. And then there was Mattie. Shy swerved the car over to the right and pulled it to a quick stop. She jerked the car door open and vomited.

It was after eight when she pulled into the driveway. Having puked down the side of her slacks, she was anxious to re-shower and change clothes. Ben had already left, and she found herself wishing that he hadn't. She needed to curl up in his arms and breathe in his assurance and security, for she was unsure how much more her nerves would be able to tolerate. Pulling off her blouse as she headed up the stairs, Shy suddenly realized how late she was going to be for work. She knew Bill would worry, so she decided to call before hopping in the shower.

As she plopped down on the bed beside the phone, she noticed that the answering machine was blinking. She had two messages- probably Ben, checking on her. She pushed the button and started unsnapping her pants. The machine told her that the first call was received this morning at five thirty.

Five-thirty? She and Ben were running at five-thirty. She hadn't noticed it blinking when they returned. Now she sat on the bed waiting to see who called.

"Shy, it's Nelson. I'm on my way out there. Stay put. I gotta talk to you." He sounded anxious. She wondered why he was coming to her house so early, and it scared her that something was wrong. Had something happened to Glorie, and he didn't want to tell her over the phone? *Please, God. No more.* She checked her watch. It was eight twenty-five. *Why wasn't he here, yet?*

Her thoughts were interrupted by the next message. It was recorded two minutes after eight, just twenty-three minutes ago.

"Baby, it's Glorie." Her voice sounded thick and pressured, "I'm at the Hot Spring County Hospital. There's been an accident, baby. Nelson's hurt real bad."

Oh, dear God! Shy's heart raced as she jumped into the same pair of vomit-stained slacks and grabbed a t-shirt out of the closet.

She left out of the house in such a panic that she didn't even bother to lock the door.

Pressure began to build under the surface of her skull as she sped to the hospital. Glorie and the rest of the family, along with half of the church were piled up in the waiting area. When Glorie saw Shy rush through the front entrance, she stood to embrace her. Swollen puffs of skin engorged the folds around Glorie's eyes. Shy could tell by her expression that Nelson was in bad shape. She found the strength to ask, "What happened?" but she wasn't sure she could tolerate the answer.

"We don't know, baby. The Saline Police Department called us just after seven. Said the Maburn police called them after they saw his name badge and saw that he was a social worker from Saline County. Said it looked like he just run off the road." She started to sob. "He hit a tree. His leg--" she stopped, trying to brace herself for the next few words she needed to say. They came out in a whisper. "He's in surgery. They had to amputate his leg."

Shy felt as if a thrust of fire had engulfed her lungs, making it almost impossible to breathe. Her legs almost gave away beneath her as she and Glorie held on to one another. Family members and church members joined them, crying, hugging, and praying. When Shy could speak, she pulled away from Glorie and cried, "He was coming to see me. That's why he was in Maburn." She started to tremble and Glorie held on to her.

"Why, Baby? Why was he coming out there that early?"

Shy was shaking her head. "I don't know. He said he needed to talk to me." Shy fell into Nelson's mother with hysterical sobs. It was two hours later before she'd gathered enough composure to call Bill and tell him the story. He cared about Nelson, too. Shy could tell that the news upset him.

"I'll hold down the fort here. Don't worry about anything. I'll be there as soon as I can. He's strong, Shy. He'll pull through."

Nelson had been in surgery for six hours when the doctor came out. Shy stood up with the rest of the family, anxious to hear what the doctor had to say. She felt dizzy, and the room began to spin. She could hear the doctor talking, but she couldn't make out the words. She tried to concentrate, but her head was pulsating. Her vision began to blur and everything before her began to give way to darkness as a numbing sensation surged through her veins. She didn't know what the doctor said. She could only remember hearing Glorie scream.

And, as she slipped into unconsciousness, she knew that Nelson was gone.

Chapter Eighteen

"Kult, this has got to stop. He's out of control. He didn't even have the vote of the rest of the group. Do we know anything about this family?"

"A woman, Traci Barett, early thirties, and her two kids. And no, Tills didn't even seek council from me. I got a phone call from him about three this morning."

Collins was running his fingers through his thinning hair and pacing the floor. "What did he think he was doing?"

"He said he was trying to compensate for the last job."

"What do you mean?"

"You know, he got the retarded girl but not the kid. Kid's in foster care running up an extensive state bill. We can't get to him, now. I told Tills that he really let us down."

"So he goes and kills a family without our consideration? We didn't even research this family." Collins was so angry that he was beginning to stutter. "What about th-the girls family? Does sh-she have an ex?"

"I'm afraid so. When I got off the phone I had one of my guys run a check. Seems that the children's dad is an attorney in Springfield."

"Oh great! That's just great."

"Calm down, John. I'm gonna have one of my guys keep an eye on him for suspicious behavior. We'll take care of it before it becomes a problem." Kult was just as calm and calculating as ever.

"And what about the bodies? Don't send them to me. I'm not gonna go around and clean up after that lunatic. It's just too damn risky."

"You don't have to worry about that, John. I'll take care of it."

"Where are the bodies right now?"

"I'm not sure. The fire marshal is holding them at an unknown location until he's finished investigating."

Collins threw his head back, "Investigating? The fire marshal is not one of us, Jack. Damn it!"

"John, it's just standard procedure. You're worrying too much. I'll take care of everything."

Collins tried to relax but couldn't. The whole thing was getting too deep. He paced the room and then turned back to Kult. "Well, what are we going to do about Tills? I'm telling you, Jack, the man is a loose cannon. He's gonna get us all taken down."

"I have concerns that you may be right. Just calm down and let me see what I can do."

Chapter Nineteen

Shy's mother, Karen, flew in from Texas as soon as she got the news. She was standing beside the hospital bed stroking Shy's hair and worrying about her little girl. Few people knew what Shy had gone through during the years following her father's death. Karen's heart ached as she remembered her daughter, age twelve, suffering from the loss of her dad and teetering on the brink of insanity from the guilt of blaming herself for the accident. She read it all in the suicide note that Shy left just before slitting her wrists.

Karen could still see the tiny scars as Shy lay sleeping in the hospital bed. They had faded quite a bit. Most people wouldn't even notice them. But for Karen, they would never disappear, even if surgically removed from Shy's wrists. They were subtle reminders of how helpless she felt when she tried to convince Shy that her daddy's death was a tragic accident and no one's fault. But Karen wasn't able to get through to her.

She and the girls moved in with Karen's parents after the fire. Everyday after school Nelson would walk the two-mile distance to Shy's grandparent's house to see his friend, only to be met at the door by Karen. She would say, "I'm sorry, sweetie. She doesn't want any company today. Just hang in there. She'll come back around."

Karen made the girls go back to school two weeks after the accident, thinking that the normal routine would be good for them. Shea did really well and readjusted easily to the school routine. Shy didn't. She began failing every subject in school, and she isolated herself from everyone around her, including Nelson.

The nightmares were horrible. Everyone in the house would awaken to Shy's screams. Try as she might, Karen could never get Shy to talk about the dreams- or anything else for that matter.

Three months after the fire, Shy weighed only eighty-nine pounds and she had dark circles under her eyes from malnutrition and sleep deprivation. Forcing Shy into therapy, that didn't work because of Shy's refusal to talk; Karen had exhausted her resources and felt helpless to help her daughter.

One week after the New Year's holiday, Karen got up late to get a drink of water. She checked on the girls and found that Shy wasn't in her bed. The suicide note was lying on her pillow. In the letter, Shy apologized for taking her dad away from everyone. She said that she couldn't stand to look in her mother's eyes, knowing what she had done.

Karen's dad found his twelve-year-old granddaughter lying in the bathtub with both wrists slit. She was barely alive. After three nights in the Intensive Care Unit and six pints of blood, Shy was transferred to the Child and Adolescent Psychiatric Unit where she stayed for three weeks. She refused to eat and lost another five pounds. The staff eventually restrained her to the hospital bed and pumped intravenous nutrients into Shy's body.

Karen was at the hospital everyday. She was exhausted and at the end of herself. Not only did she lose her husband a few months earlier, but also was forced to watch her oldest daughter slowly kill herself. And, there was nothing she could do about it. She was desperate to help Shy, but everything she tried had failed.

Glorie suggested that Shy stay with them for a few days after she was discharged from the hospital. It would give Karen a break and allow her to spend more time with Shea, who was also grieving over the loss of her dad. Glorie promised Karen that she wouldn't take her eyes off of Shy for one minute. She also encouraged Karen about Nelson's ability to get through to Shy when no one else could and vice versa.

Karen knew that Nelson was Shy's best friend, but she doubted that Nelson would make any progress with her. She wasn't talking to anyone, not even trained professionals. Nonetheless, since suffering from sheer exhaustion, Karen was willing to try just about anything. She was also aware that she had been neglecting her nine-year-old for trying to get Shy better. Shea needed her, too.

Karen talked to Shy who agreed that staying with the Jackson's for a few days might be good. But, Shy actually thought that they all needed a break from her, and she didn't blame them. Why would anyone want to look at the person who killed Dad?

When Shy was discharged from the hospital, she immediately went to the Jackson's home. She tried to isolate herself there, too, but Nelson wouldn't have it. He told her that she was selfish and only thought of herself. He said, "How would it make you feel if your mother killed herself, because she could only think about her own pain? Or, because she didn't think about you and Shea and how you would feel if you lost both your parents? Did you ever think about that?" he asked. Shy said nothing.

Nelson continued, "Well, that's what you're doing to your mom." He walked out of the guest bedroom and left her sitting there alone and miserable.

Glorie called Karen later that night and told her that Shy came out of the guest bedroom that evening. She told her that Shy had eaten half of her dinner and was watching T.V. with Nelson and Samuel. Karen was surprised and grateful.

Later, when Glorie had tucked Samuel into bed, she realized she could no longer hear the living room television. She peeked in on the kids and heard Shy say, "Nelson, did you know that I lit the centerpiece candles, and that's what caught the house on fire? I didn't have permission. Daddy died because of me."

Glorie could hear Shy crying and wanted to run in there and hold her. She felt relieved that the girl was finally able to talk about what happened that night. Standing quietly at the door, she waited for Nelson to respond. She didn't like what she heard.

"Oh, no! Here we go again." Nelson sounded exasperated. "Would you stop feeling sorry for yourself? You're giving me a headache."

Glorie was shocked by Nelson's insensitivity. She was about to rush through the door and give him a stern rebuke when she heard Shy come back angrily with, "I am NOT feeling sorry for myself."

Glorie liked the anger in Shy's voice. It was a nice respite from the dysthymic, glazed mood she had been in since her dad's death. She waited for Nelson's response.

"Then what the hell are you doing?" Nelson asked.

Glorie rolled her eyes up toward Heaven. She didn't allow cursing in her home and was surprised to hear the word "hell" come out of Nelson's mouth. Nelson continued with, "Can I ask you something, baby girl?"

Glorie's emotions ran from shock to bemusement. "Baby Girl" was her nickname for Shy. Nelson was being a tease.

"I told you not to call me that," she heard Shy say.

Nelson laughed. "Okay. Anyway, here's the question, baby girl …" He laughed and said "Hey," when Shy frogged him in the arm.

"Okay! Okay! I won't say it again. Seriously now, what would your dad have said if you had asked permission to light those candles?"

"You mean, would he have let me light them?" Nelson nodded. "Probably," she said.

"And he probably would have gone right back to sleep, huh?" Nelson asked.

Shy nodded and said, "Yes, that's why I didn't wake him up in the first place. I knew he'd probably say "yes" and then he would've gotten mad at me for waking him over something so stupid."

"And you can't see that the outcome would have been the same whether you had asked for permission or not?" Nelson rolled his eyes, thumped the side of his head, and said, "DUH!"

"Shut up, Nelson." Shy couldn't help but cheer up just a bit. Nelson's facial expressions always made her laugh.

"Well, don't you think it's kind of stupid to blame yourself for your dad's death when all you did was light a bunch of candles, something your dad would have let you do anyway? Helloooo! Earth to Shy."

Shy didn't laugh. She looked sad again. "But Nelson, I forgot about the candles."

"Well, what made you forget about them?"

Cries of the Orchids

"When I went upstairs, I saw that Shea was wearing my sweater and--"

"Whoa. Now wait a minute. See ... I didn't know about this. Shea was wearing your sweater?"

Shy nodded, wide-eyed, waiting to hear Nelson's response. Nelson was standing up now, pacing the floor. He had an angry expression on his face. He stopped suddenly and pointed at Shy like he'd just solved a mystery. His eyebrows were arched high, and he was shaking his head back and forth.

"Now, I know you ain't talking about your red sweater."

Glorie was rolling her eyes again and shaking her head. She wanted to scold that boy, but she would probably end up laughing instead. That happened a lot when Nelson was in trouble. He was a natural clown, and he'd always find a way to make one or both of his parents start laughing. Glorie thought she heard a faint giggle from Shy.

"See, baby girl," Nelson had purposefully turned his voice ghetto, "no one said nuttin' 'bout Shea runnin' around up in there wit chur red sweater on." He was waving his finger around and shaking his hips and head about, wide-eyed, much like a woman Shy had seen on the Jerry Springer Show. He stopped suddenly and started laughing asking, "Is that why Shea be standin' out there half-naked when the house was on fire?"

Shy had begun laughing so hard that her ribs ached as Nelson joined in, lying on his back and kicking his legs around. The children were cackling so loudly that Glorie was afraid they might wake Samuel up. She didn't interrupt them, though, for it was the first time she had heard Shy laugh in months.

And, the laughter only got louder when Nelson held up his hand for a high-five and said, "Got that damn sweater, didn't you, baby girl? Ha-Haa!" Shy slapped his hand and went back to holding her aching ribs.

Glorie remembered covering Shea's body with a blanket the night of the fire and had to hold her breath to keep from laughing and alerting the children that she had been listening. Covering her mouth, she tip-toed quickly to the next room where she could let out the stifled chuckle. Until now, she hadn't questioned why Shea was standing outside with no shirt on. She just assumed the girl was getting ready for a bath or changing shirts or something. *Poor Shea*, she thought, laughing so hard that tears had begun to stream down her face.

Once the laughter had ceased a bit, Nelson sat back down on the couch beside Shy. "Look, friend, centerpieces are supposed to be lit. That's the point. Folks light them at Christmas parties and let them burn all night. They walk up and down the stairs. They go to the bathroom. Nobody sits there and watches the candles all night. And do you know why? Because they ain't supposed to catch on fire. Don't you get it? You did not kill your dad. Hellooooo." Nelson had his face all drawn up. He looked hilarious.

"Stop it, Nelson." Shy said as she tried not to laugh.

Nelson purposefully made his eyes widen, and he cocked his head to the side with exaggerated impatience. "So you need to stop with the whining, baby girl. 'Cuz you gettin' on my damn nerves!"

Shy spent another week with the Jackson's, and with the help of Glorie's fried chicken, she gained another four pounds. Karen couldn't thank God enough for bringing Nelson into her daughter's life. Shy stopped isolating as much. She went back to school and eventually started bringing her grades back up.

She continued to do well except during the anniversary of her dad's death. Every year around that time, Shy would become chronically depressed. She would have nightmares and lose weight all over again. Sometimes she would become hysterical if she smelled burning leaves two blocks away. Her therapist called it Post-Traumatic Stress Disorder or PTSD. This disorder was commonly associated with war veterans who had been traumatized beyond what their bodies and/or minds could handle. They also said that Shy had a dissociative personality, also common in PTSD. What it meant was that Shy had the ability to "go away" while still being conscious. Some people called it "shell-shock," a term first coined during the Korean War, for veterans who seemed glazed and incoherent when under a great deal of stress.

Because of this disorder, Shy had had a great deal of trouble regulating her blood pressure, especially during times of stress. Sometimes her blood pressure got dangerously high. She had gotten progressively better as the years passed, but she still had terrible migraines. Karen believed that they were related, but Shy still refused to go to the doctor about the headaches.

Shy had been on and off psychiatric and blood pressure medications for years, but often became pertinacious about not needing them anymore. Nelson was always there to keep her in check, though. Karen thanked God for that. Shy would listen to Nelson before she would listen to her own mother.

Karen never had to worry much as long as Nelson was around. She even felt secure when she had to move out of state six years ago. She knew that Nelson loved Shy and would keep an eye on her. What a blessing that young man had been to her family. Karen wiped a tear from her cheek. She couldn't believe that he was gone.

Shy stirred and opened her eyes a bit asking, "Mom, what are you doing here?"

"Shh … Just rest, honey," Karen said.

Shy felt groggy and heavy. Her eyes began to fill with tears as she whispered, "Did you hear?"

"Yes," she said, trying to think of the best words, "I heard that Nelson has gone to Heaven."

A nurse walked in and seemed surprised to see that Shy was awake. "Hello, there. You gave us quite a scare, young lady." Shy didn't respond to the nurse. She felt hazy, and her head hurt. The residual shock of Nelson's death still enveloped her.

"Mom, what am I doing here?"

"You passed out in the waiting room, sweetheart. Nelson's doctor admitted you. He said your blood pressure was so high that you almost had a stroke."

Shy was hooked up to an automatic blood pressure monitor. The nurse had moved to the side of her bed and was injecting Valium into her IV tube. They were keeping her heavily sedated until the blood pressure medication stabilized her system.

Shy heard a loud, "Well, how's my baby girl?" It was Glorie, all dressed up and carrying a large quilt. She was smiling and walking to the side of the bed opposite the nurse.

Shy began to cry when she saw her. "Oh, Glorie."

"Hey, now, we'll have none of that," Glorie said as she leaned over and kissed Shy. She then started spreading the quilt out over her.

"These hospitals can get so drafty." She paused long enough to smile at Karen and give her a big bear hug. Shy thought Glorie looked elegant in the lavender print dress and matching hat. She looked radiant, as though she were the personification of God's grace in the face of tragedy. Shy wondered how anyone could be that strong.

"My, my, look at all of these beautiful flowers." She smiled at Shy and asked, "Can I take a peek?" Shy nodded as Glorie opened each card and read them out loud. One arrangement was from Bill. One was from the Department of Human Services. One was from Ben.

"Now, who is this young man saying 'I love you, Shy?' Don't think I've met him. Have you, Karen?"

Shy's mother nodded her head. "He's been here every day. Seems like a very nice young man," she grinned at Shy, "and handsome, too."

Glorie had her hand on her hip with her eyebrows cocked high. "Hmmph," she grunted. "Well, Mama Glorie hasn't met him, and we gonna have to change that. Ain't nobody sayin' 'I love you' to my baby 'til they get approved by me." Shy smiled weakly, knowing that Glorie was being chipper and strong for her sake.

"And look at this- from Sheriff Tills, telling you to get better soon. Maybe that man has changed his ways." Glorie remembered her days as a resident of Maburn when Tills harassed her family. She looked at Karen and chuckled, "The Lord can do miracles, you know?" Even Shy was surprised that Sheriff Tills had sent her flowers. Glorie sat the flowers down and headed back over to the side of Shy's bed.

"Now, sweetie, Mama Glorie's got to go, but I'll be back this afternoon." She leaned over and gave Shy a kiss on the cheek.

"Where are you going so dressed up?" Shy was beginning to feel the effects of the Valium, and her eyes felt heavy.

Glorie looked at her and realized that Shy didn't know. And, she was afraid to say where she was going for fear of upsetting her.

Glorie looked to Shy's mother for assistance, and Karen quickly came to her aid. She took Shy's hand and spoke softly, "Honey, Nelson's funeral is today."

"What?" Shy tried to sit up in the bed, but the sedative was working quickly, making her body feel heavy. Her mouth was dry, and her words were thick. "No. What day is it? How long have I been here?"

Shy's mother tried to soothe her, afraid that her blood pressure would soar, again, to a dangerous level. "Sweetheart, you need to try to stay calm. Lie back down."

"Mother, tell me what day it is!" Shy demanded.

Glorie, patting her on the hand, said, "Baby, you've been in the hospital for three days. You've been very sick. Lie down, now, you hear me." Glorie's voice rang of authority. Shy responded as Glorie continued soothingly, "That's it, baby. There you go."

Her eyes had become so heavy that Shy was having a hard time keeping them open. Her voice became slurred and slow. She was barely able to say, "But I have to go."

Glorie and Karen were relieved that the medication was taking its toll. No matter how hard she tried, Shy couldn't prevent her body from going to sleep. Her eyes had closed but her lips moved slowly, "Glorie …"

Karen and Glorie could hardly hear her. Glorie leaned over and kissed her on the cheek. "What, baby girl?" She kept her head close to Shy's mouth so that she could hear what Shy was trying to say.

As the welcoming respite of unconsciousness took over Shy's body, her words came out as whisper, taking every last effort to muster, "Take the flowers. Tell Nelson I love him."

Shy was discharged from the hospital two days later, but she didn't return to work. Bill placed her on medical leave until her doctor gave a written release for her to return. And, that wouldn't be any time soon. Her emotional state was very fragile and, while her blood pressure was now stabilized by the medication, she continued to be at high risk of a nervous breakdown.

Her mother brought plenty of clothes to stay with Shy for as long as she needed, but Shy felt she was a burden. Driving from Texas the moment Glorie had called, her mother had not gotten much sleep for worrying about her daughter.

"Mom, I promise I'm okay. Why don't you get some rest and head back home? You don't need to miss this much work."

Her mother took her up on the offer of getting rest and headed upstairs for a nap. She said she wouldn't be leaving for a few more days, that she just needed more time to make sure Shy was all right.

It was a sunny afternoon, and Shy was so glad to be home from the hospital. Ben would be coming over after work, and she was looking forward to seeing him. She curled up on the couch with the quilt that Glorie had given her. It still had the scent of Nelson's childhood home, and it made her heart ache. She felt cheated that she'd not been able to attend Nelson's funeral. Shy was told that the service was at Wilkins' Funeral Home. It was at that moment that she remembered that Mattie's body was being sent to Wilkins' on ... *Oh, no. Have I missed Mattie's funeral, too?*

She reached for the telephone and hurried to the refrigerator where she had written the number to the funeral home. Punching in the number, she heard a voice drone, "Wilkins' Funeral Home."

"Yes, hi, this is Sharon Sauze from the Department of Human Services."

"Yes, Miss Sauze, how can I help you?"

"Well, I just got out of the hospital, and I was wondering if I missed Mattie Johnson's funeral."

"No, Ma'am. They just released the body yesterday. She was transported to us this morning." Shy released a sigh of relief.

"The viewing is scheduled for tomorrow at two o'clock."

Shy thanked the woman and hung up the phone. She couldn't be there for Nelson's funeral, but she could at least be there for Mattie's. She knew Mattie's soul was in heaven, but for some reason, still felt that Mattie needed her to be there. She chose not to tell her mother or Ben that she was going. They would try to talk her out of it, and perhaps they would be right in doing so. Shy felt weak and fragmented. The very thought of seeing Mattie's lifeless body made her tremble. Unable to think on the matter anymore, she decided to make the decision tomorrow, postponing any thoughts of Mattie until then.

Ben arrived at her home after his workday. She was thankful to have him distract her thoughts. He brought pizza, but she didn't think her stomach could tolerate the grease. She fixed herself a bowl of cold cereal instead. They sat at the table and talked about everything except Nelson, Mattie, Jake, the Baretts or the Watsons. She thought, for a brief moment, that she was beginning to feel human again.

Her mother slept all evening, and Shy was glad that she was resting so well. At eight o'clock, she was ready to sleep, herself. Ben kissed her goodnight and told her he would be back tomorrow after work.

That night, she heard the infant crying again. She was running down a dark hallway, frantically trying to find him. Fire engulfed every room that she tried to enter. But, she could hear the infant crying just beyond the flames. She desperately tried to get to him, but in every room the smoke and the flames tried to consume her.

When she opened the door to the last room, the fire burned just as viciously as in all the others. But, the baby cried louder, his shrieking echoing throughout the core of her soul. Then, the shrieking suddenly stopped. Shy screamed in agony, thinking the child was killed by the fire.

Soon she saw a figure walking through the flames, untouched by the fire licking about his body. She could see that the figure was carrying the infant. She stood up and tried to see who it was. *Daddy?* When the figure moved closer and cleared itself from the blaze and smoke, she could see that he was not her father. It was Nelson. She felt tremendous joy in seeing him until she noticed he wasn't smiling. Looking at her intensely, he spoke without moving his mouth. "The mother's blood will lead the way," he said. Handing the infant to her, he disappeared. Shy cried out for Nelson while clutching the baby to her bosom, feeling a strange combination of both gratitude and grief. As Nelson's image faded in her mind, she looked down at the infant. It was the same child that she had held in the field of ravenous orchids.

Shy woke up drenched in sweat and gasping for air. Slowly reorienting herself to the bedroom, she calmed down only when she convinced herself that it was simply a dream. But, in the dream she'd seen Nelson. She began to cry, yearning to see him again. The dream seemed so real. *Was it real? Was he trying to tell her something?* She couldn't make sense of the dream. The only thing she knew for sure was that she must go to Mattie's funeral. She prayed that God would give her strength.

Chapter Twenty

Shy told her mother that she was meeting Ben for a late lunch so that Karen wouldn't be worried. She felt stronger about going to the viewing of Mattie's body but still felt a bit shaky. More than anything, she just felt pulled there. Maybe it was the dream. It was so vivid, haunting, and real. Nelson had walked through the fire to save the baby. But, what had he meant by "the mother's blood will lead the way?"

The car in front of her abruptly stopped, causing Shy to slam on her breaks so hard that her tires screeched against the pavement. She swerved to the side of the road and almost onto the median before her car came to a stop. Bracing herself, she wondered if she might be hit from behind. A moment passed. She peeked into the rearview mirror, relieved to find that there was no traffic behind her. Looking forward just in time to see a herd of three deer pass in front of the car ahead of hers, she understood why the driver stopped so suddenly. Once she was back on the highway, she made sure to keep a much safer distance between her car and the cars ahead of hers. She had an aluminum-like taste in the back of her mouth from the adrenaline rush, and her heart rate took a while to readjust to normal.

The entire event allowed enough distraction, such that it provided a brief respite from the impending turmoil that lay ahead.

Wilkins' funeral home was a restored eighteenth-century plantation home. It was a Victorian archive that looked much like a sovereign fortress behind a cluster of golden oaks. A magnificent structure, it had a steeply peeked roofline and three large white columns marking its entrance.

Skeletal remnants of ivy, aged by the hand of early winter, snaked its way up the framework. In the spring, the funeral home was a sight to behold. The lawn was lit with an array of floral vegetation. A nicely paved driveway circled around an elegant landscape of azaleas, dogwoods, sprays of graceful roses and sharply trimmed hedges.

In spite of its splendor, it was still a funeral home and could not disguise its representation of grief, sorrow, and death. For Shy, the beauty of its outer extremities was a façade for its air of darkness. It was like a beautifully decorated cake filled with dirt.

Shy parked her car near the front entrance. She was fifteen minutes early. Feeling dizzy and shaken, she grabbed her purse from the passenger's seat and mustered the courage to get out of the car. Steadily making her way to the entrance, she had to stop and brace herself on one of the large pillars. A few deep breaths later, and she was at the entrance, opening the door with a shaky hand. Inside, she was greeted by a tall, thin man who seemed to personify death. "May I help you?"

"Yes, uh, I'm here for Mattie Johnson."

"Certainly, she's in the third room to your right."

The plush red carpet had too much give and lent little in the way of support for trembling legs. Shy walked close to the wall in case she needed to reach out and steady herself. The viewing room was now directly to her right. Aided by the wall, she took two more deep breaths and reluctantly stepped into the room.

She took a moment to look upward. When she did, she was immediately surprised by the number of flower arrangements that adorned the room, as Mattie knew so few people. But, she didn't see a casket. She moved closer, wanting to identify, or at least see if she knew anyone who had sent the flowers. She soon realized that she'd stepped into the wrong room.

A tiny casket not much larger than a shoebox was drowning in the sprays of flowers that surrounded it. Shy was horrified but unable to turn away. She'd never seen a dead infant, much less in this setting. The child, obviously a girl, was adorned in a beautiful pink layette. A small teddy bear lay in the coffin beside her. The baby looked angelic, as if she were sleeping. She could have been no more than a few days old.

A picture of a young couple and a boy who appeared to be about four was taped to the inside of the coffin with a message that read:

"Our precious angel,
You were only with us but a short period, and yet
you filled us with a lifetime of joy."

"Ma'am," Shy startled and jumped as she turned around to see the funeral home director.

He continued, "I'm sorry. It appears that I have directed you to the wrong viewing room." The man appeared extremely apologetic. "Miss Johnson is two rooms down."

"Oh," Shy said, rubbing her temple in a state of semi-shock. Reflexively, she turned and looked at the infant once more before leaving the room.

"Stillborn," the director said, "such a tragedy." He escorted Shy a little way down the hallway and said, "Here we are." He gave her a gentle pat on the back and left her there alone. She steadily entered the bare room and saw an over-sized coffin that bore a grim resemblance of who she knew to be her beloved friend. She moved closer to the body and began to cry all over again as if the death had just occurred.

Mattie lay in a plain white t-shirt with stains on the sleeves. Shy felt immediate anger at the funeral home for not finding something more suitable for Mattie to be buried in. Her arms lay down by her sides as her stomach was too large to fold them over her abdomen in the customary manner.

"Oh, Mattie," the sobs were coming strongly now, "I'm sorry this happened to you. If I'd only known … I would have been there … I'm so sorry."

The funeral home did a poor job masking the bullet wound on the right side of Mattie's head. It was heavily caked with a clay-like substance and some of her hair was matted in it. The rest of her hair was combed forward in a futile effort to cover the mar. Shy tried not to look at it, as it only reminded her that Mattie had taken her life, that she was so fragile and desperate. And, her social worker didn't even know it. Shy felt extreme guilt, thinking that she should have told Mattie how much she cared about her. But, now it was too late. *Why, Mattie? Why did you do it?*

There were no flowers or cards to adorn her coffin. What irony, Shy thought. The child next door had never even taken her first breath, and yet, by appearance, she had so many to celebrate her life- as well as to mourn her death.

Mattie, a beautifully, sweet spirit, who endured years of pain and abandonment was clad only in a stained t-shirt and had only her social worker to lament her passing. Shy felt a strange, irrational sense of resentment toward the lifeless infant she had just seen. Grief and anger consumed her.

She sat her purse down and pulled out a picture from the picnic. It was of Jake, his face covered in mashed potatoes as he grinned for the camera. Just looking at it made Shy's soul groan for the little boy.

She laid it on Mattie's chest. Wiping the tears from her face, she reached into her purse and pulled out a single can of Sprite and laid it in the coffin beside Mattie. Swiping again at the tears, she reached over and gently stroked Mattie's cheek. She whispered, "I love you, Mattie. I'm going to miss you so much."

The funeral home director entered the room. He fidgeted a bit and then cleared his throat to catch her attention. Shy turned around quickly.

"I'm sorry to startle you, again, ma'am." He told Shy that, due to Mattie's limited resources, the state would be picking up the tab for the burial.

"Well, that's nice, I guess," she continued to wipe the tears from her eyes. The director appeared a bit nervous.

"Yes, well, they will only provide the burial."

She nodded while looking down at the floor. "You're telling me there will be no service?" she asked. The director shuffled from one foot to the other. His expression was solemn. "I'm afraid you're the only visitor Miss Johnson has had. We've received no phone

Cries of the Orchids

calls from anyone other than you. We were told that she had no family. This was an indigent case, I'm afraid and quite frankly," he appeared apologetic, "we really didn't expect anyone to show up."

Shy tried to contain her sudden anger. "Is that why you put her in a stained t-shirt? Because you didn't think anyone would see her or that anyone would care?"

"Let me explain and apologize." The director's eyes were kind and compassionate. "We have a selection of donated clothes in our storage room. We often have families on a limited income and we try to help out where we can. The problem was Miss Johnson's size. We just didn't have anything that would fit her."

"Why didn't any one bother to call me? I left my number with you last week." Her anger, once again replaced by grief, she began to cry, "I would have brought something for her."

"Miss Sauze, I don't know what to say. When you told me you were her social worker, well, I guess I didn't understand the degree of your relationship. You obviously cared a great deal for her."

Shy had her face in her hands but was still able to nod just enough to confirm what the man said. She whimpered, "I did. I loved her."

In all his years in the funeral home business, the director had never been so moved. Here was a state social worker who cherished a person the rest of the world had thrown away. He pondered what he could do to make the situation better. A clerk passed by to deliver some flowers to one of the viewing rooms.

"Son, put those flowers down and come here."

"Yes, sir." The boy went into one of the rooms and returned immediately. The director was writing out a check. He signed it, ripped it out of its place, and handed it to the boy. The boy looked at it, his eyes widening to the size of silver dollars.

"I need flowers for room five. I want Thomas to do them. Have them here by five o'clock."

The boy's expression seemed to deflate. "Mr. Thomas? Sir, I don't know. He keeps quite a tight schedule."

"Yes, I know. Tell him the request is from Nate, and that I really need this favor."

The boy nodded but still appeared reluctant. Nate pulled out a one hundred dollar bill and said, "I'll leave this at the front with my secretary. It will be waiting for you if you return with the flowers by five.

"Yes, sir!" The boy took off urgently.

Shy was confused. The man asked her to follow him, and she did. They walked down the corridor to a large office of beautiful antique furniture and oil paintings. A woman in her mid-thirties was rapidly typing in the corner of the room.

"Mrs. Paul," the woman stopped typing and looked up, "what would you say would be the finest dress shop in Maburn or the surrounding area?" he asked.

"Oh, I would have to say Bordeaux's in Milan. They have the most beautiful dresses." The woman looked toward Shy and said, "but I'm afraid they're quite expensive." Shy was in too much pain to be offended by this.

"Get them on the line for me, please."

Mrs. Paul raised her eyebrows and simultaneously reached for the phone book. "Yes, sir, Mr. Wilkins."

Shy jerked her head up and looked the man in the face. "You own this place?"

"Yes, this funeral home has been in my family for decades. Today, you stirred something in me that I haven't felt in years."

He took the phone from Mrs. Paul. While still looking at Shy, he put his hand over the receiver and said, "compassion." He smiled at her and took his hand off the receiver.

"Yes, this is Nethanial Wilkins of Wilkins' Funeral Home. I'm sending a young lady by the name of..." He looked at Shy.

"Sharon Sauze"

"By the name of Sharon Sauze to purchase a dress. I'll be paying for it myself and there's no limit on the purchase amount. Should I give you my credit card number? Oh, why, thank you." He handed the phone back to the secretary and said, "The lady's name is Fonday. Go ahead and issue a check when the bill arrives."

Shy was moved to tears as she said, "Mr. Wilkins, really. You don't have to do this."

"Please, do an old man a favor. I need to do this."

The fifteen-minute drive to Milan was sobering. It felt good to be doing something for Mattie. Shy was grateful to Mr. Wilkins for such a kind contribution; and, his grace erased some of the resentment she felt toward society. For the first time since Mattie's death, she didn't feel like the only person in the world honoring Mattie's memory.

She didn't have to ask for directions to Bordeaux's. She was well aware of its location as well as its reputation. They were well-known for their lavish ball gowns and formal dresses. The elaborate window displays contained individual pieces of art that often stirred childhood fantasies of parading about as a princess or ballerina adorned in sequins and silk.

Shy had never actually been in the store. She fell far beyond the outer extremities of Bordeaux's price range. She could hardly afford to admire the dresses in the window. Pulling into the parking lot, she wondered what it would have been like if Mattie were with her, picking out her own dress. She could almost see Mattie's gleeful expression which made her smile. She walked inside and found herself completely surrounded by racks of extravagant fabrics. Prom dresses and bridal gowns were elegantly displayed about the room on headless mannequins.

A tall, fashionable woman in her mid-fifties was talking with a customer and immediately turned and sized up Shy's appearance over the rim of her red-framed glasses. She looked appropriately snotty for the environment; however, she softened when Shy told her who she was. "Ms. Sauze, so nice to meet you. My name is Henriette Fonday. I'm the owner." Shy thought the woman's voice was befitting of Mrs. Howell on *Gilligan's Island*. Ms. Fonday continued with, "Let's see, you should be what? Size seven?"

"The dress isn't for me. It's for a friend of mine. She's deceased."

"My condolences." She bowed her head a few moments for dramatic effect and then spoke with luster, clasping her hands and smiling. "Now, where should we start?"

"Well, I don't know."

"What size is your friend?" Shy liked that the woman was speaking about Mattie in the present tense. It felt comforting.

"She's a very large woman. I'm afraid I'm not exactly sure of her size."

"Not a problem, darling, we'll just take a look. If we have to, we'll simply tailor the dress to her. She gave Shy a comforting smile, but Shy felt that Mr. Wilkins' wallet played a large role in the woman's charm.

Shy didn't want to spend a lot of time at the dress shop. She looked around and was thankful that only three other customers were in the store. Hopefully, Ms. Fonday could help her pick out something quickly. For some reason she felt a need to get Mattie changed into something more dignified as soon as possible. It was a final tribute to her friend.

The women walked over to a rack that contained plus-size dresses. Shy thumbed through them, ignoring the woman as she held out the more expensive dresses. The customer whom Ms. Fonday abandoned immediately after Shy introduced herself, stood at the register and coughed politely to signal that she was ready to pay for her purchase.

Ms. Fonday cocked her eyebrows to not-so-politely signal her annoyance. She leaned over and whispered, "I'm sorry, darling. I'll be right back." She made a one-hundred-and-eighty-degree pivot and turned on the charm. Shy thought she fashioned a fifty-five-year-old runway model or a beauty pageant contestant, prancing and gliding her way to the cash register. If today had not been one of the most horrible days of her life, Shy would have found the whole thing quite entertaining.

"Ahh, you've made your selection?" Ms. Fonday asked as the customer held up a pale yellow, taffeta dress with sheer sleeves and beaded bodice. "Yes," Ms. Fonday cooed, "marvelous selection. And won't it be gorgeous in your daughter's wedding?"

Shy's curiosity got the best of her. She turned to see the customer with a dress which was obviously designed for a teenage girl's high school prom. Holding it to her short, frumpy body, she looked hideous, Shy thought. Turning back around, Shy continued to forage through dresses until she finally spotted one that she thought

Cries of the Orchids

Mattie would have loved. It was pale pink with soft blue accents. Shy wasn't sure what the fabric was, but it was soft and light. It felt a lot like a silk nightgown.

Ms. Fonday walked toward Shy while waving the other customer out the door. Holding up the pink dress, Shy said, "I like this one." The woman frowned at her with burrowed eyebrows.

"Are you quite certain? Mr. Wilkins said there was no limit."

Shy could tell by the woman's expression that the dress she selected was not very expensive. It didn't matter, for Mattie would have loved it. That's all Shy cared about. "This one will do just fine."

The woman took the dress with a "hmm" and went behind the counter where the register was located. She scribbled on an invoice. "Please sign here to show that you picked up the purchase." She flipped the invoice around without even looking up. Shy signed it, noticing that the dress cost a grand total of fifty-three dollars and forty-two cents, a drop in a bucket considering that she saw one dress that cost over two thousand. The woman took Mattie's dress, wadded it up, and threw it carelessly in a plastic bag. She then set the bag on the counter in front of Shy.

Startled by the abrupt rudeness, the mistreatment of the dress was viewed by Shy as mistreatment of Mattie. It was Mattie's dress, and this hateful woman was throwing it around as if it meant nothing. "Would you please hang it up?" she asked, unable to contain the anger in her voice. "I don't want it to get wrinkled on the way to the funeral home. " But the woman continued about her business as if she didn't hear her.

Mrs. Fonday put the receipt on the counter with a pop and spoke to Shy curtly, "We normally reserve our hangers for our more expensive purchases."

That was it. Shy could take no more. Anger, one of the six stages of grief, came forth unleashed and violent. Before she realized it, Shy was screaming at the top of her lungs, "PUT IT ON A HANGER!" She took the dress out of the bag and threw it at the woman. Ms. Fonday jerked back reflexively and displayed an expression of total shock.

Twelve days of inconsolable tragedy and pain swirled together into one moment of fury that caused the very pigment of Shy's skin to turn blood red. Her body shook as she glared at the woman. Mrs. Fonday jerked back again when Shy screamed, "NOW!"

The two remaining customers stopped browsing to see what was going on. In an effort to salvage a bit of dignity, Ms. Fonday quietly uttered, "Well, I never…" as she took the bag from Shy's hand. Her eyes were wide with fear, and she futilely tried to disguise it with poised anger. Ms. Fonday snatched a plastic hanger from the dress rack behind her and flippantly adorned it with the dress. She then grabbed a clear plastic bag, draped it over the dress, and tied a knot at the bottom.

After the dress was hung and secured she thrust it over the counter with her nose up, her eyes looking over the rim of her glasses. Shy snatched the dress away from her and turned to leave. Ms. Fonday, feeling completely humiliated and much safer now that Shy had her back to her, stepped out from behind the register. Having never in her entire life succumbed to not having the last word, she raised her voice with strong fortitude, a last effort at saving face in front of the astonished customers.

"Young lady…" she was about to tell Shy to never step foot in her store again when Shy turned around quickly and held her finger toward the woman's face, her eyes searing and dangerous. The words came out slowly and angrily, through clenched teeth. Barely able to hold herself back from committing bodily harm, she said, "Say one more word, lady, and I'll cram one of those hangers down your throat."

Ms. Fonday stood quietly in fear, with more egg on her face than she could have consumed in a lifetime. Shy turned and walked out the door.

The return to the funeral home was much more relaxing thanks to the good scream at Ms. Fonday. Shy needed the release and, quite frankly, so did Ms. Fonday. She pulled into the drive of Wilkins' Funeral Home, stopped, and reached for her cell phone. Not having returned home as soon as her mom would have expected, she punched in her home number.

Cries of the Orchids

"Mom? What are you doing?" She felt fortified by her rage toward Mrs. Fonday and was able to deliver her voice in such a way as to not concern her mother. Her mother asked her if she and Ben had a good lunch.

"Yes, we had a nice time. I'm feeling so much better," she lied. "I'm going to run by the grocery store. Do you need anything?" Another lie. She needed more time. Her mother sounded exhausted and Shy felt both concerned and guilty that she was the root of it. "Mom, you sound tired. Why don't you take a quick nap. I'll wake you up when I get home so that you'll still be able to sleep tonight. We really haven't gotten to have some girl talk since you got here, anyway." She waited for her mother's response and then added, "All right. I'll see you in a bit. Love you, too."

Shy walked into the building with the dress draped neatly over her left arm. She didn't feel quite as nervous entering the funeral home the second time. The secretary looked up and smiled as she walked through the door. "One moment," she said picking up the phone to call her boss. "Mr. Wilkins, Ms. Sauze is here."

Within seconds, the director was out of his office and greeting Shy. His smile, warm and sincere, comforted her. Gratitude and appreciation replaced the cruel hearted first impression of the man.

"Did you find something suitable for Ms. Johnson?" he asked.

She nodded and held it up for his viewing. "Mattie would have loved this dress. I don't know how to thank you."

"You just did," he smiled at her and then added, "My secretary told me that Kenny Thomas arrived early with the flowers. I haven't been back there yet. Would you like to take a peek?" Shy nodded eagerly. Mr. Wilkins held his hand out as if to say, "After you."

Unlike her first trip down the hallway to Mattie's viewing room, Shy felt a bit of anticipation to get there. She wanted to see the flowers and drape the dress over Mattie's body. At the very least, she could go to bed tonight with a different image of Mattie's final farewell.

Nearing the room, Mr. Wilkins stopped her and said, "I should probably warn you that, although Mr. Thomas is a well-respected decorator among our wealthy clientele, he can be a bit, shall we say, eccentric." He winked at her when he said this.

Mr. Wilkins had worked with Kenny Thomas for many years and had become quite attuned to Thomas' personality and haughty air. Any time he did arrangements at the funeral home, he expected all things to work around one central theme, that being his flowers. Thomas had even been known to have a corpse re-attired because "it didn't go" with "his work". And his clients didn't mind. They were getting the best designer that Arkansas had to offer, and they dared not argue lest he gather his things and walk out. One could either love his work, or they could scrounge in the grunge of the less talented. It made no difference to him.

Shy followed Mr. Wilkins into Mattie's room and was immediately overcome by what she saw. Six people busied themselves around the most extraordinary display of flowers she had ever seen. There were at least nine different arrangements, each of them exceptional and elegantly different from the other. Pheasant feathers jutted out behind long grasses and date palms. All intermingled with an assortment of blooms from flowers she had never seen before. It took her breath away.

A chicly-dressed man, clad only in black, stood in the center of the room and barked at a young woman who was fixing pink roses in and about the casket centerpiece. "Absolutely not! Have you ever seen pink roses in a Kenny Thomas Design? Take them out, and get me the Catalyas. Quickly now!" He clapped his hands as he spoke, and this seemed to make his subjects move faster, like a small swarm of buzzing bees around their royal counterpart.

Mr. Wilkins smiled and winked at Shy again as if to say, "What did I tell you?" And then he said, "Mr. Thomas, what extraordinary work."

Kenny turned. His facial expression softened as he walked toward Mr. Wilkins and held out his hand. "Yes, isn't it, though?" Kenny Thomas was never timid about telling someone how much they should love his work. "It's always nice to see you, Nate."

Mr. Wilkins shook Kenny's hand and continued to look about the room. "Every time I think I've seen your best work, you surprise me with something else. This is absolutely magnificent."

"Yes, some of these flowers were imported from Egypt for Fionna Stephenson's annual hoopla. We got them in last week. Quite beautiful, aren't they?" Kenny spoke fast and used his hands a lot to express himself. He didn't give Mr. Wilkins an opportunity to speak. "Anyway, the delivery boy said that you had an emergency situation here. And quite frankly, Nate, this is more than an emergency."

He walked toward Mattie's coffin and held his hand out toward her body. "Have you seen what this poor girl is wearing?" He didn't give Mr. Wilkins a chance to respond. "And this hair. It just won't do." He primped around on Mattie's hair and then noticed the Sprite can lying beside her. Kenny snatched up the can with hostility. "Look at this!" He held the can up high so Mr. Wilkins could see it clearly and then spoke as slow and patronizingly as possible. "It is a can of Sprite." He said this with distinct emphasis on each word as if Wilkins were a complete idiot. Shy wanted to run up and grab the can away from him. He continued, "In the coffin of all places!" He sighed with as much drama as possible. "I'm extremely disappointed in your people, Nate."

He started to throw the can in the trash when Shy yelled, "No!" Kenny looked at her with a perplexed expression. It seemed to be the first time he even noticed she was in the room. Mr. Wilkins, still flushing from the berating he'd just gotten, cleared his throat and said, "Mr. Thomas, I'd like you to meet Sharon Sauze. She was Mrs. Johnson's social worker."

Kenny's expression lost its arrogant edge but only for a second. He started clapping his hands while yelling, "Out! Everybody out! Quickly, people! We don't have all day!"

Within seconds the only people remaining in the room were Shy, Wilkins, and Kenny. Kenny looked at Wilkins with his eyebrows arched and said, "Will there be anything else?" Mr. Wilkins flushed and politely excused himself from the room. Shy could tell that, unlike Ms. Fonday, Kenny Thomas didn't give a damn about the size of Mr. Wilkins' wallet or anyone else's for that matter. He was the master of his world, and he played the game by his rules, period.

Kenny's arrogance was immediately lost as the door shut behind Mr. Wilkins. He looked perplexed again. "What was her first name?"

"Mattie," she whispered.

"You were more than just her social worker, weren't you?" He was staring into her eyes as he spoke; it made her feel uncomfortable. She nodded.

"Well, honey, why in the world did you put a can of Sprite in her coffin?"

Shy felt a bit defensive. She didn't expect a name brand, ritzy, decorator like Mr. Thomas to understand why she put it in there. She was irritated that he would even ask. It was personal. She answered with a mere, "Because she loved it."

Kenny held a hand to his chest. "That's the most beautiful thing I've ever heard." He seemed genuinely moved. "And you know what else?" he asked, clasping his hands together with excitement, "All of my flowers are procured with Sprite! They love it and blossom better when they drink it." His face gleamed. "Don't you get it? My flowers and your Mattie- they just belong together! Isn't that beautiful?" He took in a deep sigh but didn't give Shy a chance to respond. The drama was over, and he'd moved on.

"Now, let's see what you have here." He snatched the dress from Shy and studied it, looking periodically at the coffin centerpiece.

"Hmmm. I think this will work." He walked to the door and opened it with all the haughtiness of twenty minutes earlier. "I need Catalyas, please. And I'm getting annoyed!" He said this in a curt, singsong manner. He was about to shut the door but then reopened it and added, "Tell Nate I need a brush, curling iron and some spray. Quickly now! I don't have all day!" He shut the door and pranced back to the front of the room, holding the dress out in front of him and eyeing the casket, as an artist to his canvas.

"Do you mind if I put this on her? I need to see if the Catalyas will go with it." Shy shook her head but turned around. She didn't think she could stomach seeing Mattie's stiff body being moved about.

Kenny hummed and talked to himself throughout the course of re-dressing Mattie. It was obvious that this was not the first time he had handled a corpse. Shy turned around when she heard him say, "Now, this is much better."

The dress looked very pretty on Mattie, but her hair was ruffled and pulled back during the process of changing her clothes. Until now, Shy was able to avoid the full extent of the damage done to Mattie's skull. Bone fragments still lay at the hairline around a gaping hole that was at least four inches in diameter. She turned away from it quickly and started to cry.

"Oh, honey, don't cry." He began brushing Mattie's hair down with his fingers saying, "Nothing a little hairspray won't take care of. Look, much better, see?"

Shy turned around, this time forcing her eyes only on the dress. She wiped the tears on her cheeks and nodded at Kenny. There was a soft knock on the door. Kenny clapped his hands together with glee. "That must be my Catalyas. Wait 'til you see them. You'll feel so much better. They're just gorgeous! Now, turn around. I want to put them in the arrangement before you look. Okay, don't peek." Shy turned to the wall.

He skipped to the door and found two of his people standing on the other side. One carried a large vase of flowers and the other carried a sack of beauty supplies. Kenny returned to the casket and quickly inserted the flowers into the arrangement on top of it.

"Okay, Sharon, on the count of three." Shy hadn't been called Sharon in a long time, and it took a moment for her to realize that he was talking to her. "One ... two ... three." Shy turned around and saw orchids- large purple orchids the size of small dinner plates with bright yellow throats and veins. She heard herself gasp.

"I know. Aren't they gorgeous?" Kenny moved to the sack and grabbed a brush. It seemed that the delicate petals of the orchids moved with every waft of air that encountered them. They were alive, calling to her, taunting her. Shy was entranced by them and half expected them to grow teeth and leap out at her, as did the orchids in her nightmares. She could feel her eyes glazing. Something's wrong.

Kenny kept rattling on as he brushed Mattie's hair, but Shy couldn't hear him. Things were spinning inside her head causing her stomach muscles to knot. She closed her eyes tightly and brought a hand up to her temple, trying to convince herself that everything was okay, that she wasn't going insane.

The dreams came back to her in a swirl of confusing scenes. The flowers and the fire were one and the same, screeching, burning, and killing. And Nelson, holding the baby. His voice rang out, *The mother's blood will lead the way ... The mother's blood will lead the way,* over and over inside her head until she thought she would explode.

She prayed silently, *God, show me.* What is it that you want me to see? She opened her eyes and saw Kenny brushing the hair on Mattie's right side. He pulled it up and away from the wound and coiled it up into the curling iron, obliviously chatting as he worked. Shy forced herself to look at Mattie's shattered skull. The largest part of the exposed gash was caked with some type of mud.

Shy wanted to run from the room, but she couldn't. Her eyes were drawn to the ghastly wound. Closing her eyes tightly, she prayed, *what do you want me to see?* When she opened her eyes, it came to her. With one terrifying jolt of reality, she knew. Horror replaced fear, and she found herself running from the room, leaving a confused Kenny wondering what he had said to upset her. She ran down the hallway, passing Mr. Wilkins.

"Miss Sauze, are you okay?"

She couldn't hear him. The director shook his head with sympathy, thinking she was simply overcome with grief. He had seen this sort of thing often and felt sorry for her.

Shy found herself out on the parking lot fidgeting with her keys, trying nervously to get the door open. Once inside, she locked the doors and looked around nervously. Taking several deep breaths to try to calm down, she instead found herself gasping and gulping for air in the midst of complete panic. Reaching over to the glove compartment, she pulled it open and dug around until she located the envelope of pictures she'd taken of Mattie and Jake. She looked through all of them and found that they only confirmed what she already knew.

Mattie had been murdered. Shy had the proof.

Chapter Twenty-One

Ben cautiously looked around the first floor of the courthouse. It was unusually busy for a Thursday afternoon. He was finding it increasingly more difficult to think and felt sick to his stomach. What had he gotten himself into?

Looking at his watch, he leaned into the office to his right. A young, pretty secretary was typing on the word processor in front of her. She chomped viciously at a piece of bright orange bubblegum.

"Has Tills made it back?" he asked.

The woman didn't look up. "No, said he's got some kind of meeting to go to. Said he'd be back late this afternoon. Didn't give a time."

"Thanks, I'll try to catch him later." She kept typing, unresponsive to the world outside of the project at hand. Ben stepped back into the hallway and then jutted his head back into the office.

"Hey, I'm gonna go ahead and catch some lunch. I'm starving. I won't be long."

The girl nodded but never looked up.

Ben's heart began to race. This was dangerous. But they'd decided he was a lot less likely to be watched while on duty, under the eyes of his co-workers, than when he was out and about in his private life. They bargained that the brand new courtroom had not yet been bugged. Even still, he couldn't make an error. Not even one. By now, they were all watching. He headed for the stairwell as Percy leaned out of the office door, holding a file in his hand. He tried to wave Ben down, "Hey, Crossno." But Ben didn't hear him. Percy looked down at the file and shook his head, mumbling something that no one else could understand. He turned and stepped back into the office.

The third floor had been under heavy construction for nearly eight weeks. The courtroom was completely finished and some furniture was moved in this morning. Trim work and minor incidentals were still lacking in some of the offices. The entire project was expected to be completed at the end of next week.

Drop cloths, spray cans, and a lot of border trim were littered about the corridor. Ben made his way around the outer hallway, careful not to turn on any lights or trip on a stray bucket or board. The layout of the third floor was reconstructed such that the outer corridor made a square around the soon-to-be juvenile court room. So, at least, Ben had a sense of where he was going as he inched around it, looking for any remnant of human life.

He checked all of the offices to the right of the hall. All were open and vacant. He made his way around the second corner and felt the door to the judge's chambers. He opened it just far enough to check for lights or movement. Nothing. It was the only office that was placed on the left side of the corridor, and he knew he was at the halfway point. He continued the venture, checking each office and standing still every few minutes to see if he could hear movement.

He rounded the third corner and finally worked his way to the front doors of the courtroom. He was grateful for the faint glow of the stairwell light. The queasy tension in his stomach intensified as the large French doors of the courtroom loomed in front of him.

Ben entered into the darkness of the courtroom, wondering again what the hell he'd gotten himself into. He felt the cold wood of the first pew and moved slowly from the back of the room, touching each of the pews until they seemed to have disappeared. He continued to feel in front of him, checking to see if there were any more pews. There were none. He knew that he was now at the front of the courtroom.

Ben walked back, feeling for the last seating he had touched. He knew from seeing the courtroom in daylight that this pew sat closest to the judge's bench as well as directly to the side of what would soon be the jury box. He felt his way to the center of the pew and sat down.

Hearing only the sound of his own breath, Ben felt secure that he was alone. No one would look for him here nor would anyone else have a reason to be on this floor. He sat in the darkness and gathered his thoughts, periodically looking back toward the large French doors in the back of the courtroom. As his eyes began to adjust, he could see tiny, fragmented rays of dim light seeping in from the stairwell through the tiny cracks in the doors. He would be able to see if anyone entered. As the steady rhythm of his heartbeat pounded within his chest cavity, he waited.

A tall man wearing a T-shirt and jeans blotched with white paint walked into the courthouse and began inching his way through the obstacle of people on the first floor. He wore a hard hat and carried a large drum of what looked to be paint thinner over his left shoulder.

People who headed his direction, and saw him, stepped politely to the side. Others were oblivious to the world, and he would have to stop, grimacing as he held the heavy drum, and say, "Excuse me, please." No one stopped him to ask how the construction on the third floor was going or when it would be ready; and he was relieved. He headed toward the stairwell that read, "Authorized Personnel Only."

Chapter Twenty-Two

Shy couldn't get to the courthouse fast enough. She had to show Ben the pictures. Her thoughts were spinning, and she felt desperation and pain, so agonizing that it threatened to choke her. Deep down, she always knew that Mattie hadn't killed herself. It was more than just knowing Mattie wouldn't commit suicide, leaving her baby behind. There had always been something her unconscious mind was picking up. Until now, she wasn't able to figure out what it was. It was the picnic. In almost every picture Mattie was reaching for either Jake or food with her left hand. The bullet wound was just behind Mattie's right temple. Not only did it not make sense for a left-handed person to twist her neck and body around to shoot themselves in the right temple, it would have been nearly impossible for Mattie because of the size of her girth. Someone killed her. What other explanation could there be?

But who? Shy began to cry again, only this time it wasn't just grief. She felt an odd combination of pain, confusion, and fury. Why would someone kill Mattie? Why? She must have asked herself this question a hundred times in the short distance from the funeral home to the courthouse. Did someone hate Mattie so much that they wanted her dead? She thought about it from every angle. Mattie had nothing of any value. Nothing was reported stolen from her house. It just didn't make sense.

Shy wondered if it were too late to have Mattie's body sent to the state crime lab to see if there were any sign of struggle or rape. She almost choked on her own air as she allowed herself to process this last thought, remembering the torment on Mattie's face as she tried to explain that Jake's daddy was not her boyfriend. Shy shuddered the thought away, refusing to even entertain the idea that someone would hurt her that way again.

And what about Jake? What if the murderer had found him? She shook her head and squinted through the tears, trying hard to stop her thoughts from spiraling around all of the horrible possibilities. She pulled into the heavily congested courthouse parking lot. She found a vacant parking space in the second row and inched her way into it. After turning off the ignition, Shy adjusted the rearview mirror so that she could see how she looked. The skin underneath her eyes and down her cheeks had been saturated with a mixture of tears and mascara. Shy was able to wipe most of the mascara off, but she still couldn't conceal the fact that she had been crying all day.

She didn't want anyone to see her like this. They all thought she was losing it or was about to have a nervous breakdown. She certainly didn't want to give them any more reasons to talk. Maybe she could find Ben without being seen by the other deputies. There was a large crowd today. She could find him and ask him if he could come outside for fifteen minutes. They could sit in the car or go for a drive. She would show him the pictures when she told him how she knew that Mattie was murdered.

Thoughts of the pictures stimulated her mind to unconsciously flash through the horror that had occurred over the last two-and-a-half-months. And, her thoughts allowed each tragic story to unfold, as they had a hundred times, repetitively tormenting her soul. Her best friend and soul mate was gone forever. Mattie was killed and Jake was placed in foster care. Mothers and their precious children were burned to death in their own homes, leaving their loved ones to face the world without them. She thought of Mr. Border standing before the burned remains of the rental house. It was at this point that she felt the subtle jarring of her psyche. *Smoke alarms! Didn't Mr. Border tell me that he'd just installed smoke alarms? Dear God, is it possible that the Barett's had been murdered too?* She pulled her cell phone from her purse and dialed information.

"Glen Rosen. Carl Border, please. Thank you."

She knew she should probably wait until later when she could talk to him person-to-person. When the operator connected her, Shy became laden with self-doubt. *Why am I doing this? What do I hope to accomplish by asking about the fire alarms or, worse yet, by insinuating that his loved ones had been murdered?* It was only a hunch. She certainly didn't have enough information to justify upsetting him. She was about to hang up the phone when he answered. "Hello," his voice sounded frail and weak.

"Mr. Border, this is Sharon Sauze."

"Yes?"

Shy fidgeted nervously with the strap of her purse, wondering how to ask him about the smoke alarms without upsetting him. It was a futile effort. She rubbed the wetness that was beginning to form in the corner of her eyes.

"Uh, I was wondering if I was remembering correctly ... Did you tell me that you recently installed fire alarms in the rent house?" She paused, uncertain how he would react to the question.

"Yes, I put them in two weeks before the fire."

"Well, are you sure they had batteries?"

"Yes. Why are you asking me these questions?" he asked suspiciously.

Shy rubbed her temple. "Mr. Border, I'd like to come out and talk with you if that's alright. I don't think it's a good idea to talk over the phone, until I know more about what's going on. It may be nothing at all."

"When can I expect you?"

"In about an hour or so."

"Miss Sauze," his voice sounded stronger and more authoritative, "is this something we should get the sheriff involved in?"

"Mr. Border, I need to stress that it's probably nothing at all. I don't want to upset you for no reason."

"Something's got you upset. I hear it in your voice."

"Yes, sir." Shy heard her voice break. "It's about another client." Tears began to wet her lashes. "Something's wrong, but I can't talk about it now. I'll tell you when I get there. It may be completely unrelated to Traci and the kids. I just need to make sure."

"This sounds serious."

"Yes, sir. I'm going to talk to a friend of mine, right now. He's a deputy. I may bring him with me when I come out there, if that's okay."

"What ever you need to do. You say you'll be here in about an hour or so?"

"Yes, sir."

"I'll see you then. Keep yourself safe, young 'un."

"I will. Thank you."

She laid the phone in the passenger's seat and sat in her car, trying to think of the best way to approach Ben with the information. She would tell him about Mattie and show him the pictures. They would support the fact that Mattie didn't kill herself. It was physically impossible. Mattie was left- handed and so large that the funeral home was unable to position her hands together over her belly in the customary manner. There was no possible way that she could have twisted her head and body in such a way as to have allowed a straight pattern of travel of the bullet from her right temple.

Shy knew all along that Mattie didn't kill herself. She had never known Mattie to have a gun and didn't think Mattie could successfully make it through the registration process without assistance. And most of all, Mattie wouldn't have left Jake.

Ben would probably think she was being irrational if she suggested that the Barett family had been murdered too. She had no evidence of that, nor did she have any reason to even entertain the notion. Shy decided to take one thing at a time. She would tell him about Mattie, and then she would go talk to Mr. Border alone. Maybe Carl could think of something else or, at least, tell her if he had any reason to believe that someone would want to kill them. *Maybe her ex-husband?* Even this possibility didn't make sense. During the initial interview Traci had told Shy that her husband fought for custody of the kids during the divorce dispute and lost. Even during the greatest fit of rage toward Traci, why would he kill the children for whom he had fought less than a year-and-a-half ago? It didn't make sense!

She squinted her eyes and shook the thought from her head. Maybe she was losing it. Maybe this was just an over-indulged state of denial. What if Mattie had hidden the gun somewhere? Maybe someone had given it to her. What if she had been playing with the gun and dropped it or something? Was that possible? Would Ben think she was going crazy? Self-doubt had sunk in hard. Now, she couldn't make herself get out of the car.

Shy had been here before. When her dad died years ago, she teetered on the brink of insanity several times. She thought everyone around her was going to die, or that the house was going to catch on fire every time someone lit a match. Shy wondered if she should call Mr. Border back and tell him…well, she didn't know what she would tell him. She felt guilty for upsetting him further.

Shy closed her eyes and prayed for God to help her calm down. *God, don't let me go crazy!* She felt a numbing sensation as her body began to go limp. The world outside of her seemed far away. She could no longer hear the sounds of traffic passing on the street in front of her or the wind breezing against her windshield. The world seemed but a blurred memory which was no longer enforced with the power to hurt her. It felt like the night she passed out at the hospital when Nelson died, only this time she was alert.

The dream she'd had last night returned to her in the form of a vision. She saw Nelson, once again, holding the baby, the same baby she had repeatedly seen in her dreams- the one whom she didn't recognize but loved so much that she would have given her own life to save it. It was her baby. And, this time, when Nelson spoke to her … when he said, "The mother's blood will lead the way," he held the baby out to her and, for the first time, she recognized the child. His face was no longer blurred but vivid, clear, and beautiful. It was Jake, and he reached out to her as Nelson put him in her arms and disappeared.

Shy opened her eyes free of doubt and clear about what she needed to do. It was Mattie's blood that would lead the way. That's what Nelson was trying to tell her. Shy needed to find out who killed Mattie, and while she didn't know exactly how to do that, she knew Ben would help her. He had a good rapport with Sheriff Tills. They could reopen the case and send Mattie's body to the state crime lab before she was buried. Baby Jake was her new-found strength. She opened the car's door and got out. Her legs weren't shaking anymore.

As she entered the crowded building and headed for the sheriff's office, she felt conspicuous, as if everyone were looking at her swollen eyes and red cheeks. She tried to keep her head down to avoid eye contact as she squirmed between groups of people standing in front of the door to the sheriff's office.

"Excuse me, please," she said.

A couple moved out of her way, but no one replied to her polite gesture. She leaned in the doorway and asked for deputy Crossno. The secretary typed furiously at the keyboard in front of her. She didn't look up. "He's gone to lunch."

This was not what Shy wanted to hear. She looked at her watch. "But it's four o'clock."

"Yep, it's been hectic around here." The brunette looked up for a millisecond and then returned to her typing. "You want to leave a message?"

She didn't, and she didn't want to wait. As much as she didn't like Sheriff Tills, she needed to talk to someone. At some point Ben would have to tell him anyway.

"Is the sheriff in?" she asked.

Percy walked in with a stack of papers and plopped them down beside the secretary. She looked up at him, released a large sigh, and rolled her eyes. The deputy chuckled as the secretary became consumed with her work once again, never responding to Shy's question. Percy turned to go into the back hallway and saw Shy standing in the doorway.

"Hey Shy, you out here on a case?"

She wondered if he could tell that she'd been crying and tried to overcompensate with a big smile. "No, I was actually trying to catch Ben, but it looks like he's gone to lunch."

"I just saw him a bit ago. He was heading up the stairs, probably going to the file room. You know where it's at? Second floor?"

She lied with a quick nod, as she didn't feel like having an escort. "Thanks, I'll go see if he's there." Smiling, she walked out the door.

Percy followed her asking, "Shy, are you okay?"

She made a silly face and pointed to her nose. "Allergies." He smiled and gave her a sympathetic nod which told her that he didn't buy her story but would pretend as if he did. Percy's sincerity reminded Shy that decent people still existed.

"Let me know if you can't find him."

"All right." She nodded.

Knowing that Ben might still be in the building gave Shy a tidbit of relief. She knew that Ben often went straight from lunch to patrolling, usually not returning to the courthouse until he was off duty. She walked up the first flight of stairs and was on the second floor in a matter of seconds. The entrance to the third floor was blocked off with two large doors and a poster that read, "Authorized Personnel Only." The second floor appeared to be almost abandoned.

Stacks of boxes and old furniture littered the foyer and both sides of the hallway of the second floor. The only evidence of human life was the light that poured into the hall from an open office three doors down. Shy could hear movement generating from that direction and she headed toward it. In the office, she saw a woman with thick glasses and a butch haircut thumbing through papers behind an old oak desk. Shy tried to talk softly, hoping not to startle the woman.

"Could you please tell me where the file room is?"

The woman did not jump as Shy expected. She smiled and said, "And you're going to the file room because?" She let the "because" linger.

"Oh, I'm sorry. I'm looking for Deputy Crossno. I was told that he might be in the file room." The woman stacked the papers neatly in front of her and stood up.

"I'll need to take you. Only authorized personnel are allowed in there."

The woman brushed by Shy and led her down the hallway. There wasn't as much congestion here as there had been on the first floor. In fact it was very quiet, and the woman's chunky shoes echoed about the barren walls. The file room was the last door to the right. The woman stopped in the doorway as if to barricade it from Shy.

"Have any of you seen Deputy Crossno." Shy heard rustling. Someone inside repeated the question to others. Shy heard several "no's."

"No one has seen him. Are you sure he came to the file room?"

"No. Someone thought they saw him coming upstairs. Is there any other place he might be on this floor?"

"I don't think so. Most of these offices have been turned into storage until they get everything remodeled upstairs. The clerk's office, the treasurer's and the probation officers' were all moved downstairs. It's a big mess right now."

She walked Shy to the stairwell around the corner from her office. It wasn't the same way she came up, but she could certainly find her way back to the front entrance of the courthouse. The woman opened the old, steel door for her. "Is this an emergency? For Crossno, I mean?"

"Uh, no, I just wanted to chat with him for a bit." Shy smiled, but it was weak.

"Do you know where the sheriff's office is? It's downstairs just past the--"

"I know where it is," Shy interrupted, "I just came from there."

"Oh," the woman had a pleasant smile, "well, just go down there and leave a message for him. I'm sure he'll get back with you as soon as he can."

Shy nodded and thanked her. The woman closed the steel door to the stairwell behind her and the noise of it clanked about the walls above her and resounded downward to the first floor. She looked up and remembered the restoration going on upstairs. It looked dark but surely people would be working up there. There were no doors barricading the steps to the third floor.

The deputy said that he saw Ben heading up the stairs and that he wasn't in the file room. *Could he have gone to the third floor? Perhaps to look around and see how the new courtroom was coming along?*

Shy eased her way up the stairs, feeling a jump in her internal organs. It was much like the butterflies she felt in her stomach as a child that had cautioned her from mischief. She knew that she had no business going up there with all of the construction going on. If anyone questioned her, she would tell them she wanted to check out the new renovations. The worst that could happen is someone might tell her to leave, she reassured herself.

As she moved up onto the final step of the stairwell, she was puzzled. No sound or movement emanated from the third floor. This was certainly not what she expected. For the last several weeks, juvenile court was often disrupted from all the constructional noises. One time she was on the witness stand for an hour and a half because she had to keep stopping. No one, including the judge, could hear her. (And that was all the way down on the first floor.) But here, just outside the door to the third floor, she heard nothing. *Perhaps they finished early today.*

Shy opened the door about twelve inches and saw nothing but darkness. She peered through the opening hoping, maybe, to see solitary rays of light coming through an open office. Nothing. As she started to close the door, she thought she heard a low mumble and stopped to listened. Yes, she was sure of it. Someone was talking. It was definitely a man's voice, but she couldn't make out the words. She listened again. Two men, she thought, sitting in the would-be courtroom.

Shy slipped through the opening, careful not to make a sound and inched her way down the hall to the right. She didn't want to peek inside the large French doors because they were directly in front of the stairwell. She was afraid that just enough light would pour into the room and startle whoever was in there. *Was that Ben's voice? And who else's? Why were they sitting in the dark?*

As Shy rounded the first corner, the hallway became darker. She waited a moment for her eyes to adjust, careful to keep one hand on the wall as a guide in the darkness. Momentarily, she came to a swinging door that she thought was probably an exit to the side of the courtroom. Moving it slightly, she was pleased to find that the door was freshly oiled and didn't squeak. Shy peered inside and could barely make out an outline of two people. They were sitting quite a distance away, toward the front of the courtroom.

She concentrated, trying to make out the words or recognize a voice, but she couldn't. She had to get closer. Feeling a bit childish for spying, her urgency to speak to Ben kept moving her forward. If she could get to the front of the courtroom and see that Ben wasn't one of the two men, she would simply find her way back and try to find Tills. And, if he were in there, she would sit by the stairwell and wait until he was finished talking to whomever he was talking. But, she wasn't going to know unless she got closer.

She closed the door slowly and began to inch her way further up the hallway and around the next corner. Her hand grazed the molding of another door. This one, she thought, must lead to the center of the courtroom, but it didn't have a swinging door like the one she'd just left. She turned the knob carefully, crunched up her face reflexively, and braced herself for the noise it might make. It didn't. She put a slight amount of pressure on the door, and it opened without a squeak.

She wondered what she would tell someone if they caught her sneaking around up here. What could she tell them? *I was just looking around? In the dark?* Shy forced the thought away. She just needed to talk to Ben and nothing else mattered right now.

The door didn't lead to the courtroom, as she expected. It was an office, the only one she had discovered on the right side of the hallway. *Judges chambers?* Directly across from her, Shy could see light. She waited a moment to let her eyes adjust and realized she was looking through a two-way mirror. The light was coming from the stairwell, maybe through the cracks of the large doors. She thought she must be directly at the front of the courtroom, and if the light were coming in from the French doors, she could only assume that she was right in the center. That would mean that the two men would be sitting in front of her and to the left.

Her eyes adjusted a bit more, and she was finally able to make out the outline of the two men. One of them was indeed Ben. She could barely see him, but she was sure it was him and felt immediate relief. She didn't recognize the tall man to whom he was talking. He was wearing some type of a hat. *A construction hat maybe?* She couldn't understand what they were saying. Or, why they would be sitting in the dark.

Her curiosity got the better of her, as she moved closer to the mirror. She wondered if it had an intercom button like the one back at the office. If it did, she should be able to hear the men clearly even if they were whispering. She felt the wall to the right of the mirror and moved her hand carefully to the base of the seal until she felt a plastic protrusion. *There it is.* It wasn't a button, though. She'd seen this kind before in newer DHS buildings. It was a knob that had volume control.

Shy wondered if the microphones had been installed yet, thinking they probably hadn't been. She turned the knob one notch to the right and was surprised to hear mumbling. As she moved it two more notches, she could immediately make out the words of the conversation. The man with the hat was talking. She slowed her breath so that she could hear every word.

"So you don't have to worry about the Baretts just yet," a male voice said. Shy stiffened, thinking she had not heard him clearly. *Did he say Baretts?* Maybe he was talking about someone else.

"And who was the last?" the man continued.

"Mattie Johnson was the last, but they didn't get the kid."

"They didn't? Why not?"

Shy froze. Her legs wanted to give way beneath her. She hung on to the molding of the two-way mirror to steady herself. She had to hear more.

"The baby was asleep in one of the bedroom closets."

"No kidding? Lucky little fellow. Where is he now?"

"He's in foster care, but I'm not sure what town."

"The social worker knows, doesn't she?" Shy stood in horror. She heard Ben say, "Yeah, but she hasn't said anything. I think he'll be hard to get to."

"Are you sure? There's not as much of a cut unless they get him, too."

"I'll try to see what I can find out."

Shy held a hand to her mouth, trying hard not to gasp or cry out. Was she really hearing this? The man in the hat continued to talk saying, "How's everything with Tills?"

"Cool. I think he trusts me."

"Good. Keep him happy."

"Yes, sir."

"Any word on who's next?"

"Not yet. Haven't heard anything. I'll keep you posted."

"Yeah, we can't have another case end up like the Johnsons'. One more thing, about your social worker ..."

"What about her?"

"Think she knows too much?" Shy's heart began to race, and she took deep breaths to try to slow it.

"No. Don't worry about her." Ben said.

"Just keep an eye on her, Matt. She may become too much of a liability. You know what happened to the social worker in Saline who became a problem."

Shy jolted backward and choked on a suppressed gasp. *Nelson...they're talking about Nelson!* Her heart was beating so fast now that she feared they might hear her. She had to get out of there! Her foot brushed a paint bucket that sat beside a drip pan in the middle of the room. It made a slight clunk. She looked to see Ben jump into a standing position and look in her direction. Shy couldn't move. She reminded herself that he couldn't see her and found it to be a challenge to slow her breath.

Ben looked toward the man with the hat. "I'm sure it's nothing. I'll go check it out." He headed toward the swinging door to the side of the courtroom where she'd been at just minutes ago. The tall man stood up and headed for the back of the courtroom. She'd be trapped. Turning around as quickly and quietly as possible, she groped for the door by frantically moving her hands in front of her until she could feel the door molding. She slipped through the opening headed in the opposite direction from which she had come.

She fumbled blindly in the darkness and moved as fast as she could without making a sound. Ben was coming down the hallway just as she rounded the corner. She could hear him go into the judge's chambers. She didn't know where to go next. The stairwell had been just around the next corner, but she knew that the tall man, with whom Ben had been talking, could have been standing at the French doors. Beside herself, she thought, *If they catch me they will kill me, too!* She thought about screaming- maybe someone would hear her. Then she remembered what the men had said about Tills. He was also involved. They were all involved, even Ben.

She heard Ben leave the judge's chambers. Standing stone still, she allowed short, inaudible breaths. Hearing another door open, she knew he was checking the offices on the right side of the corridor. As she heard the last office door open, she remembered the other set of stairs, the ones she had been on when she went to the file room on the second floor.

From the position of where she was on the second floor, they should be close and they would be on the right side of the hall. She could hear Ben moving closer, so she progressed quickly to the other side of the corridor. *Please God, help me find the stairs!*

Removing her heels and continuing in stockings, Shy moved hastily and quietly, desperately hoping that the floor beneath her wouldn't creak. She let her hand brush the wall lightly, praying that it would brush over the molding that led to the hallway. Ben had just rounded the last corner and was straight behind her at the end of the hall. Shy couldn't see him, but she could hear his footsteps. She moved faster while praying that her foot would not hit a stray board or walk over a loud plastic drop-cloth.

The wall ended and she felt a large opening. It had to be the stairs. Shy felt with her foot for the first step down and positioned herself for balance. She could hear Ben who was only about fifteen feet away. When she gained firm footing, she moved into the opening and inched down three steps. She couldn't move any further, for he was too close and would hear her.

Shy tried not to breath, not to cry. Ben was moving closer. Had he heard her? Would he know that she was on the stairs? She heard a slight brushing sound and could tell that he was letting one hand slide against the wall, just as she had, to guide his way through the darkness. He came to the opening of the hallway, and Shy held her breath. She knew that if he reached far enough, he could touch her. She froze in place. *Please, God, don't let him find me!*

He stopped briefly then inched his way forward. His hand was extended out into the stairwell. Shy felt a slight waft of coolness against her cheek as his hand brushed by, stirring the air in front of her. If she had been on the second step, he would have caught her. He moved to where the wall began again and rounded the next corner before Shy began her quiet decent down the stairs.

Once down the first flight, she could feel the large doors that barricaded people from getting to the third floor, and she thanked God for them. Had they not been there, the light from the second floor would have radiated upward, and Ben would have seen her. The doors were locked from the inside, and Shy frenetically searched for the latch. Once she opened one of the doors, she slipped through it and began to move faster, caring less about the noise she made. A man and woman were walking up the stairs, each carrying a box of files. They were chatting about a court procedure. Shy was relieved to see them. Neither Ben nor the man with the hat would hurt her in front of witnesses.

On the first floor, Shy put her shoes back on and darted around people, not caring what they thought as she shoved past them. She had to get to safety! But, where would she go? Percy, standing beside the door to the sheriff's office, was trying to wave her down. Shy did not see him. When she saw a clearing in the crowd of people, she began to run.

Chapter Twenty-Three

The man in the construction hat went down the stairwell. Ben went down the other set of stairs and waited until he couldn't hear rustling movement on the other side of the barricaded doors. When he was sure no one was on the stairs heading to the file room, he opened one of the doors and slipped out.

He hesitated on the stairs. *Why weren't the doors locked?* He realized that he had not checked them earlier. A bit of paranoia arose, but he dismissed it. Construction workers moved in and out of the doors all day; they probably just forgot to lock them.

Ben headed down the stairs and was glad to see the diminished traffic on the first floor of the courtroom. As he headed for the office, he checked his watch. It was nearly five o'clock. The secretary had already gone home. In an effort to appear as though he had been in there toiling a while, Ben scrambled for one of his files and perched himself at the desk.

Sheriff Tills stepped out of his office and heavily trudged down the hallway. When he saw Ben in the front office, he bellowed, "Boy, you still here?"

"Afraid so, boss. I'm fixin' to head out, though."

It was quiet in the office. The new shift was out on patrol and most of the office staff had gone home. Tills looked about the empty room and planted both palms on the desk in front of Ben so that he could look him square in the eyes.

"We got our meetin' Friday night, boy. You in?"

Ben looked at him and cracked a wicked smile, "Hell, yeah, I'm in. I want to know more about it. Like, what's my role?" He fished but Tills wasn't biting.

"In due time, son."

Percy walked in with another small stack of papers that he promptly put in the secretary's "to do" box. "I'm afraid I'm about to work that poor girl to death." he chuckled. Then, he turned his attention toward Ben. "Hey, Crossno, did Shy catch you earlier?"

"What do you mean?"

"She was in here looking for you about an hour ago. I told her I saw you going up the stairs and that she might catch you in the file room. Where were you, anyway?"

Ben stiffened and thought he caught the same in Tills. He purposefully made the pitch of his voice relax. "File room," he answered calmly.

"For what?" the sheriff asked with his head cocked to the side.

Ben tried to think fast. He made a conscious effort to relax. "Oh, I pulled a guy over today for a traffic violation. Thought I'd seen him in here before. There wasn't anything from dispatch. I just thought I'd see if he had a history but wasn't charged. Thought I might need to keep a closer eye on the guy is all."

"Did you find what you was looking for?" the sheriff asked.

Ben didn't like what he was seeing in Tills' eyes. Trying to stay cool, he said, "Yes, sir, the guy was clean."

Tills nodded and added, "You know we got a secretary to take care of stuff like that."

Ben faked a smile and said, "Loretta? Trust me, boss, I didn't want to ask Loretta for nothin'. She was a little on the cranky side today, wasn't she, Percy?"

Ben was grateful when Percy started laughing and said, "Sure was. I thought she was going to bite my head off a time or two. That girl can get downright nasty when you give her extra work to do."

Ben thought he saw Tills relax. The sheriff smiled a bit and nodded that he understood. Loretta could be touchy sometimes. He started clicking at the computer in front of him.

Ben felt his gut settle a bit. He turned to Percy and asked, "Did she say what she wanted?"

"Who?" Percy asked.

"Miss Sauze."

Percy shook his head. "No. I saw her come back down. Sure was in a hurry to get out of here. I hollered at her to see if she found you, but she didn't hear me. She looked upset and was darn near runnin'."

Ben felt as if a knife had pierced near his heart. He knew now that someone had, indeed, been in the judge's chambers. It was Shy. She'd heard him talking to Burns. That was why the doors to the second floor were unlocked. She must have been hiding on the stairs when he was searching about, looking for a possible intruder. *Dear God, she knows!*

He wondered if Percy could see his forehead perspire. Tills sat at the secretary's desk, fiddling with the computer. Ben wanted to dart out the door to go find Shy, but he had to be cool. His mind raced to access his imagination. He forced his facial muscles to relax and looked at Percy slyly. "Yeah, I guess she's a little upset," he smiled awkwardly and tapped his fingers on the stack of papers in front of him, "told her last night that we needed to slow things down. You know how it goes."

Percy looked at Ben intensely, "I think you're a fool, man. She's a good woman. Pretty, too."

"I know, I'm just not ready for anything permanent." Tills continued to be consumed by the task at hand.

Ben stood up and stretched. "Well, boys, I'm gonna go grab a bite and hit the hay. Tomorrow morning comes early." Percy gave him a wave, as he headed for the door.

"See ya later, Sheriff."

Tills cocked his eyebrows. "Thought you just ate, boy. That's what Loretta said, anyway."

Ben tried to think fast. "Only had time for a little cheeseburger, boss. It's been one of those days, you know what I mean?"

Tills nodded but Ben wasn't sure if he bought it. He thought quickly and added, "Hey don't forget, Sheriff, about the case you want me to look at on Friday." He was talking in code about the meeting, and Tills nodded that he understood saying, "See you in the morning."

Ben headed out the door, and Percy began to gather his things. "You want to go get a beer?"

"No, thanks. Got things I've got to get done here." Percy said.

"Okay, man, see ya bright 'n' early."

Tills didn't respond. He sat motionless in front of the monitor until he heard the front doors of the courthouse close behind Percy. He picked up the phone and asked the operator to connect him to the file room. "Linda, this is Sheriff Tills. I'm following up on a report for Crossno. Can you look at the sign out sheet and tell me what chart he pulled. I'm gonna need to take a look at it. Thank you, sugar." Tills waited, tapping his forefinger on the desk.

The woman came back on the phone and Tills listened intently. "Is that right? No where on the flow sheet, huh? Hmmph. Guess I'm gonna' have to have another meeting with the boys about signing out those charts when they're lookin' at them. Thank you, darlin'." Tills pushed the receiver button down and listened for the dial tone. He called the operator.

"Yes, I need the number to the L.A. Police Department. Thanks." He scrambled for a pen and wrote the number down. He waited for the dial tone again and then punched in the number.

"Yes, ma'am, this is Sheriff Wayne Tills of the Maburn County Sheriff's office in Arkansas." He was staring at the computer monitor.

"I'm looking at a file here on an officer that worked for you all several years ago. Social Security number's 431-55-5899. Can you verify that name and date of birth for me? Yes 'um." He waited. "Uh-huh, that's what I got, too. 'preciate your time." He was about to hang up, but the operator kept talking. "No, ma'am, I sure didn't. Tragic. Well, thank you so much." He hung up the phone and sat quietly, thinking and staring at the screen.

It appeared that Ben Crossno, formerly of the LAPD, had died ten years before in the line of fire. He was fifty-two-years-old and had a wife and three kids. The boy had played him for a fool. He had not looked it up before now, because he thought he could depend on his good judge of character. He had been wrong. Now he had to find out who this guy really was.

He picked up the phone and dialed the mayor. He knew Kult would be pissed. And, this made him even more angry.

Chapter Twenty-Four

The fall weather had almost completely chilled the earth in Arkansas, but Shy was unable to feel the icy water that lapped about her ankles. The moon was full and hypnotic. At some point while driving away from the courthouse, Shy's emotions had capsized. Her thoughts flew from one horrible notion to the next.

The man that she loved- would likely have spent the rest of her life with- had somehow been involved with the murder of Mattie and Nelson, along with countless other innocent people. How had he held her when she grieved over Mattie and consoled her when they put Jake in foster care when all the while he was ruthlessly plotting to kill Jake for a "bigger cut?" What the hell did that mean? Was he getting paid for the people he killed? By whom?

Her thoughts rushed to Jake, and she panicked, wondering if he was safe. Ben even knew the names of Jake's foster parents. Her only consolation was that she didn't think she had ever told him where they lived. She picked up her cell phone and dialed Bill at home. After three rings the answering machine picked up and recorded her message, "Bill, it's Shy. I need to talk to you, but I may not be back in the office for a few days. Something very serious is going on. I have reason to believe that Mattie was murdered, and the same people are trying to find Jake. I know it sounds crazy, but I need you to trust me! You've got to move Jake to another home. Don't tell anyone where he is. Please, Bill, I'm begging--" The answering machine cut her off.

She tried to catch her breath. She loved Ben, and he had used her to get information about people he would murder? But why? What did anyone have to gain by murdering these people? And what about Nelson? What did the man mean when he said that Nelson had become a problem?

She cried hysterically as her thoughts spun rampantly. She didn't know to whom she could turn. From what Ben said to the other man, Tills was involved, too. She couldn't turn to the police. Who else was there? How far up the ladder of bureaucracy did the evil reach? The numbness started at her fingertips and prickled its way up to her neck and down her spine. It was the welcoming warmth of shock, and she embraced it to the point that she could no longer focus on the road ahead of her or the thoughts that swirled about in her head. Everything went blank, and with it, the confusion, the heartbreak, the tears, and the pain ceased. Disassociated and numb, she found herself at Lennox Marcus; standing in the comforting, dark waters of Lake Degray.

Ben sped down the highway to Shy's apartment knowing full well that she would not be there. He also knew that she wouldn't be with any of her family if she thought he was dangerous and might harm them to get to her. When he drove by her house and didn't see her car, he kept going.

Never in his life had he felt so desperate to find someone. There was no telling what she had overheard in his meeting with Burns, or what she thought of him. He tried to tell himself that maybe she had not been on the third floor, but he had heard the noise coming from inside the judge's chambers. It was quite possible, if someone had been in there, for them to go down the opposite hall and slip out before he had even had the chance to find them. And, Percy said she was nearly running when she left the courthouse. He knew in his heart that she had been there.

He knew he should have never fallen in love with Shy. It was a selfish act that put her at risk. Until now, he had been able to subdue her. He had comforted her and tried to re-direct her thoughts from the idea that someone might have murdered her clients. He never wanted her to know that there was an intricate, evil plan designed by the mayor, himself, to reduce a vast portion of the population living off of welfare. He did not want her to know that a number of the political offices across the state of Arkansas were involved. Now, she knew too much. If she told anyone what she had heard, both their lives would be in grave danger. *God, please help me find her!*

Tills called up one of his loyal subjects who had helped him out a time or two. He didn't mind calling him because he had given the guy a number of "get out of jail free cards" since his parole over a year ago. The man's name was Lester Crumb, but his friends called him Bug.

Bug was not only a murdering psychopath but also an ingenious computer hack. Tills gave him the directions to both Ben's and Shy's apartments with specific instructions. If anyone was at home, kill them, but make it look like a burglary. Otherwise, Bug was only to enter the apartments and destroy any information that might be incriminating.

Just before his conversation with Bug, the mayor had returned Tills' call on a secured line. Kult called him a "blithering idiot," among other things, for not checking the boy out sooner. The mayor was right, but Tills was not likely to admit it any time soon. He hung up the phone just after Kult told him to kill Ben as well as the girl.

Chapter Twenty-Five

It took Ben almost two hours to find Shy. He pulled into Lennox Marcus, the campsite that Shy had taken him to on their first date. Carefully scanning the water, he could see the outline of her figure standing against the pale of the moon. Pulling his jeep to a stop, he got out, not bothering to shut the door, and hurried toward her. The point had been abandoned for the fall and winter seasons. Having disturbed the calm of the deserted campsite with the noise of his vehicle, Ben was concerned that Shy had not turned around. She did not seem to notice that anyone was there.

She was standing shin-deep in the chilly waters of Lake Degray, shoes and all. Ben walked toward her at an angle and was soon able to see her face in the moonlight. Her eyes were glazed, staring listlessly at nothing. She appeared to be in shock. He walked to the water's edge and soothingly called her name. She didn't turn around, flinch, or give any indication that she was aware of her surroundings.

Ben immediately became concerned about her blood pressure and mental state. He desperately wanted to get her to the hospital but wasn't sure how to approach her without terrifying her. It pained him to know that she was in this condition because of what she had heard at the courthouse. He could only assume that it was enough to put her in this glazed, disoriented state. It sickened him that he, albeit unknowingly, had played a role in it.

He stepped into the lake and couldn't help but wince as the icy water soaked through his socks and shoes and began inching its way up his shins. He moved slowly hoping that he wouldn't startle her. Recalling the mental status of her adolescent years, Ben remembered Shy's episodes of hypertension. *Was her blood pressure already so high as to cause the state she was in?* He inched closer and softly spoke her name, trying to get her attention without alarming her, "Shy?" He was about five feet away and inched closer. The water sloshing about his shins failed to orient her. "Honey?" he said gently, moving closer still until he was only two feet away and just to the side of her.

She looked very fragile and pale. Her cheeks were sunken below her hollow eyes. Until now, he'd not realized how much weight she'd lost over the last several weeks. Tears began to form in the corner of his eyes. He wanted so badly to gather her up and hold her. He said her name again as he extended his hand and gently touched her on the back. She flinched. It was the first sign of movement he'd seen since he got there. She turned to look at him, and he smiled gently.

Shy stared at Ben, focusing with an expression that seemed almost puzzled. Her eyes moved about his face, and he wondered if she even recognized him. He spoke to her soothingly. "Shy, honey … it's me … Ben."

Shy's expression turned from confusion to horror. She began flailing about, pushing him away from her and screaming. He tried to reach for her, but she hit him hard with a closed fist just under his left eye. The force of the blow threw him off balance and gave her the chance to get away from him.

After regaining his balance, Ben splashed from the water after her. It killed him to see her so frightened of him. He had to catch her and make her understand. "Shy, come back! I'm not gonna hurt you, honey. It's not what you think. Please!" He secured his gun more firmly in the holster.

Shy was running like a wild animal toward the woods. She was about thirty feet away, and he thought she was running for the hiking trail that she had shown him the first time they came here together. He started after her but then remembered the shortcut she had shown him to the bridge. He ran to it, sprinting as fast as he could through the woods, and was grateful that the moon was bright so he could see where he was going.

In just three minutes he had reached the intersection of the other trail, stopped, and listened. In the distance he could hear her whimpers. Poor baby, he thought, she's so scared. He knew that jumping out at her would scare her even more, but how else would he be able to catch her and make her understand?

He felt his eyes water and swallowed hard. Ben had only cried once in his entire life, at his grandfather's funeral. But even then, it wasn't much of a cry. Until now, he'd never loved anyone with such intensity.

The frightened whimpers were getting closer, and he could hear the steady rhythm of her feet hitting the ground as she ran. He ducked low. The throb under his eye reminded him that she had a pretty mean left hook. He braced himself.

The running sounds moved closer, closer, closer. Ben jumped out of the woods and grabbed Shy, causing her to shriek and cry out. He had his arms tightly wrapped around her, forcing her arms flat to her sides. He fell to his back with her on top of him then rolled over and let the brunt of his weight hold her down.

With one of her hands freed, she clawed at his back, neck, and face until he was able to restrain her hand. His bulletproof vest took most of the damage, but he could already feel blood begin to ooze from the wounds on his neck and face. He managed to get her other hand and hold them both firmly to the ground.

"Honey, it's okay!" He was yelling loudly, trying desperately to get her to hear him over her screams. "I'm not going to hurt you. Please calm down, Shy! Listen to me!" He was afraid she might pass out, or worse.

Shy tried to butt her head against him and tried to bite, all the while screaming and furiously trying to squirm her way free. For the first time, Ben truly saw the terror in her eyes. He could tell that she really thought he would hurt her. No amount of strength could keep his tears at bay.

"I'm not going to hurt you, Shy!" He was nearly screaming now, desperate to get her to stop struggling and hear him out. "Don't you understand? I love you. I know you heard me at the courthouse.

I know you were there. But it's not what you think. I'm a Fed, Shy. Do you hear me? I'm in the F.B.I!" He hadn't noticed that she'd quit squirming. He let go of her hands so he could cup his hands around her face. "God knows I love you. I would never hurt you, baby."

Shy wasn't crying anymore. She no longer felt the serenity of shell shock. She was back, and fighting for her life. Somehow, she had managed to rip the pistol from Ben's holster. Holding it up to his nose, she screamed, "Get off of me, right now, or I'll blow your head off!"

Ben was confused. How did she get a gun? It took him a minute before he realized it was his. He scrambled to his feet, quaking with fear from the fury in her eyes, and held his hands up where she could see them.

"Prove it!" she demanded.

"Prove what?" Ben was still trying to figure out what had just transpired. He thought he had gotten through to her. Now, she was pointing his gun at him.

"Prove to me that you're in the F.B.I."

"Okay, just put the gun down and I'll--"

"I'm not putting the damn gun down. And, if you don't show me proof in five seconds, I'm pulling the trigger.

Ben spoke softly, "Shy, put the gun down," as he took a step toward her, holding his hand out for the gun. The explosion from the pistol made him jump and crouch in fear as the blast whizzed by his head and snapped a tree limb behind him.

"Shit, Shy!" he said half angry and half scared to death.

"Five seconds," she said, "One…"

Ben could see her eyes in the moonlight, and the look on her face scared him. "Okay! Wait!" He scrambled to pull his wallet out of his pocket. As he unfolded it, half of its contents dropped to the ground. Shy was at number four.

"Wait! Look!" He held the badge out in front of her. "This is my real badge." She moved closer, as he held his credentials in the moonlight.

She couldn't read it and said, "Walk to the car, Ben."

"What?"

"I said walk to the car. And, put your hands on your head." She held both hands firmly on the gun and waved it as if telling him to move. Ben put both of hands on his head and intertwined his fingers as he inched through the trail that led out of the woods. "Shy, your blood pressure…"

She interrupted with fury, "Shut up! Just keep moving!"

Ben walked out of the woods and up to Shy's car. He turned and looked at her. "Open the car." He did. "Now, put the badge in the light where I can see it."

Ben moved one hand slowly to the pocket containing the badge. He took it out carefully and held it toward the light. Shy moved toward it, carefully pointing the gun at Ben. She diverted her attention just long enough to read the badge.

"That doesn't say Ben Crossno." She gripped the gun more firmly and squinted her eyes at him.

"I'm undercover, Shy. My real name is Matt Hollingsworth. What can I do to prove it to you? Get your cell phone. I'll let you call my mom."

It wasn't necessary. Shy remembered the man in the courtroom calling Ben "Matt." It made sense. She was starting to believe him.

"Shy, please put the gun down."

Bug had not found anything to speak of in Ben's house. He had figured as much. If the guy was a Fed as Tills suspected, surely he was smart enough not to leave sensitive data lying about the house. Just to be on the safe side, Bug plugged a virus into the hard drive. The minute Ben booted up the computer, the whole system would shut down, permanently. The place looked spotless, and Bug left feeling certain that there was nothing to be found. He climbed out of the back window and closed it carefully.

Maybe Tills would let him come back and kill the Narc. Tills always let Bug do the dirty work. He walked behind a series of houses until he saw his buddies circling the block. Waving them down, he stepped out onto the road and waited for them to pull up beside him.

After thirty minutes of questioning, Shy was finally convinced that Ben was legitimate. She was no longer holding the gun to Ben's face, but she wasn't quite ready to turn it back over to him. She said, "Ben, you've got to tell me what's going on."

"Shy, I have to be very careful with what I tell you. Knowing everything that I know could get you killed."

"I understand and I will be very careful with whatever you tell me. Ben, I'm already involved in this mess. How can I play a game when I don't even know who the players are?" Ben thought about this last statement. She was right. He couldn't imagine her being in any more danger than she was already, but he did not want to risk it.

Shy continued to pry, "Well, what about you? I guess your life is already in a great deal of jeopardy." He nodded in agreement. This scared her. She had almost forgotten how much she loved him, despite the fact that she had been willing to kill him just moments earlier.

"Is anyone on to you?" she asked.

"I don't know. It's hard to tell sometimes. I'm sure Tills is keeping a close eye on me, being the new guy and all. He asked me if I wanted to attend a meeting Friday night. I'm pretty sure that it's about the plan. If it is, all the key players will be there."

"The plan?" Shy was looking at him with her head cocked to one side. He had momentarily forgotten that she didn't know the motive behind all the murders. He took a deep breath knowing that she would not take the information well.

"Last year, the federal government noticed a significant decline in the number of funds that it doled out to Arkansas for public services such as food stamps and Medicaid. The state has gotten a number of grant dollars that has been distributed among certain counties to help dependent woman and children become productive members of society. The federal government initially thought that the programs established by the grants were working well and wanted further research. They hired an independent contractor out of California to check into it. What they found out was that a number of welfare families had died that year."

Cries of the Orchids

Shy felt the muscles in her stomach recoil. "Don't tell me our state was killing innocent people to reduce taxes."

"We don't know. That's why I'm here, Shy. Arkansas' state government has no idea that it's being watched. At least, we don't think so. Anyway, there are several agents who have gotten themselves hired as deputies across the state."

"So, a lot of the counties' sheriffs are involved?"

"That's the theory."

"But what do they gain? I don't get it."

"The Bureau thinks that the plan goes something like this: The sheriff or one of his guys murders a family. They mostly go after the families that are inter-generational welfare clients." Shy nodded as if she understood. He continued, "The coroner, another politically-appointed position, goes in and pronounces the family dead. Afterwards, he validates the sheriff's documentation regarding the manner in which each family member died."

Shy began to tremble but tried to not let Ben see for fear that he would withhold information to protect her. She wanted to know everything that was going on and didn't want to give Ben a reason to not tell her every detail.

"The bodies may, at that point, be sent to the state crime lab for examination. This would happen if there was any reason to suspect foul play. The state crime lab examiner, another politically-appointed position, then files a report supporting both the sheriff's and the coroner's findings. For each family homicide, depending on the size, of course, the state saves thousands, sometimes hundreds of thousands each year. In addition to this, the accountability of millions of dollars in grant monies is under heavy scrutiny."

She shook her head in disbelief, taking a moment to digest what she had just heard. "But what's your theory? On everything, I mean. Do you actually believe all of these people are being murdered?" Pausing briefly to weigh the benefits of his answer, he nodded and said, "Yes."

Shy's face went momentarily ashen then flushed with rage as she looked at Ben incredulously asking, "Then why aren't they being stopped? How come the F.B.I. hasn't done something?"

"We've got almost enough information to nail Tills. It's just a matter of time. And, we had a strong lead on the sheriff in Saline, but we lost our informant." Ben looked down. He couldn't hold Shy's gaze.

"Nelson ... you're talking about Nelson, aren't you? He was the informant," she gasped. Forcing back tears, she said, "that's what he wanted to talk to me about the night of his wreck. They killed him, didn't they?" It was not possible to stop the tears which swelled up in her eyes and began to freely dribble down her cheeks. Ben didn't answer. He wondered if knowing the truth was in her best interest right now.

"Ben, answer me!" she demanded.

"I'm sorry, honey." He tried to gather her up into his arms, but she pulled away and looked directly into his eyes.

"And they killed Mattie, too." She didn't present this as a question. She already knew the answer. She just needed him to confirm it.

He nodded and reached out for her, hugging her tightly. She began to wail and shake uncontrollably, "Damn them ... Damn them all to hell!" Ben didn't know how to console her. He let her cry, curse, and violently threaten Sheriff Tills and whoever else might be involved, including the F.B.I. for not overtly intervening. Then, she directed the anger upon herself. "Oh, Ben, do you know how they found out about Mattie? Oh, God! It's because of me!"

Ben tried to soothe her. "Honey, what are you talking about? How could it possibly have been your fault?"

"If I hadn't gotten her hooked into all the services, they wouldn't have even known about her. She'd still be here. All of them would be ... the Watsons, the Baretts, all of them." She let her head fall to his shoulder and sobbed uncontrollably.

"Shy, Mattie couldn't have lived without those services and you know that. She needed every one of them. Our government designed those programs just for people like Mattie, and the Baretts, and the Watsons."

She asked him to give her a moment alone. Giving him his gun, she walked to the water's edge to try to process all that she had heard. Ben put the gun back into his holster and waited patiently by the jeep. He could hear her mournful crying and wished so badly that she would let him be with her.

After a long period of time, Shy came back toward him. Defensively, her arms were folded just below her breasts. She moved close enough to him so that she was able to look him square in the eyes. "You used me, didn't you?" she demanded. Ben was once again thrown off by her accusations. "What?"

"You used me to get information about Tills' victims in Hot Spring County. You're no better than they are, you son of a bitch!" She pushed him with all of her might. As he stumbled backwards, she moved forward and socked him in the face again shrieking, "You never loved me!"

Ben defensively held his hands upward, but it didn't do much good. She hit and clawed him while he shielded his face. He couldn't blame her for thinking that he used her. It wasn't his intent, but he could see how she might think it. He finally grabbed both of her hands, pinned her against a tree, and yelled, "Listen to me! I fell in love with you the day I met you! Don't you know that? I met you under an alias, but the feelings are no less real." He looked deep into her eyes. "I want to love you forever."

Shy started crying, for she truly wanted to believe him. This, their love for each other, had to be real. She didn't know if she could live through all the pain and tragedy if their love was a façade. She wrapped her arms around his waist and buried her face in his chest. All of the agony and anger were somehow tempered by this one, solitary moment. And, they held on to one another until they both felt safe enough to let go.

"I want to love you forever, too, Ben, uh, I mean, Matt." They couldn't help but laugh at how ridiculous it sounded, and laughter was a nice break from the excruciating intensity of the situation. Shy stopped laughing when Ben looked at her seriously saying, "Tell me you will be mine forever."

Bug climbed up on the air conditioner and slipped easily into the side window of Shy's apartment. It was dark outside now, so he didn't have to worry as much about being seen. He had a pocket flashlight that did a good job getting him around in the dark.

He was in the girl's bedroom and couldn't resist opening the top drawer of the chest sitting to the right of the light switch. It was filled with an array of silky panties in a variety of colors, just what he'd expected.

Tills didn't tell him anything about the girl, but he did tell Bug he could kill her if she happened to be home. He was disappointed when he originally drove to the house. All the lights were out. No car in the driveway. He wouldn't get to kill tonight.

He took a pair of black panties out of the chest and rubbed them against his cheek. Flashing his light at the photo sitting on top of the chest, he saw a picture of Shy and her best friend from college. They were hugged up to each other and smiling for the camera. He put the panties back in the drawer, closed it, and reached for the picture, holding it close to get a better look. He wasn't sure which one of the girls lived in this apartment. Perhaps he would come back another time to find out. They were both lookers.

Another picture lay on the chest. It wasn't in a frame. It was a fat chick holding a baby. She looked familiar. He didn't know where he'd seen her but then suddenly realized that this was the lady Tills wanted him to kill last week. *Huh! Wonder why there's a picture of her here?* He made a mental note to tell Tills.

He followed the same procedure as he had in the other house and found nothing remarkable. Searching through her computer downstairs, he found nothing. Nonetheless, he programmed the same virus into it just as a precautionary measure.

Bug was headed upstairs and was back in the bedroom in minutes. He was nearly to the window before he realized that the bed wasn't un-made. Someone was asleep in it. He had thought, from looking at the exterior of the house, that no one was home. The idea that he had been rummaging about in the girl's house for nearly an hour without waking her was quite entertaining.

He inched toward the form and felt the rush that he always felt before he took the life from someone. It made him tingle and sweat. He moved closer to the bed, pulled the knife from his pocket and opened the blade. Putting the knife in his right hand, Bug leaned over the form, moving slowly as to not disturb her. Not yet. He wanted to hear her breath first, soft ... and quiet.

He moved close to her face and heard a slow, rhythmic heaving as her lungs filled with air. He embraced the moment, holding the tiny flashlight to the side of the bed but not on her. She didn't even stir. This wasn't one of the chicks in the picture. This woman was older. She had similar features as one of the girls. Maybe it was her mother. No matter to Bug. Her breath sounds were just as alluring. He began to feel a slight buzz.

He was ready to watch her wake up and find him over her. Ready to watch her eyes widen in shock as she tried to scream with his hand over her mouth while showing her the knife with his free hand. He pulled the blade forward feeling aroused and excited ... but then he heard the sirens. They were far away and probably not coming for him, but he wasn't going to risk it.

Bug darted out the window and hid in the darkness, periodically flicking the flashlight on and off. After the third time of flicking the light, he saw his friends flash their headlights up the road. In a matter of seconds he was back in the car with them and heading in the opposite direction from the sirens which seemed to be moving closer.

He grabbed the cell phone from a buddy and punched in Tills' number. He was still at the office. Bug's breathing was still labored from the escape. "Nothin' there either, man, 'cept for a picture of the case you wanted me to take last week. Yeah, I'm sure, man. Just sittin' there holdin' her baby or somethin'. No, she wasn't home either. Nowhere in sight."

He opted not to tell Tills about the older broad. What was the point? "Yeah. Where can we pick up the stuff? Yeah, okay, man. Thanks." He shut the phone off and reached for a beer in the small ice chest perched in the front seat. He lit up a cigarette and smiled at his friends. For the last job, Tills only paid him one kilo of coke. But he was able to sell it and make just over two thousand an ounce. He made a total of eighty-five thousand dollars after he and his buddies rolled on it for a couple of days. Tills had two for him this time. Bug was thrilled!

"Said he got the bomb this time. Picked it off some dealers Friday night." His buddies hollered and bumped hands.

Bug sat smugly, "Ya'll ready to roll, or what? 'At's what I'm sayin."

Karen was startled when she was awakened by loud pummeling on the door and a booming voice that yelled, "Police. Open up!" Grabbing the bathrobe she'd borrowed from her daughter, she slung it on and headed downstairs.

Having fallen asleep around two o'clock, she hadn't even realized that it was nearly eight. She had gotten her days and nights mixed up since tending to Shy in the hospital. None of the lights were on. While in a state of unconsciousness, she hadn't even realized that Shy had not come home from her lunch date with Ben. Now the police were banging on the door and she found herself suddenly feeling afraid. She rushed downstairs, frantic that something had happened to her daughter. The jolt of adrenaline had shaken any ounce of grogginess from her deep sleep. She opened the door so quickly that it startled one of the officers.

"Yes, sir. What's wrong?" Her eyes were wide with panic.

The taller of the two spoke first. "Ma'am. We were called out here on a possible intruder."

"What? What do you mean?" The panic subsided and confusion took its place.

"We got a call from your neighbors. One of the kids said they saw someone in your bedroom. Are you Miss Sharon Sauze?"

"No, she's not here. I'm her mother."

The officers looked at one another and gave each other a quick nod as if they may have solved the problem. Now, the shorter officer spoke. "Ma'am, have you been here all night?"

"Yes, sir."

He smiled at her. "Well, I think, with your daughter's car being gone, maybe one of the neighbor kids saw you in the bedroom and thought there was a burglar in the home."

"Oh," she laughed nervously. She wanted to ask them about her daughter but opted not to. Perhaps Shy had called when she was asleep, and she hadn't heard the phone ring.

"Well, ma'am," said the tall officer, "we're sorry for scaring you. Just wanted to make sure everything was okay."

She thanked them, grateful to have the neighbors watching out for her daughter. She shut the door and locked it behind her. Trying not to worry, she headed for the living room to see if there were any phone messages. There were none. Maybe she and Ben went somewhere. But why didn't she call? She knew Shy would get angry with her for making a fuss. After all, she was a grown woman. But her mind wandered back to the fragile child with cuts and blood spurting from both wrists. She forced the thought away. It was a long time ago. Shy was much better now.

Karen went upstairs to take a bath hoping a warm soak would soothe her nerves. She went straight to the bathroom and turned on the tap until steam began seeping upward from the tub. She took off the robe and was immediately chilled by a cold draft that she had not noticed in her frantic rush to answer the door. *What in the world?*

Putting the bathrobe back on, she went back through Shy's room to the hallway. The heater was going full blast. She checked the thermostat and saw that it was set on seventy-two, but the gauge securely stood at a chilly, sixty-three degrees. Hoping the heater wasn't going out, she considered calling Shy's landlord but couldn't recall his name, much less his number. She checked her watch and decided to go ahead and go to Wal-Mart before it closed. She wondered if Maburn had a taxi service. Maybe she could find a good electric heater for a reasonable price. She didn't have a lot of money, but she feared that she and her daughter would be sleeping in the cold until the landlord could get out there. Besides, getting out of the house would help distract her from where Shy might be- and the urge to call the police.

Walking back to the bathroom, she turned the water off. Karen kept her belongings in a suitcase at the end of Shy's bed. Flipping on the light to the bedroom that, until now, had only been lit by the soft hue of the hallway and Shy's bathroom, fear swelled up in her lungs. She stared with disbelief at the opened window with its curtains flowing in the breeze.

Chapter Twenty-Six

"So what happens, now?" Shy asked.

"We wait."

"Wait for what? More deaths?"

"So far, we don't have enough information to convict anyone. It's too early in the investigation." "But what about Sheriff Tills? I thought you said you have enough information to nail him."

"No, I said that we're close. We've pulled some of his prints from the remains of the Barett's house.

"But can't he argue that his prints were there because he was out there with the fire department?"

"Yes, he can argue that in all the murder cases. We're hoping that this meeting he invited me to Friday night is about the next hit. He's made several references about a family in Dower Mill, but he hasn't given me any solid leads. We're hoping this will happen Friday night with all the club members present. I'd be willing to wager that Kult will be there."

"But what about you? What if they're onto you and setting you up?"

"I'll be wired. The Bureau's setting up a sting. I'll be fine."

"But, if this is going on over the entire state, more people could die before the meeting."

"We can't just jump in there and make arrests, right now, Shy. We have no proof that these people are being murdered. If we jump now, the system shuts down. Everyone gets away. Can't you understand that?" She nodded and started to tremble again. She suddenly remembered the pictures.

"I have proof, Matt. This is why I came to the courthouse to find you, today." She ran to her car and pulled the pictures from the glove compartment. "Come over here so that you can see in the light."

Matt was puzzled, wondering what she could possibly have that would serve as proof. He walked into the dim light emanating from inside the car and looked down at the pictures.

"Mattie was left handed. She couldn't have made a clean shot directly into her right temple. See how she's reaching for everything with her left hand. The bullet wound was above her right temple."

Matt held the pictures up. "Incredible! Well," he had to admit, "it certainly does suggest foul play. But how do we link our guys to it?"

Shy slumped down into the car's seat and shook her head in frustration. She knew she was grasping at straws but opted to tell Matt anyway, hoping that the extra information might give him some type of inspiration. "Well, also, there's the Barett's house. Mr. Border told me that he had just installed smoke alarms two weeks ago. Now, why didn't the alarms wake Traci or the kids?"

"When did he tell you that?"

"The morning the house burned down. And, I also called him today to confirm…" She jerked her hands up to her chest and exclaimed, "Oh, Dear God!"

"What?"

"Matt, I called Mr. Border from the courthouse and told him that I was coming out to talk to him. He knows that I suspect foul play. He may have called the sheriff when I didn't show up. Oh, Matt, he might be in danger!" She scrambled over the passenger's seat, looking on the floor and reaching under the passenger's seat in an attempt to locate her phone.

"I can't find my phone."

"You probably can't get a signal out here, anyway. Scoot over!"

Shy tucked her legs in and over the console as Matt tumbled into the front seat behind the steering wheel. He took off, throwing rocks and dust behind the rear wheels.

"What all did you tell him, Shy?"

"Uh, I can't remember. I, I told him enough to make him suspicious." she said in panic.

"Shit!"

"He asked me if we should call the sheriff and get him involved. I told him that I wanted to talk to him first."

"Well, let's hope he didn't get the willies after you didn't show up. We'd better pray he didn't call Tills."

"Do you think they would kill Mr. Border?"

"I don't know."

Even the air smelled evil as they pulled in several yards ahead and just to the right of what used to be the Barett's home. They decided to park the car and walk to Border's house as a precautionary measure, not wanting to alarm anyone who might be on the property looking for them. With a full moon's glow, they had enough light to see yards ahead. The burning stench of lost lives permeated the air. As they neared the charred ghost of a house, Shy grabbed Matt's hand and slowed.

"Did you hear something?" She looked back toward the car. She could see it, beyond running distance, and there were no trees or bushes in which they could hide.

"It's okay, honey. Even if Mr. Border did call Tills, it's doubtful that he gave him enough information to make him suspicious."

A voice growled from somewhere among the trees, startling them both. "Yeah, I guess it'd take a lot more than the paranoia of an old man to make me suspicious." Shy gasped and jumped backwards as the voice continued, "Like maybe a fake birth certificate and social security number. You reckon, Agent Hollingsworth?" Tills stepped into the moonlight. His cowboy hat sat low on his forehead. He had a long piece of what appeared to be grass hanging between his teeth and a steel-barreled, three-fifty-seven Magnum pointed at Matt's face. Matt held his hands, palms forward, toward Tills, as Shy stood just in front and to the left of him. Wanting to push her behind himself, Matt felt an urgency to protect Shy. "Where's Mr. Border?" she demanded.

"Now don't you go worryin' your pretty little head over him. He'll be dyin' of natural causes tonight. But it'll be quick. Don't you worry."

Shy started to cry. "Please don't hurt him. He's not a threat to you, Tills."

"Well, you can thank your boyfriend for that. Nobody would have died tonight."

Matt stiffened, his blood boiling to the surface of his neck and cheeks. "What about all the innocent people you killed before tonight, Tills? The children, innocent babies."

"Now, you shut up, boy!" He gripped the Magnum tighter, aiming it higher. "Those people were nothing but leeches to our fine country."

"But what did they ever do to you? Did you even know any of them?" Shy was trembling and crying through her words.

"You wanna' know what I know, Miss Sauze? I know that my daddy served two years in combat in World War II. He retired as captain of the Bearden Police Department where he served for thirty years. He never took one red cent from his government. But when he got cancer and the radiation burned up his kidneys, our same government, the one he risked his life for, somehow couldn't afford to help him buy his life-saving medication."

He cocked his head to the side and continued venomously, "We got the money to feed ever' nigger in Arkansas, but we can't help a hard-working white man stay alive. Now don't that make sense?" He laughed in a hostile, almost psychotic manner. With the gun still pointed at Matt, he continued to speak, "Ain't it somethin'? You can lay around and not earn an honest day's pay in your entire life, and our government will pay you to live, give your kids an education, pay for their medical bills, feed the damn bunch of 'em. Problem is … they ain't got enough money to go around, and hard working white Americans do without. Our fine mayor saw it, and he devised a plan to fix it. I'm part of that plan."

He held his head high with racist, redneck pride. His eyes were cold and cruel. Looking at Shy, he watched her tremble. He had no sympathy. There might have been before he found out she was a nigger- lover. He gave Shy a little wink equivalent to the one she gave him at the café as she and Nelson walked out of the Chinese restaurant. "But, at least we got one less nigger to feed now don't we, Miss Sauze?"

Shy shrieked with violent rage as she realized he was talking about Nelson. She rushed for Tills, wanting desperately to tear his eyes from their sockets. But, before she could reach him the gun fired twice. Shy winced, covered her ears, and looked back as Matt fell to the ground. "Matt!" Shy screamed. With her stomach recoiling, she ran to him, fell on her knees, and pleaded, "Oh, God, please! Please, Matt. Don't leave me!" She was oblivious to Tills' demented reeling of words behind her. Shy could see thick blood, which was shimmering in the moonlight, dribble from the wound on Matt's upper thigh. Then, she saw the other bullet hole. It was directly in the center of his chest. "Matt, stay with me! Stay with me! *Dear God, help him!*"

Matt, rigid with pain and gasping for oxygen, looked into her eyes, unable to speak. He grabbed her right hand sternly and moved it to the wound at his chest. Taking her forefinger, he forced it into the hole and looked deeply into her eyes while continuing to gasp for air. She could feel the bullet. *The vest...The bulletproof vest!* Matt was trying to tell her that he was okay. Tills had been yelling for Shy to stand up and face him. She continued to look into Matt's eyes as he guided her hand down his chest to his hip. She looked at him knowingly.

Tills continued, "I wouldn't leave you here to face this world without your little boyfriend, Miss Sauze. I just thought we could have a little fun first." He chuckled and lowered his gun just long enough to unbutton the top of his trousers. Too late. She had turned around.

The glint of the nine millimeter was no match for the murderous glare in Shy's eyes. It was as if all of her feelings had been emitted with a fiery, volcanic eruption that left her cold, numb, and sociopathic. There was no pondering of consequences. There was no consideration of human life. The cold steel of the pistol seemed but an extension of her own flesh and bone... as though it would fire if she merely willed it to do so.

Tills, in all his thirty-two years of law enforcement, could not remember feeling the level of fear he felt now, looking into the face of a woman who wanted nothing more than to see him dead. It was too late to try for even the tiniest movement of his gun. She would kill him. He had no doubt about that. Trying to reason with her, he stammered, "Now, uh, Miss Sauze," as he fidgeted, held the pistol's butt forward, and extended it toward her. Slowly, he inched it down and dropped it to the ground. Then, he held both hands, palms forward, toward her. Shy did not divert her attention. His pants hung around his hips from his opened fly. Cautiously, he continued, "You see, there. I dropped my gun. You know I wasn't gonna' hurt ya."

In one quick sweep, she cocked the chamber back. Tills began to stutter, "Now, M-Miss Sauze, I-I know, you bein' a Christian woman and all ... I mean, n-now think about what you're doing."

"Sheriff," she spoke softly and methodically. The tone of her voice sent an icy chill up Tills' spine. It was all he could do to contain the urine from spilling out of his bladder. He listened, hoping that what Shy had to say would offer him some remnant of hope. Someone surely heard the shots earlier. *Maybe the old man. Yeah, that's it!* Or maybe she would hold him at gunpoint until the police arrived. She wasn't the type to pull the trigger, he reasoned, as his heart painfully pounded in his chest cavity. He'd never go to jail. Kult would get him out of this mess.

"Sheriff," she repeated, bracing her shoulders and tensing her arms, eyes burning right through his soul, "go to Hell."

One shot echoed through the valley.

Chapter Twenty-Seven

It was a brisk morning in September. The mountain air was fresh and swirled through golden, orange-colored trees as it carried their aging leaves to the ground. Shy loved it here. The mountains were tranquil and serene.

She walked outside to get the mail that had been in the box since yesterday. Nothing was ever a rush in her new life. She retrieved her mail and the morning paper as the wind whirled her hair about. A single leaf managed to make its way in before she closed the door to the modest cabin, courtesy of the F.B.I. She walked from the living room into the kitchen which had a nice, double fireplace that allowed one to see the fire from both rooms. Besides its location, the fireplace was her favorite part of the cabin.

A wedding portrait of Matt and her was displayed beautifully above the mantel. She recalled her wedding day. Agents stood at every entrance, armed of course. And there was an agent on either side of them. It all happened so quickly that her mother and Glorie were the only guests able to attend. Just as they said their "I do's," they were whisked away into the witness protection program.

Matt was in the back yard rolling around in the leaves with the son they'd adopted two and a half years ago. They were wearing matching flannel shirts which were probably not enough, Shy thought, having just walked outside. She made a mental note to get the boy's jacket after she thumbed through the mail. But, she found it difficult to take her eyes off of them.

Watching the two of them squealing and wrestling about made her heart melt. The chubby little boy would be four years old next month. And he was definitely Daddy's boy. It amazed her that, although adopted, he had taken up so many of Matt's characteristics such as the way he cocked his head to the left when he was asking a question and the way he walked around with his hand on his hip when he was angry.

Matt was now galloping around the hilly backyard, with the little one yelling, "Whoa, horsey!" She smiled and wondered how she'd ever lived one moment in her life before them. Sitting at the dining room table, she turned her gaze to the letters in front of her.

Rarely corresponding with the outside world, she and Matt had to go to great lengths to protect the family's identity. Just the mailing of a letter was quite an ordeal. Only a handful of people knew where they were or what their new names were.

Matt set up an intricate system of protection with some of his friends. In order to send a letter, she had to send it in code names to a post office box in California. An F.B.I. agent picked the letters up once a month and laundered them through another F.B.I. official in New Orleans. After this, the letters are, finally, mailed out to the perspective people, all of whom have a post office box under a different name. Sometimes, it took three or four months before the letter actually arrived at its destination.

Occasionally, she and Matt were able to use a secured telephone through the F.B.I., but it was rare. Shy usually called her mother but wasn't able to talk very long because of the possibility of putting her mother in danger. She missed her mother and sister very much.

She spoke with Bill once, two years ago. She had worried about him when she heard that the F.B.I. suspected that the DHS administrators in Arkansas were being paid off by Kult to give statistical data regarding a potential hit. It was suspected that Nelson was killed because he had overheard someone talking at the facility where he worked. Unfortunately, this had not been proven.

Bill was fine and still working at the Department of Human Services. He had told her that Brice's grandmother had attended parenting classes and counseling. She was awarded full custody of Brice. Shy was so pleased for the little boy. She had always wondered what had happened to him- as well as the other cases she was forced to abandon. Shy never told Bill why she left or where she was. When he asked, she told him only that she had to go and that she wished him well.

Shy began thumbing through the mail. The first of the letters she viewed were addressed to "Greg and Michelle Laster," their new names. It was basically junk mail, but she was happy to even get that. The last envelope was green and looked like some type of card. It was also addressed to Greg and Michelle. There was no return address.

She opened it carefully, hoping it was from family or friends. It contained a "Wishing You Well" card, so she opened it quickly to see who had sent it. A picture fell to the floor. She picked it up and immediately recognized the Baretts, amazed at how much the children had grown.

Hannah, now six, sat perched in Mr. Border's lap. Piersen stood to the left of Mr. Border. Traci was kneeling beside Hannah to Border's right. Each gleaming expression was a reflection of sunlight during a very dark hour, an hour that still haunted Shy's dreams. It seemed only yesterday. Three years' time was hardly enough time to heal the wounds that scarred her so deeply. And, she was still unable to prevent her thoughts from going back to that dark, dark night.

She was standing near the burned rubble of the Barett's home, holding the pistol to Tills' face. He had just shot Matt. All Shy wanted to do was watch this man suffer as he died. She didn't remember when she had first heard the police sirens. However, she did recall the red and blue flashes of light from Percy's squad car reflecting from Tills' face as she told him to go to hell.

Thank God, Mr. Border had heard the commotion and called the police. She remembered hearing, "Put the weapon down!" three times before she realized Percy was referring to her. Feeling relieved to see Percy's kind face, she lowered her gun to the ground and stood back up.

It was at this point that Tills threw his head back and burst into laughter. He started walking toward Percy. "Hey, bud, glad you got here early. What, did the old man call?"

"Yes, sir. I was patrolling in the area and was able to get here faster than the others. The other units will be here soon."

"Good." Tills was about twenty yards from Percy when he threw his thumb over his shoulder and said, "Clip her before they get here."

Shy's heart filled with both fear and sadness when she realized what was going on. Percy was a member of the plan. And now he was going to kill her. Tills was ten feet away from Percy.

"Boy, you gonna clip her or you want me to do it?"

"I got it, sir."

Shy looked helplessly at Percy but didn't try to run or escape. Percy aimed his gun at her. Tills was five feet away. "Boy, what're you waiting on?" Tills asked with irritation.

Percy aimed the gun at Tills' face with only two-and-a-half feet between them. "I'm waiting on you, sir," he replied. One shot sent a patch of Tills' skull flying two feet from the area where his body landed. Pieces of gray matter, blood, and bone fragments littered the earth around his shattered face. Shy ran toward the body wanting to make sure he was dead. He was. The whole back portion of Tills' head was gone, and its slushy contents emptied onto the ground.

Shy remembered Percy standing just in front of her with Tills' dead body lying between them. His gun was smoking in the crisp air from the fatal bullet wound. They looked at one another as other police units pulled up, sharing a moment that each of them understood perfectly and that no one else would understand for a lifetime.

She looked at him with deep sorrow as he stepped over Tills' dead body and embraced her forcefully. Putting his mouth to her ear, he whispered, "Get out of Arkansas, Shy. You're not safe here." He pulled away, looked at her miserably, and turned without saying another word.

It was later rumored through the F.B.I. that Percy had been ordered by Kult to follow Tills and kill him, preferably after Tills shot Matt and Shy. Tills had become too great a risk to the rest of the group. If caught, he would have squealed on all of them for lighter sentencing. The newspapers reported that Percy was a hero. One month later Percy hung himself off the side of the deck in his back yard.

Shy refused to believe that Percy was anything but a good and decent man. She recalled the article in the newspaper about Sheriff Tills and the Hot Spring County Sheriff's Office supplying the generous donation that enabled Clare to have her bone marrow transplant. Shy now knew that it wasn't a donation after all. Percy had made a deal with the devil to save his daughter's life, probably not even realizing it.

Percy's daughter continues to do well. She and her mother moved to Texas after Percy's death to be closer to family. Shy heard that Clare was in her freshman year of college at Texas State. Occasionally, Shy and Matt send anonymous donations to help support her education.

Shy remembered a chill in the air that mid-fall night, the night Matt was shot, and Tills was killed. She remembered a warm blanket being draped around her. It was Mr. Border. He'd covered Matt and put a pillow under his head. The ambulance team quickly assessed him. One of the wounds was deep but not fatal. If he had not been wearing the vest, he would have surely died. Shy couldn't bear to think about that possibility, even now. Within minutes he was being whisked off to the nearest hospital.

Mr. Border, who seemed a bit wobbly, even with his cane, put his free hand on Shy's back to provide what little support he could to her. "Why don't you come on back to my house and rest a spell."

"Thank you, Mr. Border, but I've got to get to the hospital and be with Matt."

"Why don't you let me drive you?"

Shakily, she said, "I'll be fine, Mr. Border. Thank you. You know, if it weren't for you, Matt and I might both be dead, right now. You saved our lives." She hugged him as her heart continued to ache for the loss of his adopted family. She wondered how he was doing but couldn't bring herself to ask, afraid of dredging up more pain for him.

He patted her shoulder and walked away. Stopping at Tills' bloody corpse several yards away, he turned back to Shy, and they held each other's gaze for several minutes. He knew. Shy closed her eyes, which released the swells of tears that had formed. She looked back at Mr. Border and nodded in confirmation. Border looked down at the man who killed his family and spat on him with contempt. Shy watched him with a heavy heart. His limping shadow seemed frail and miserable. The pain she had for him was smothering.

She was just about to get into her car when another car pulled up. It looked to be some type of un-marked patrol car. The door to the right back seat popped open, and Shy immediately saw Barney slippers and bright pink pajamas tumble out of the car. And then Shy heard the angelic sound of three-year old Hannah yelling, "Pa-Pa! Pa-Paaaaaw!"

Her brother followed, both of them running, ignoring the remains of what used to be their home. Shy began to cry as she saw the limping shadow freeze and stiffen. He turned and let out a wail as he realized that his babies were still alive. He grabbed them, held on to them, and sobbed. Traci was now on her knees beside him, crying against his shoulder.

Shy continued to choke up as she remembered watching the family holding on to one another. Mr. Border couldn't even speak between the sobbing and kissing. At one point Shy heard him try to muster "I love you," but even those words failed him. It was the most touching sight she had ever seen.

Shy later came to know that the Barett family was the next on the hit list. Matt had heard about it one night when Tills was talking to Percy. The F.B.I. shuttled the family out the back door in the middle of the night but set the house up to look as if someone were home. For their own safety, no one could know that they were not in the house as it burned to the ground. The F.B.I. worked closely with the fire marshal to insure that Tills would think he'd killed them.

The F.B.I. camped out in the woods that night and saw Tills set the fire. It was certainly enough information to incriminate Tills for arson, but they held out on the arrest waiting for information that might link his actions to others. That never happened. The Sheriff was killed along with any hope of catching the others involved.

Kult publicly grieved on national television for the families who lost their lives due to the deranged mentality of Sheriff Tills. He offered a message of hope and encouragement to the families and residents of Arkansas. Also, he promised to develop services to help and protect the needy of his fine state. He received national coverage and public favor sky-rocketed. This sickened Shy as much as it would have if Hitler were resurrected and became leader over the free world- or perhaps the anti-christ. She tried not to think about it.

She returned her gaze to the picture and smiled. What a beautiful family! Traci had written a few notes about how the children were doing and how they were all looking forward to another wonderful Christmas together. Mr. Border had written a large "Howdy, Friends!" at the bottom of the letter, causing Shy to chuckle. She went to the refrigerator and hung the picture up with a small magnet. She stared at it a moment longer. It was the picture of a miracle.

The chatter of a four-year-old boy chasing his dad down the hill broke her attention. She'd forgotten about the boy's jacket and went to the living room's coat closet. Grabbing the tiny red jacket, she held it to her face, loving the smell of her little boy.

As she closed the closet door, the glint of a gold frame caught her attention. She reached up to the top shelf and pulled it down. The image was so familiar to her that it was eternally etched in her memory; but, somehow, just looking at it, made it all real again. It was Mattie and Jake on the day of the picnic. An adoring Mattie was holding her baby high above her, both of them smiling and cooing at one another.

She thought of Jake. How his world had been torn away from him. How he was made to live among strangers in the cold foster care system. Running a finger over the picture, she touched both Mattie then Jake, as she had done a hundred times before. She couldn't cry, anymore. It was as though there were no more tears inside of her. She returned the picture to the same spot in the closet and closed the door, thinking once again of Baby Jake. She wondered if he would ever know how much his mother adored him.

Someday, she would tell him. Someday, he would know everything. Walking back to the kitchen, she gave the sliding glass door a tug. "Matt," she smiled sweetly, "Jake needs his coat on."

The final dream found her in the same sea of orchids. She and the child were running and playing in and about the flowers. The flowers didn't recognize them. And they went about doing the things that flowers do, waving in the soft air and basking in the sun. Shy was swinging the boy by the arms around and around as he laughed and squealed. They were safe. And Shy was happy.

A voice behind them disrupted the play. It said, "You did it, baby girl." Shy turned to find Nelson. He was smiling at her and wearing the same red jacket he had always worn. She walked toward Nelson until she could almost reach out and touch him. And, she wanted to cry, to grieve all over again.

"How can I make it through the journey without you?" she asked.

Nelson didn't speak. He was looking over Shy's shoulder to the child playing about in the meadow. Shy turned to look also. A woman, the most beautiful woman Shy had ever seen, stood vigilant over the boy and watched him play. Her skin was golden and translucent. She had long brown hair that flowed in waves with the wind. Her eyes glowed a soft blue and her lips were the faintest of pink. It seemed to Shy that the woman radiated light from her core that seeped out through the pores of her flawless skin. She had to squint her eyes from the woman's brilliance.

Shy turned back to Nelson. "Who is she?"

Again, Nelson did not speak. He nodded toward the woman as if to tell Shy to take another look. Shy turned and watched as the woman moved her head to one side and arched her back. Great golden tipped wings with silver etching unfolded behind the woman and stretched a span of nearly fourteen feet. She lifted the wings up and over the boy as if to shade him from the sun.

The vision of the celestial woman hovering over the child was a glorious sight to behold, leaving Shy speechless and in complete awe. "She's an angel. She's the most beautiful thing I've ever seen."

Nelson nodded and said, "Look closer."

The woman held her wings over the boy and watched him with sheer delight. For a brief moment she looked up at Shy, then tucked her wings and began moving forward. Shy's knees began to tremble, as she had never seen a heavenly being, much less one so close. As the woman moved closer, Shy held her hand up in an attempt to block the light which increased with each step the woman took.

Shy heard Nelson say, "Don't be afraid of her. She is kind and won't hurt you." Shy put her hand down and stood face-to-face with the heavenly creature.

The woman's eyes were transparent, and Shy was almost able to see straight through them. Her spirit was gentle and child-like. It was at this time that Shy realized that she knew the woman. And she mustered the courage to utter, "Mattie?"

The woman did not speak. She only smiled. Then, she turned away from Shy and repositioned herself over the boy. Slowly, she disappeared from human sight.

"Did you see that, Nelson? She was an angel! Mattie was an angel!"

"Yes," he said with a smile, "she always was." With this, Nelson turned and walked away.

Shy cried out to him, asking once again, "How can I make it through the journey without you?"

Nelson turned around and stared at her. He looked serene and joyful. After a few moments he smiled at her and said, "I never left you."

And, this was the last time she saw him.

Printed in the United States
32665LVS00006B/187-198